Last Call

Coffee Girl Series Book 4

Sophie Sinclair

Dear Reader,

Music plays a big part in my life and my writing. I post the playlists on Spotify for all my books under their titles. The Coffee Girl series was created after I went to a summer concert series, so each book has a playlist. You don't have to listen along with the book, but sometimes it adds an extra element if you love music while you read. I also recommend listening to Pink's song after you finish the last chapter. Enjoy!

Doing Life With Me – Eric Church
Good As Hell – Lizzo
You Need To Calm Down – Taylor Swift
Treat People With Kindness – Harry Styles
I Was Born To Love You – Ray LaMontagne
Rock & Roll – Eric Hutchinson
Nonsense – Sabrina Carpenter
Little Rain – Morgan Wallen
Lucky – Jason Mraz, Colbie Caillat
Gloria – Laura Branigan
Lost In The Light – Bahamas
Players – Coi Leray
Best Friend – Saweetie, Doja Cat
Fast Car – Tracy Chapman

My Man – Maddie & Tae
Songbird Instumental, Take 10 – Fleetwood Mac
Danny's Song – Loggins & Messina
Thank God – Kane Brown, Katelyn Brown
Can't Take My Eyes Off Of You – Straught No Chaser
Man In The Mirror – James Morrison
Never Gonna Not Dance Again – Pink

"I've had to go against all kinds of people through the years just to be myself. I think everybody should be allowed to be who they are, and to love who they love."

– Dolly Parton

"A lot of people don't understand my enthusiasm or my love for everything that sparkles. They think I'm zany and overly dramatic, or God forbid…a stereotypically *gay* man. I admit, I can be a little extra at times, but that just makes life more fun, right? Who wants to be boring? Not me, honey. I'm here to dance to my own beat, and if that's irritating to some, they can take that negativity and shove it where the sun doesn't shine. I apologize to no one, bitches."

—TJ Ryan, *The Nashville Spotlight*

Chapter 1

Connor

LAST CALL. SOME say it's the last alcoholic beverage to be served before the bar closes. Others think of it as the last chance to make plans with your friends to head somewhere else before you're kicked out. And for some, it's the warning right before the lights are about to come on, ruining your fantasy of the sexy girl or guy you've been trying to land for the last hour. *Slainte.*

Last call is tricky because no one wants to go home when they're drunk and having a good time. They want the party to keep going and they expect those behind the bar to be the ringmaster in their circus. But, like everything else in life, there comes a point when the fun has to end.

The gold tequila sloshes over the ice in the tumbler before I slide it across the bar to the pair of giggling brunettes who have been shamelessly flirting with me for the last two hours.

"Last call, ladies. Ye don't have to go home, but ye can't stay here."

"Boo. You're no fun, Connor. Can't we hang out with you a little longer after closing?" the long-haired brunette slurs while trying to bat her fake eyelashes. "Your accent is sooo sexy." Her lips pucker into a pout right before she tips sideways and falls off the barstool. Her friend turns and throws her head back, laughing like a hyena. She offers a hand to her friend, but isn't in any shape to help. They're both giggling hysterically as they try to right themselves in their seats. I shake my head, drying a mug. I nod goodbye to some patrons as they leave.

"I'll call ye a Jo Maxi," I grunt as my cell phone buzzes in my back pocket.

"Who's Joe? Is he as cute as you?" the short-haired brunette asks, slurping her drink.

"It's a taxi." I slide my cell out and see my brother's name. Turning my back, I answer.

"What's the craic?" Lex asks.

"I'm almost done. Come on in."

"Is it crowded?"

"Not too bad. Come help me move these two pissed geebags out of here."

"Ye know, when I offered ye a ride home tonight, it didn't mean I wanted to deal with a bunch of half-cut arseholes."

"Would ye come on to fuck? Quit being a narkey hole and get yer arse in here."

"Fine, ye ungrateful gobshite," Lex grumbles.

I call a cab for the two women and a few minutes later Lex saunters in wearing a baseball hat pulled down low and a peacoat with the collar up. I snort and shake my head while he keeps a low profile, maneuvering his way through the crowd. Mr. Incognito is causing more of a reaction by trying to hide himself than he would if he walked in like a normal person.

"Ye feckin' eejit, it's not empty in here, this place is jointed," he gripes, pulling off his coat and joining me behind the bar. "I'm fucking sweatin' donkey balls in here."

"Emily, I think we need to go home." The short-haired brunette's eyes widen. "I'm seeing double of that hottie bartender."

"Yo sexy bartender! One more, pleeeaase?" The one called Emily waves her hand in the air as if I can't see or hear her.

Lex smirks. "Christ, she's off her trolley."

"Wanna have some fun with these two? They've been hittin' on me all night."

His grin stretches wide and he pulls off his hat, running his fingers through his hair. We're both wearing black t-shirts and jeans. "Like old times?"

We fist-bump, then walk over to the bar where the duo is sitting. "Okay, ladies, time to close out," I say, leaning on the bar in the exact same position as Lex.

"Wait, hold up. There are two of you?" The long-haired one looks like she's about to vomit.

"Can ye pick yer tongue up off the bar? I just cleaned it," Lex says while he and I take a washcloth and wipe the bar in a slow, circular motion at the same time. The ladies' eyes track our movements with fascination.

"Wait, I'm so confused. Have you both been here all night?" the short-haired one asks.

"I don't know what yer talking about, Love, it's just been me," I say.

"Emily, you see two, don't you?" she asks her friend.

"I think I'm going to be sick. They're making me dizzy."

"It's just me, Love," Lex says. Their eyes swivel back to him. "I think yer Jo Maxi is here. It's time to call it a night."

"I am never drinking again." Emily clunks her head down on the bar. I motion for our bouncer, Kyle, to come help them out.

"Have a nice night, ladies," Lex and I say at the same time.

"I didn't think I drank that much. I've never seen double before." The short-haired brunette shakes her head while digging in her purse. She slaps two twenties on the bar.

"Liz, do you think we've been drugged?" the long-haired one, *Emily*, evidently, slurs as Kyle helps her off the stool.

"Probably if we're seeing double." Liz looks over her shoulder and we both grin and wave. "Not by our sexy Irish hottie, though. Probably that creep from earlier who was hitting on you."

Emily peers back at us and we both blow her an air-kiss. She trips over her feet and crashes into a table and chairs.

Kyle manages to get them both out the door. Lex shakes his head and loads the glasses in the dishwasher. "God-damned rat-arsed, they are."

Gina and Mac, our two servers, count their tips after wiping down all the tables. I look at my watch and groan. It's one a.m. I told TJ it would be an early night. I turn and look over my shoulder.

"Sorry it's so late."

"No worries," Lex says. "Sunshine knew I'd be coming home later tonight after I told her I was driving ye home."

I nod and close out the register. "How is Sare doing?"

"She's grand." Lex wipes the bar down one last time. He pauses and shakes his head. "Fuck, that's a lie. She's feckin' stressed over balancing work and the kids."

"What's wrong with the kids?"

"Wyatt has started therapy because he keeps having meltdowns at school. Ye know, his anxiety pretty much cripples him."

"Poor fella."

We wave goodnight to Gina and Mac and I shut off the lights and turn to lock the door.

"Yeah, it's crazy. He's always been fussy. We can't figure out what triggers it. Sarah is hoping therapy will help."

"What do ye think?"

"About therapy? I think it's a bunch of baloney, personally. But Sunshine thinks it will help, so I support it."

We turn and walk down the hallway out to the parking lot. I hate that Lex and Sarah are going through this. "Sickner for ya, brother." I slap Lex on the back. "I'm here for ye both if ye need anything."

"Thanks, bro. Appreciate that. Be thankful ye and TJ are kid-free. It's a lot harder raising kids than we thought it would be."

I smile and slide into his car. I love my niece and nephews to death, but there is no way I'm ready to take on the responsibility and stress of raising a child.

Chapter 2

MY UNRULY HAIR has always been a point of contention for me, which is funny considering everything else in my life is totally off the cuff. Pink pants paired with a silk cheetah-print button-down, and purple suede loafers? I'm down with that. Red rhinestone boots with seersucker shorts? Hell to the yes. Black leather pants with a handknit vest made by my Nana Rose? Girlfriend, that look landed me the hottest husband in the world, besides Andie's husband, Cam, of course. I'll always hold a special place in my heart for my first crush. The point is, I can dress as crazy as I feel, but my hair has to be perfectly coiffed for me to feel my best.

Patting down the wayward curl that refuses to conform with my man-of-steel hair gel, I take a deep breath before the elevator doors glide open to our cute, trendy loft in downtown Nashville.

Inhaling deeply, I step off. "It's showtime, ladies. I'm thinking we play Lizzo's 'Good As Hell' for this entrance scene."

Andie looks up from the desk and smiles. "Morning, TJ." Her smile slips a little as she notices the three men behind me. "What's going on?"

I wink at her and hold up a finger. "Sare Bear, Kinky! Get your asses out here *étutto pronto*. That means 'now'!"

Andie raises an eyebrow, her eyes skimming to the two men setting up their equipment behind me. "Actually, it means 'it's ready'."

Ignoring little *miss-know-it-all*, I toss my coat and bag on her desk.

"Ugh, TJ. I'm not your freaking coatrack." She frowns, dumping my things on the floor. "You almost tipped my coffee over."

I give her my best pouty smile. "But *mi casa es su casa*, Shorts. I don't have an office in here, so…wait, why don't I have my own office again?"

"Because you're always throwing your shit around everyone else's?" she grumbles, holding her coffee cup up and wiping down her desk.

"Oh, Shorts, you're so adorbs, but a little cranky this morning. Maybe this calls for a little *café* fetch? I'll take a double whip, caramel macchiato, half sweetened with extra foam. Oh, and can you ask Marco to make a star with the cinnamon, like he did last time? Ooh, and make sure he adds the cute little sprinkles. *Muchas dinero*. You're a doll."

"I'm not going for a coffee run. And its *muchas gracias*, not *dinero*. That means money. God, I hope you don't converse with Marco in Spanish."

Ignoring her, I sweep past her desk, annoyed that Kiki and Sarah haven't come running from their offices. It's been six years since we started Nashville Stylists, and we are busier than we've ever been. Andie still runs the office and keeps our appointments in order, but she also has a lucrative photography business, shooting family portraits and photos for Kiki's blog. She's also published four coffee-table books with her best friend, Mandy, as they travel through Europe showcasing her eye for majestic landscapes and Mandy's witty writing.

Andie keeps us all organized and focused. I'd never tell her because it would go to her head, but she's the reason our business has tripled in the last year. She and Cam have been blissfully happy raising their two children, Enzo and sweet, beautiful Charleigh.

My other two besties, Kiki and Sarah, are my styling partners. Three years ago, Kiki started designing wedding dresses and they took off like hotcakes. Her designs have been shown in *In Style Weddings*, and she was featured in the *Harper's Bazaar* wedding section as the next rising star. She has over two million followers on her style blog, *City Girl in the Heart of Country*, and she's married to the hottest country-music star, Tatum Reed. They have their hands full with their two boys, Chase and Drew, who couldn't be more opposite. Kiki is desperate for a girl, but with Tatum touring and her hectic schedule, they can't seem to find time for a third.

Sarah continues to slay as a makeup stylist for several celebrities and is often jetting off to awards shows and photo shoots for her craft. She's married to Lex Ryan, my hubby's identical twin and the lead guitarist for Tatum's band. Together, they are raising Jax, the fifteen-year-old product of

Lex's crazy ex-girlfriend, Alana, and his deadbeat cousin on his dad's side, Liam. They stepped up and adopted Jax a few years ago when Alana ditched town and left her son without a parent. They also have the four-and-a-half-year-old twins, Alexis and Wyatt. Sarah is passionate about photography and has brought national attention to their ranch of rescued horses helping children with trauma with her compassionate photos of the children and animals.

Touching a Dior velvet smoking jacket on a rolling rack in the back corner of the office, I smile. I've come a long way from working as the assistant to that creepsadoodle loser, Jonathon, at *Cufflinks* magazine, who got his kicks by calling me kitten and fetching him disgusting tuna sandwiches. I'm in charge of the men's side of styling here at Nashville Stylists and have several Nashville-based A-listers in my appointment book on the regular. I'd like to add home décor to our services, but I've been so busy styling, I haven't had the chance to get it rolling.

I shimmy into the jacket and look at myself in the floor-length mirror, pressing down on the lapels. "Looking sharp, you sexy beast." I blow a kiss to my reflection, my ring glinting in the morning light streaming through the windows. Connor and I celebrated our five-year wedding anniversary last week and not a day goes by that I'm not grateful for my sexy Irishman.

I can't complain, life is good for all of us, and honestly, it's about to get a lot better.

"Good morning, bestie! Rise and shine!" I stick my head in Kiki's office, looking for her amongst the racks of clothes. Movement behind a wedding dress catches my eye. "It's a mess in here. Are you ever going to take my advice and hire an assistant? Chop chop, early morning meeting out in the main area."

Kiki pops up, her eyes narrowing. "I've been here since seven a.m. Don't pretend like the day's starting because you rolled into work at ten."

"Well, someone's grumpy this A to the M. Shake it like a polaroid picture and get your ass out here." I leave Miss Sourpuss to stew and duck into Sarah's room. "Knock knock? Good morning, Sare Bear!"

Sarah looks up from her phone and smiles. "Morning, TJ."

"Can you come out to the main area for an important meeting, *por favor?*"

"Oh, sure." She sets her phone down and follows me out to Andie's desk. "Hey, when do you think that rack of fabrics you rolled into my office two months ago will go away?"

"Times that by six."

"A year? TJ, come on…"

"Well, maybe we need to look for a new space, Sare Bear. I've been telling y'all for months. If we keep growing like we are, we're all going to need assistants with our own space."

"I know. This place holds so many special memories for us," she says. "But you're right, we've outgrown it."

I look around the tiny, cramped area, nostalgia tightening my throat. This was where our humbling beginnings began. But that's a discussion for a different day. Today I need to talk about *my* news.

We don't have room for a conference table, so we all take

our usual spots around Andie's desk. Sarah sits on a loveseat by the windows where Kiki's cat Oreo is sunning himself. Kiki walks over to the Nespresso machine, while Andie sits officially behind her desk.

I spin in a circle and clap my hands, garnering the three women's attention. "Ladies…and Kinky." Kiki flips me off while she makes a latte. "I'd like you to meet Cal, Brody, Tina, and Sam. They're with *Nashville Next* and they are doing an exclusive exposé on yours truly. They're filming us in our natural environment, like zebras in the Sahara. Isn't that exciting?"

"I think you mean the Serengeti," Andie says, tapping a pen to her lips.

"Okay, Miss World Traveler." I roll my eyes. "It's the same thing. Anyway, they'll be filming me. You three will just happen to always be around. Like little insignificant planets orbiting the bright, beautiful sun."

"Did he really say that?" Kiki huffs while taking her seat.

"Why are they filming you again?" Andie asks.

"Great question, Shorts. Because I pitched them a story and they said yes."

"What is *Nashville Next*? I've never heard of it." Sarah's eyes widen as she looks over at Brody, Cal, Tina, and Sam. "Sorry, no offense."

"Oh my gawd, Sunshine, do you live under a rock? *Nashville Next* is the show that follows celebrities around Nashville, documenting their lives. It's like Oprah's exclusive interviews."

"Except there's no Oprah and you're not a celebrity," Kiki chimes in.

I pinch the bridge of my nose, close my eyes, and count to three.

"What's wrong with him?" Andie asks.

"Oh no, he got this look when he belted out the whole soundtrack to *Cats* the other day," Sarah replies. "It sounded like a bunch of cats in heat."

"TJ, please don't sing 'Memories' again. It will cause another migraine," Kiki bitches.

"I'm not going to sing," I snap. "Although Oreo did enjoy my repertoire. Ugh, stop getting me offtrack. *Nashville Next* did a piece last month with that girl…wearing the cowboy hat. Melody-what's-her-name? No, maybe it was Rebecca. She recently came out of the closet. You know who I'm talking about." I snap my fingers, my brain fizzling.

Sarah looks at me helplessly. "I have no clue who or what you're talking about. So wait, they only interview gay celebrities around Nashville?"

"No, I was just trying to give you a glimpse of what *my* documentary would be like. Really, it doesn't matter. It's going to be fabuloso."

"Wait, I'm confused. Why you?" Kiki's brows knit together while Andie suppresses a giggle.

"Kinky, don't be jelly." I sit on the edge of Andie's desk and rub my hands together. "So, I pitched a storyline and they jumped at the idea, and now we're all going to be on the show!"

"What if we don't want to be on camera?" Ugh, my bestie can be such a mood-killer sometimes.

"Kiki, don't be a Tic Tac. This will be uh-maze publicity for our business."

Andie side-eyes Sarah. "What's a Tic Tac supposed to mean?"

"Nothing, ignore him. It's a piece of candy," Kiki says.

"A Tic Tac, *Andie*, means someone can be colorful and sweet on the outside, but one crunch and they're over in a hot second." I glare at Kiki.

Andie scrunches her forehead. "I'm sorry, I still don't understand."

"He's trying to call me basic," Kiki says.

"But with colorful flair." I nod supportively. "Anyway, all three of you have to be on the show, or else my life will be completely ruined and Connor will leave me and I'll end up in a gutter drinking decaf coffee, wearing last year's Ferragamo and eating Subway for the rest of my life." I shudder at the image I evoked. "I could never be that guy who lost a ton of weight and got caught with porn on his computer…" I whisper.

"Ooh-kay…this just took a weird turn." Andie adorably wrinkles her nose. "So, what do you need us to do?"

"Just act like your fab selves." I motion my finger at Kiki. "We'll bring in some help for you."

"Ha-ha. Very funny. What's the story idea you pitched?"

"Two gay men in the heart of Nashville with very busy, successful careers navigating the challenges of having a baby!"

All three of their mouths drop open. I squeal and do jazz hands, snapping them out of their shock. "We're having a baby!"

"You and Connor are adopting?" Andie perks up, a beautiful smile lighting up her face.

"I can't believe Connor didn't say anything last night

when he was over." Sarah furrows her brows.

"Well, he's, um…" I flutter my hands, anxious about the girls' reaction. "He doesn't know yet."

"Uh, don't you think this is something you should discuss with Connor first? He should be involved in this decision," Kiki says, her eyes cutting to the camera crew.

And there's my little dark thundercloud, electrocuting my good vibe.

"Yeah, I agree with Kiks, TJ," Sarah says and Andie nods along. "This is definitely something you should talk over with Connor before making such a big decision."

"Sare-ugh! Not you, too. Come on guys, we *have* talked about it, but we can't agree on what we want to do, so if I bring it up on camera, he'll have to move forward with it. He can't say no."

"That sounds like a terrible idea," Kiki says while the other two nod their heads in agreement.

"Don't you want to be involved in your little niece or nephew's conceive-ment?"

"Is that even a thing?" Andie asks the room.

"Strangely, I do." Kiki smiles with wide eyes, the rusty cogs in her mind slowly churning. I knew I could hook her in. And if she's in, the other two will cave shortly.

I grab my bag and pull out four sparkly purple binders with "Baby Ryan" bedazzled on the fronts and hand them each one. I look back to make sure Cal, Sam, Tina, and Brody are filming.

"Oh, and one more thing, try to not look at the camera. Breaking the fourth wall is *très* tragic and makes you look desperado. I'm looking at you, Kinky." I give her the two fingers to my eye and point at her. She flips me off in response before turning her attention to the binder.

"Now, I've divided it up into three sections. We're not sure which avenue we want to pursue, so I wanted to run it by my besties to help us decide. The first tab is fostering where we get to try a kid out from the prison system."

"You mean foster system, I hope? They're not like in juvie, right?" Andie looks at the other two, her eyes wide.

"Is there really a difference, Shorts?" I ask.

"Uh, actually yes, a big diff—"

"Eyes on the prize, ladies." I flip the page. "Fostering will be like a trial period for us, to see if we can handle having a kid in our lives."

"Perhaps you should get a dog first," Kiki mumbles.

"Tragically, *Kiki*, most fosters don't work out because they have a hard time trusting their new family or Grandma Pearl decides she wants them back."

Sarah coughs as she takes a sip of tea. "TJ, a child is not something you can order off Amazon and return if it's damaged or you don't like it."

"Okay, maybe *'try out'* is the wrong word"—I finger-quote—"but you know what I mean. We get to have little Gino in our house and be a family of three. But then his mom gets out of jail because she's no longer on *the drugs* and wants to do better…she comes for a visit and Gino loves his mommy, but he's torn because he loves Uncle TJ and Uncle Coco too. But we all know the streets are mean and she's going to fall right back into the crack. Pun intended—"

"Jesus," Kiki groans.

"Uh, are you sure we should be filming this? It's probably not PC to say..." Andie looks hesitantly over at the cameras, but I can't stop now. I get up and pace back and forth, making sure to stay in the camera's frame.

"But sweet little Gino has a loving home where he's allowed to wear ascots and suede shoes and gets to ride a sparkly unicorn for family picture day. They know his mom can't handle the pressure. She's back on the D-R-U-G-S and forgets to show up to his custodial hearing. The judge loves Uncle TJ's suave style and Uncle Coco's sexy accent, so he says they can keep him and rename him Bartholomew. Sweet little Bartie. Can't you picture him?" I press my hands to my heart.

"That's so not how this works!" Kiki snaps, slamming her binder shut. "He's not a doll you can dress up, for fuck's sake. You can't foster a kid and then return them back into the system if they don't work out. And why the fuck are you calling yourselves Uncle TJ and Uncle Coco to your own foster child? It's creepy. A judge isn't going to give a fuck if you're wearing Gucci or TJ Maxx, and he certainly isn't going to base his decision off of an Irish accent, as incredible as it is. And as his totally awesome aunt *and* godmother, I put my foot down on renaming poor sweet imaginary Gino, Bartholomew."

"Bartie for short," I remind her.

"That's even worse."

"You and Connor watched that movie, didn't you?" Sarah asks.

"The one with Mark Wahlberg..." Andie snaps her fingers. "*Instant Family*! I loved that movie."

I shoot them all a dirty look. "It was very educational

and eye-opening."

"Clearly." Kiki sips her coffee.

"Okay, so I guess fostering is at the bottom of our list."

"Thank God for poor little Gino," Sarah mumbles. I roll my eyes and flip the page.

"Our next possibility is having a surrogate. Andie, this is where you come in."

"Wait, what?" Her eyes widen comically. "No. Absolutely not. I love you guys, but I'm not carrying a baby for you. Those days are done."

"Jeez, good to know we can't count on you…but that's not what I need. Can you take pictures of Connor and me? We'd like to put a look-book together for potential birth moms and surrogates. Maybe Mandy could write little tidbits throughout since you guys are now *New York Times* best-selling authors?"

"Oh, not *New York Times*." Andie laughs nervously, her eyes ping-ponging from me to the camera. "But, I'd be honored. I know Mandy will make time. She just finished up the Spain book I photographed last summer."

"Ex-cellent-o. Okay ladies, flip to surrogate number one. I gathered these bios from a surrogate website, but I'm not sure about them, which is why I'm asking for your help."

"Wait, why aren't you asking me or Sarah to be a surrogate?" Kiki asks.

"Kinks, no offense, but you're not exactly a spring chicken anymore."

"I'm thirty-two—"

"And let's be honest, your children are the devils incarnate. I love them, but cheese and rice, *no thank you*. Besides,

I've seen what you consume when you're preggers, and you get super cranky and bloated. It's not a good look for you." I sigh and smile at sweet, lovable Sarah, placing my hand over my heart. "And Sare Bear, I totes love you, but your kids are kind of weird, and Wyatt cries a lot. I hope you understand."

"I didn't want to be a surrogate, anyway." Sarah looks miffed.

"I think I can speak for the both of us when I say we're totally offended. You have officially lost your bestie card." Kiki folds her arms over her chest and looks right at the camera.

I sigh and look up at the ceiling. "Kinky, you're killing my mojo vibe right now. Can we continue? Okay, so this one is *not* my favorite, but I think Connor will like her. Her name is Amy and she's from Seattle. She started as a surrogate when her best friend couldn't have a baby, and has since carried two more. She's very selective and *super* expensive, in my opinion."

"How much are we talking?" Andie arches an eyebrow.

"Well, she's on the high end. Around a hundred and fifty thousand plus expenses and the IVF." I bite my lip, avoiding eye contact.

Sarah splutters tea on her shirt, causing Oreo to jump down off the loveseat.

"Holy crap, that's a lot of money! And you'd have to go to Seattle, or would she live here with you?" Andie asks.

"Seattle. She's not willing to leave. We would have to do a lot of flying back and forth, which I'm not crazy about, but I'd do it if she were the perfect fit for us. I'm worried she'll drink a lot of coffee while on the job."

"Is that in her bio?" Kiki scans the sheet, her brows knitted.

"No, but she lives in the coffee mecca of the United States. She probably works at Starbucks or that horrid seawater they call Seattle's Best." I shiver in disgust.

"Did you even read her bio? She works for a tech start-up," Andie points out.

I flip the page, ignoring her. "K, next! Rebecca from Indiana, who has never been a surrogate before, but she's less expensive, coming in at forty-five thousand plus expenses and she's very enthusiastic about the job. One major problem, she doesn't have insurance."

"No offense, TJ, but she doesn't look very healthy, either." Sarah frowns at the picture.

"She looks like she drinks Mountain Dew on the regular," Kiki says.

"Why do you say that?" I ask.

"Because she's holding a bottle of Mountain Dew."

"Is that a bag of fast food on her car behind her? I don't mean to be judgy, but do you want her carrying your baby for nine months?" Sarah asks.

"I'd take Starbucks girl over her. It says here, she works at Wendy's," Andie observes.

"Well, we can't all be at tech start-ups, can we, girls? She did promise us free Frosties and fries every Friday, so that's a win in my book." I clear my throat and flip the page. "The next one is my personal fave, Penny from Van Nuys, California. We'd be her last clients because she's getting too old."

"She seems vibrant and fun. How old *is* she?" Andie

frowns.

"She's thirty-four, but she recently quit her job and said she'd be willing to move to Nashville. We'd, of course, move her in with us. She's a bit pricey too, but she's experienced. And isn't she so sassy with her bikini and leg warmers? I love her."

"Yeah, she screams classy," Kiki deadpans while perusing her bio.

"All I can think of is the movie *Baby Mama* when Amy Poehler's character was pretending to be pregnant. What if you get someone like that?" Sarah's brows crease with concern.

"Sare Bear, you don't think I can spot a fake a mile away? Do I even need to bring up Lex's psycho ex?"

"I'm worried you guys will invest all this money and it doesn't work out. Then you have this stranger in your house living with you, and she won't leave. So now you have a squatter that's eating all your food while you and Connor are at work—"

"Dial it down a notch, Betty. That's not going to happen. I think you need to cut back on the chamomile and stop watching *Baby Mama*," I whisper loudly while side-eyeing Kiki. "Okay, moving on to the last section, which is adoption."

"Is adoption as expensive as hiring a surrogate?" Andie asks.

"Well, it depends on if you go through a private lawyer or an agency. Personally, I'd rather go through a private adoption, but it can also be riskier doing it that way. It's gotten a lot better in the last decade, but it's still not easy for two gay men to adopt. A lot of foreign countries won't allow it, so we'll be looking in the United States, but that also means it could be a longer process. It could take years. It's definitely cheaper than surrogate, that's for sure, but at least with surrogate it's a sure thing."

"I don't know if I would want to go through the process of surrogacy," Sarah says. "I mean, what if the in vitro doesn't take? Do you want your and Connor's sperm with some unknown female?"

"Oh, we don't care if our baby has our DNA or not. We just want it to be healthy. Although it would be totes adorbs if he came out speaking with an Irish accent, wouldn't it?"

"Tammy Jean, you do realize the baby isn't going to be talking with an accent, right?" Kiki raises her eyebrows.

"Talking, crying, whatevs." I brush her off while she tilts her head, staring at me quizzically.

"Then I vote for adoption," Sarah says decisively. "Lex and I are so happy we have Jax in our lives. I mean, sure, it was difficult at first, but with therapy and having a stable home, he's adjusted incredibly. I can't imagine our family without him."

I think about Lex's looney-tunes ex-fiancée, Alana, who claimed Jax was his son, but after taking a paternity test it was revealed Jax's dad was a cousin of Lex and Connor's. "Jax is a pretty cool kid, but I think I want a baby. Is that wrong to want?"

"Does Connor want a baby too?" Sarah asks.

"I don't think he knows what he wants," I say, brusquely.

The three women exchange looks. "Don't you think y'all

should be on the same page about this?" Andie asks.

I glance quickly at the cameras. "We are, we are…don't worry. He wants me to be happy, so whatever goes." I snap my fingers above my head. "Snapsies, we made a decision! Adoption it is. Isn't this exciting? It's like *Three Men and a Baby*, except there's only two of us…"

"And you're gay. And some lady didn't leave the baby on your doorstep. And you're not Tom Selleck. More like Steve Guttenberg," Kiki says, scribbling in the binder I gave her.

"Kiki, please don't deface my binders." I snatch it out of her hands. "I would *so* be Tom, by the way. I could totally rock the stache. Ugh, you're getting me off track again. Okay, listen up, this means we need to get started on our adoption book pronto! Andie, can we borrow Enzo and Charleigh as child props for our family photos for the look-book? We need to look like we're experienced child handlers. You know, like we know how to hold them? Oh, and Sare, maybe Connor could hold the twins. That would be so adorbs."

"Uh, sure?"

"You can use Chase and Drew." Kiki's brow furrows. "They love Uncle TJ and Uncle Coco."

"That will be a hard pass. Remember the last time you guys had photos done and Chase smeared mud all over your dress and Drew threw up on Tatum?"

"Oh, come on. That was one time."

"Remember when you had Christmas photos done and Chase pulled Santa's beard off and Drew threw up on Tatum?"

"Okay, he did get a little feisty with Santa and Drew had

a stomach bug that day—"

"Or the time Chase kicked Andie in the shin and Drew threw up on Tatum? Or—"

"Okay fine. Point taken," Kiki grumbles.

"Sare Bear, I'll need you for hair and makeup."

Sarah gives me a thumbs-up.

"Might want to get a haircut." Kiki squints at my hair. "You're looking a little Ronald-like."

"Kinky, you know that's the worst thing you can say to me," I hiss, looking over my shoulder at the camera. I quickly pat my hair down.

She grins evilly while I beckon them to gather in for a huddle. I stick my hand in the center and waggle it until they do the same. Kiki groans in protest, like she always does.

"Bitches, let the baby planning begin. Baby Ryan Campaign commences now! Give me a razzle dazzle, snizzle my shizzle, TJ's the most awesomeness out of everyone and we couldn't live—"

"Please end this," Kiki rudely interrupts.

"Fine, mood-killer. On three. One, two, three!"

"Baby Ryan!" the three shout.

"Okay, enough of that. Who's going to go get me a mocha whip with two shots of vanilla, a drizzle of caramel, and sprinkles on top?" I ask the room.

A magazine goes whizzing past my head before my three besties disappear in the back.

"Don't forget, Tina, Cal, Sam, and Brody have the authority to follow you around. And don't break the fourth wall. You won't even know they are here! Are you bitches listening to me?"

I look around at the empty loft and sigh. "Okay guys, that's a wrap for now."

I sit down on the couch and run my finger along the purple, sparkly binder. "Well, little Gino, I guess this is really happening."

Now I have to go convince Connor that we need to adopt a baby.

Chapter 3

Connor

I SCOOT PAST the throng of women clad in tight athletic gear, trying like hell not to knock into any of them. These hallways weren't built for six-foot-three guys with broad shoulders. Scanning the names along the built-in cubbies, I ignore the pointed stares and whispers happening behind me. I find Alexis's name and grab her Hello Kitty sequined backpack and then look for Wyatt's Superman backpack. Rearing my head back, I practically run over the woman who has suddenly materialized right in front of me.

"Hi, I'm Jennifer. You have the twins? My Austin adores Wyatt. He's all he can talk about," she gushes before taking a gulp of her pumpkin spice latte.

"Oh, I'm actually their—"

"Grace Stevens." A hand juts out, blocking me from moving forward. I look down at the dark-haired woman who has sidled up next to Jennifer. Her smile is frozen on her face as she zeros in on my hands. I smile politely and nod, unable to shake her hand because of the backpacks.

"Oh my god, your accent is to-die-for! Is it British?" Jennifer croons.

"Uh, Irish, actually."

"So dreamy." She smiles, cradling her drink next to her chin. Her undivided attention has me searching for the first available exit where I can get a leg up, the hallway suddenly feeling hot and claustrophobic. "You look sooo familiar."

Grace bumps her elbow, causing coffee to slosh onto Jennifer's white tank top. "What she's trying to say is that we've never seen you here before. Normally, the nanny picks up the twins. My daughter is *best* friends with Alexis."

"I'm glad the kids have friends," I say. Two more women push their way next to Grace. I'm deeply regretting saying yes to this trip to pick up my niece and nephew as more women gather around, forming a small mob. I'm pretty sure one ran her hand along my ass in passing. No wonder Sarah and Lex send their nanny to get them. They're like piranhas circling an innocent animal in murky water.

Heat crawls up my neck while the women look at me curiously. Grace grabs the Superman backpack. "Here, let me help you."

"No, I'm fine, thanks." I try to hold onto Wyatt's strap, but she yanks it out of my grasp with surprising strength.

"Did you hear that accent?" someone murmurs.

"To-die-for."

"I insist." Grace grins, all her teeth showing like a great white shark and I'm a little nervous she might bite me.

"Oh my god, it's Lex Ryan! Lex, can I have an autograph?" One woman brazenly thrusts a crinkled receipt and a pen in my face.

"Don't be so desperate, Anna!" Grace smacks her hand down, causing the pen and paper to fly out of her grasp.

"Actually, Lex is my brother." I lean down to pick up her pen, and hand it back to her.

"Ah! It's his identical brother. The *gay* one," a woman behind me in line whispers loudly. I get mistaken for Lex, my identical twin, a lot. Unfortunately, because he's the lead guitarist for the hottest country band in the United States, it's not easy for me to go out in public without women and men thinking I'm him. We both have black hair, blue eyes, and the Celtic cross tattooed on our arms. But you can tell us apart because my brother has *'Sunshine'* tattooed on his inner wrist for his wife Sarah and I have *'TJ'* scripted behind my ear.

"I've always wanted a gay guy friend," pumpkin-spice-latte Jennifer says wistfully.

"Me too!" a woman chimes from the back.

"That's nice." I grin, but it feels more like a grimace. *Shite, this is my worst feckin' nightmare. Where is TJ when I need him?*

"He looks just like Lex. It's uncanny. I didn't realize he was the father." A voluptuous brunette squeezes her way into the throng of women to get a closer look. *What in the bloody hell is taking the teacher so long to release these kids?* "Maybe our kids could have a playdate? Here's my number." A piece of paper is shoved into the back pocket of my jeans with a little extra squeeze.

"What's it like being a gay dad?" Jennifer asks.

"Oh uh, they aren't—"

"Jennifer, you can't ask him *that*." Grace frowns.

"But I bet it's really hard. What will you do when Alexis has issues that men don't know anything about, like getting her period? What are you going to do then? It's not natural for her not to have a mom."

Jesus, help me. "She has a—"

"Poor thing, she can always come to me with questions," the woman in back says.

"She's four!" I blurt out.

"He's clueless." Another mom shakes her head. "What's going to happen to Wyatt when he says he has two dads?"

"Absolutely fucking nothing," I grind out.

"Wow, potty mouth on that one. Let's hope the other dad is more sensitive." They all nod sagely, their lips pursed. I'm itching to go hide in the jacks until school is out. I run my finger along the collar of my sweater and tug on it.

"Wait, isn't he married to TJ?" someone asks behind me. "I'm confused. Are the twins theirs?"

Jesus, Mary, and Joseph, I'm drowning right now, trapped, and I can barely get a word in to explain to these *geebags* that I'm not the twins' parent. I just want to get to the preschool room door, grab the kids, and be on me fecking way.

"Out of my way, skanks." TJ pushes his way through the women circling me. "Halloween's over, bitches, put your broomsticks away."

"Where've ye been?" I grab his arm and hang on for dear life.

"TJ, is this your husband? He's delicious!" the brunette preens.

"Back off, Trish, he only likes dick."

Someone gasps then whispers, "I told you."

"I thought ye were getting Chase and Drew?" I ask.

"They're still out on the playground, so I thought I'd help you fight off the vultures." TJ winks.

"Hey TJ, playdate next week?" Jennifer asks.

"Let me check my planner." He takes his index finger and pretends to leaf through an imaginary planner while Jennifer eagerly awaits. "Yeah, no can do-sey. I'm all booked until the end of summer."

"Darn, maybe next year." Jennifer pouts and I wonder how many lattes she's consumed this morning.

"Do ye know these women?" I ask.

"TJ, don't forget the PTO meeting next week. You're in charge of cupcakes," Grace says, her beady eyes raking over us.

"I know, Grace. I got your twenty emails reminding me." TJ grabs Wyatt's backpack from her hands and rolls his eyes, whispering to me, "She's a tiger mom. Stay clear of that one."

"Why are ye on the PTO?" I look at him incredulously. How the hell did I not know how involved TJ was with the twins' and Kiki's kids' schooling?

"Kiki volunteered me last time I came to help her pick up the kids, but I don't mind. Preschool gossip is *lit*. Did you know they have a private Facebook group? It's like an underground fight club at this school. Everyone is constantly stabbing each other in the back. It's seriously the shnizzle."

"Please don't get any ideas," I grumble as we step toward the teacher. "I can easily picture ye organizing a fight club for preschool moms."

A middle-aged jovial woman walks to the door from inside the classroom. "Hi, you must be Connor, the twins' uncle. I'm Debbie, their teacher. TJ, looking posh as ever!" Debbie fawns over TJ before air-kissing him.

"Thanks, Debbie. Had to look my best for my gal! Love the festive fall sweater. So fab."

Debbie titters and blushes, smacking TJ playfully on the arm.

"Sarah wanted me to ask how the kids were today?" I interrupt the strange little love fest happening between Debbie and TJ.

"Oh, they were…um…better than yesterday. Alexis, as always, was quite inquisitive. She's going to be a cross-examiner one day." Debbie chuckles. "But our attention was mainly focused on Wyatt because he cried the whole time."

"Sounds about right." TJ bends down and scoops Alexis into his arms. She hugs his neck and kisses his cheek. It makes my heart melt. I take Wyatt by the hand as he sniffles.

"Thanks, Debbie. Hey buddy, rough day?" Wyatt nods and rubs his hand over his nose. It breaks my heart that he has so much anxiety at school. "Maybe we can go to—"

"Rahhhhhh! Uncle Teeeeee-J. Uncle Cooooco!"

"Chase Reed! Get back in line this instant!" a teacher shouts from down the hall.

Kiki's eldest bulldozes past the moms standing in line, right into my legs, and wraps his arms around them, almost taking me down.

"We've got him, Meg!" TJ calls to the teacher wearing a sour expression, standing with her hands on her hips. She shakes her head and follows the rest of the kids into her classroom.

"Hey, little dude. Next time, do what your teacher asks you to do, okay?" I pat his back.

"I want lunch!" Chase screams as I grab his hand. "McDonald's!"

"He's like a little pterodactyl." TJ laughs as we turn to leave. "You know the drill, Chase. We need to pick up Drew from the threes' room and then we can get lunch."

"You're not actually going to feed him McDonald's, are you?" Grace wrinkles her nose. I forgot she was still standing next to us. "Studies have shown that fast food is the number one culprit of obesity in children."

"Well, Grace, not that it's any of your biz, but yes, we are getting them McDonald's and then we're going to make them run a mile until they puke it up. That way, everyone wins."

I struggle not to laugh as TJ pulls me along, leaving Grace sputtering.

"TJ, call me!" Pumpkin-spice Jennifer bounces on her feet. He waves without turning around.

"I hate those bitches. They only want a token gay friend. I can spot their desperation a mile away. And Grace trying to act all high and mighty, like she's fucking mom of the year."

"I hate those bitches!" Alexis pipes up.

I glance at TJ and we both cough into our fists, smothering our laughter. I let go of Chase's hand and touch her cheek to get her attention. "Alexis, ye can't repeat those words to yer mum and da. They aren't nice to say." I try saying it in a serious tone.

"Then why did Uncle TJ say them?"

"Because some people, sweetie, are a nuisance and deserve to be called out on it," TJ explains.

"What does noosend mean?"

"You know how your cousin Chase makes a lot of noise during your favorite show, *Bluey*?" TJ asks and Alexis nods. "That's what a nuisance means."

I peer up at him and twist my mouth into a frown. "Not help'n, Uncle TJ."

"Right, right, sorry. Alexis, let's not repeat those no-no words to Mommy and Daddy. It will get Uncle TJ into some serious trouble."

Alexis nods her head solemnly. "Okay, Uncle TJ."

We stop by Drew's room and quickly collect him before Chase can cause any disruptions. Drew reminds me of the *Peanuts* character Linus, the little boy who sucks his thumb, always holding his blanket. I pick him up while Chase and Wyatt race out of the building.

"Bitches, bitches, bitches!" Chase spins around in a circle, throwing his arms up in the air like he's just been released from prison. An elderly grandmother stumbles, her features morphing into shock. She glares at us, shaking her head before entering the school.

"That is exactly why we should never have kids," I joke.

"Never say never," TJ singsongs. "Despite the minor snag of teaching our niece and nephews the word 'bitches', I think we'd be excellent parents."

"TJ, we make excellent uncles. But kids of our own? We're not ready."

TJ groans. "Connor, don't be such a wet blanket. You always say that. We're totes ready."

I shake my head. "We are constantly goin' in different directions. Didn' ye want to travel with Cam and Andie this summer to Greece? I'm thinkin' we should look into getting a dog before a baby."

"We're too busy to have a dog."

"Exactly my point."

"You're no fun." TJ pouts.

"Are we seriously having this conversation again? We've talked about this, *mo fhíorghrá.*"

"Oh, don't pull out the, my true love, soul-mate bullshit in that sexy Irish accent on me, mister." He looks around and whispers, "You know it makes me horny."

Ignoring him, I unlock the car. "I don't think we're in a position to have kids right now."

"Look, I've always loved kids and you are so good with Lex's little monsters. Studies have shown that most gay parents are more successful at raising children because it's a choice that we're making, not one we're forced into."

"Yeah, and our choice is not right now." I chew the inside of my cheek as I buckle Wyatt into his car seat. The echoes of what the preschool moms said earlier make me self-doubt. "What if they get made fun of for having two dads? What if we have a girl and she needs a woman's guidance? A mother figure, so to speak?"

"Then she'll have three mommies to help her out. Hello? Have you already forgotten Aunt Kiki, Aunt Sarah, and Auntie Andie? Earmuffs, kids!" TJ barks over his shoulder. Buckling my seat belt, I glance in the rearview mirror while the three in the back obediently cover their ears, all except for Drew, who has fallen asleep already. "I'll take down any punk-ass kid who tries to make fun of ours for having two fabulous, incredibly good-looking, well-dressed dads," he stage-whispers, folding his arms over his chest.

"Yer going to beat up a six-year-old for making fun of our kid?"

"Probably not beat up. I'm not the physically violent sort, but he'll wish he never messed with Bartie, I guarantee. I have zero boundaries."

"I'm aware," I say dryly. "Who is Bartie?"

"A conversation for another time." TJ pats my thigh.

"Okay guys, earmuffs off," I tell the kids. "You'd have to give up yer Jeep, y'know."

"What? Why?"

"Because it's not safe. What if ye roll it and the baby falls out? Ye know yer a shite driver."

"What do you propose?"

"I dunno. A minivan? Why are ye givin' me that face?"

"I'm not driving a minivan. That would kill my whole hot-dad vibe. No way in hell will I be caught dead in one, so don't even go there."

"It's called being a responsible parent and minivans have a lot of cool gadgets that make yer life easier gettin' kids in and out of the car. Lots of cargo space for work."

"Hmm, I'll agree to disagree. You know, Connor, there's never a 'right time' to have a baby, but I think if any two gay men can do it, you and I can. My clock is ticking."

I bark out a laugh. "Yer clock is tickin'? I hate to break it to ye, babe, but ye done have a clock. Men can have babies into their seventies. Hell, probably in their eighties if they can still get it up."

"I'm not going to be like David Foster having kids in my seventies. I'm serious, Connor. We're not getting any younger. If we wait too long, we're going to be past our prime and no adoption agency will consider us."

I glance over at TJ as I pull out of the parking lot and notice his taut jaw. "Yer serious about this?"

"Deadly."

"So, what do ye propose? How do we go about having one of our own?"

TJ squeals, giddily clapping his hands, swiveling his body to face me. "Oh my god, for real? Does that mean we can start? Because I've already researched surrogates and adoption lawyers—"

I gently lay a hand on his thigh and squeeze, trying to keep my eyes on the road and calm him down. "No, we're discussin' it, is what we're doin'. I'm only askin' questions."

TJ reaches down into his bag and pulls out a binder. "We can go through a private lawyer or go through an adoption agency. Another alternative is fostering a child to see if they are a good fit for us, or we can use a surrogate. Penny is my favorite. She seems like a real go-getter, although between you and me, I think she's going to be going through the change soon. Poor thing. She's like thirty-five, so it's a risk, but if she's willing…"

"Whoa, whoa, wait a damn minute. Who's Penny?"

TJ stabs his finger at the eight-by-ten glossy of a redhead, smiling and waving as she rollerblades in a bikini somewhere with palm trees. "This is Penny. Isn't she fab? I love that she's a rollerblader."

"Mary, Jesus, and Joseph, I can't believe we're doin'

this." I shake my head and grip the steering wheel while I try to wrap my brain around everything that is spewing out of TJ's mouth. "Who will be the donor egg and sperm?"

"I don't know, but we can pick out someone that will match our lifestyle and personalities. Obviously, she'll have to have a flair for fashion and be smart. Maybe red hair to match your Irish heritage and my hair? I think we should use your little swimmer."

"My little swimmer?"

"You know what this means?"

I cast a look at him, dread filling my belly. "We're not throwin' a party."

"No, silly, not yet, at least. We'll have to have *Nashville Next* follow us while we choose a donor. Do you care if they film you at the sperm bank? I mean, not actually watch you spank one off, but film you going in and doing the paperwork. If that's the course of action we choose to take, of course." TJ squirms in his seat, texting on his phone.

"Hold up. What is *Nashville Next*?"

"Oh, didn't I tell you? I swear I did, babe," he says distractedly, rummaging through his bag. "They're making a documentary of our journey."

"What do ye mean, 'documentary'? And what journey?"

"Uncle Connor? I'm hungry!" Chase whines from the third-row seat.

"Okay, we're almost there, buddy," I say.

"But I'm hungry now!"

TJ turns around. "We'll grab something at home. Two shakes and we'll be there."

"But you promised we could play on the McDonald's

playground! I want French fries!"

"I did no such thing, mister. You know Uncle TJ refuses to go into McDonald's. The guy with the red hair is scary and all those germs on everything? No way, Jose. You should eat something healthy anyway, like tofu."

"Who's Jose?" Alexis asks.

"But I don't want tofe-froo! I'm hungry now!"

"And I don't want to see their creepy mascot clown, but you don't hear me whining about it," TJ snaps back.

"I don't want to see the scarewee musk crown eider!" Wyatt wails, waking Drew up from his nap.

"I want Mama." Drew sniffles. "Where's Bankie? I need Bankie!"

"It's right here, bud." TJ picks up Drew's blanket off the floor and hands it to him.

Chase yells louder to be heard over the crying, "I'm hungreeee! French fries! French fries!"

"Uncle TJ, who is Jose?" Alexis shouts over the boys in the back.

"Jesus Christ, how do Sarah and Kiki put up with this?" TJ asks.

I give him a pointed look as I pull into the McDonald's drive-thru. "I'm not sure we're ready for this, Love."

"Oh, no, don't base how our kids will behave off those hooligans back there. Drew is very obedient when his brother doesn't stir him up and Alexis is normally quiet—"

"Uncle TJ, who is—"

"For the love of God, Alexis, it's an *expression*! There's no one named Jose. It just rhymes and sounds catchy. Everyone quiet or no one gets fries and you'll all have Brussel sprouts for dinner!"

"Way to keep yer cool there, Love." I bite down on my lip to keep from laughing.

Chase immediately erupts into cheers when he sees where we are. Wyatt howls about seeing the scary clown. TJ assures him we're not going inside and there will be no Ronald McDonald clowns.

"Yer doin' great, Thomas. Keep it up. Parentin' is a snap." I laugh before placing everyone's order.

"These monsters are the exception to the rule," TJ says, woefully. "Besides, we'll only have one to contend with. There are four of them."

Once the Happy Meals are passed through the window and we pull away from the curb, TJ hands out the boxes. "Do not spill any food, especially fries, in this car. Uncle TJ just had it cleaned and it's spotless."

I look over at him and chuckle. "Yer in for a rude awakenin' if ye want babógs."

He shoots me a dirty look. "Hey, I like nice things, and I don't need ketchup and greasy fries ground into our Range Rover's leather upholstery. Our kids will be well-trained angels like Drew and Alexis. Ooh, what do you think of the name Benny?"

"Benny? For what?"

"No, you're right. It sounds like a Jersey Shore musclehead."

I shake my spinning head and enjoy a few minutes of silence before a strange noise emits from that back seat. "Eeeew!" Chase shrieks. "Drew puked!"

I mutter an expletive and pull over. TJ looks back, making vomiting noises of his own. "Oh my god, I can't! Why does he always throw up? He's like the exorcist baby back there. Bhlep."

"Fuckin' Christ," I breathe out, rolling my eyes as I get out and open Drew's door.

"I want Mommy." Drew's bottom lip trembles.

"I know, buddy."

"Uncle Coco, I need help," Wyatt cries, while he tries to open his apples. He's upended all his fries onto the floor of the back seat.

"Give me a second, bud." I unbuckle Drew and stand him up on the sidewalk while I strip off his t-shirt. Alexis reaches into the baby bag and hands me a pack of wet wipes. "Thank you, Love."

TJ squirms in the front seat, pinching his nose. "I can't. I'm sorry, babe, but I can't do vomit." He leans over and rolls down all the windows. "Blurrep."

I ignore his dramatic retching noises as I wipe off Drew. Luckily, his car seat is okay since he only threw up on his t-shirt. I crouch down and feel his forehead. He isn't warm, which is a relief. "Get a little car sick?"

He nods his head as his bottom lip trembles. "I frew up on Bankie."

"S'okay. Let's get ye home and we'll wash him." I buckle him back in and throw the wipes in the fast-food bag. I grab Wyatt's apples and tear them open before he turns into a puddle of tears. TJ hangs his head out the window while I pull away from the curb. "A bit dramatic, done ye think?"

He pulls his head back in. "I had a tragic experience with vomiting once. Never fully recovered from it. Back in high school, I was part of an a cappella group. We were in the middle of a performance and the girl next to me vomited all over the microphone." He shivers. "I've never been the same."

"Uh-huh." I side-eye him, recalling the movie Kiki made us watch a few weekends ago where the exact scene played out. "Sounds vaguely familiar. I didn't know ye were in an a cappella group." I key in the gate code as we arrive at Kiki's house.

"Hello? It took years to train this voice into perfection."

TJ's the worst singer I know, but I chuckle, because I love his confidence. "Wasn't that vomiting scene from the movie Kiki made us watch? *Pitch Perfect?*"

"Oh look, we're here!" He unsnaps his seat belt and bolts from the car before I can even turn off the engine. "Bet I can beat you to the front door, Chase!"

Chase hurtles out of the car, running to catch up to TJ. I unbuckle the remaining three and grab their bags as they clamber out of the SUV. Surveying the damage of strewn fries and half-eaten cheeseburgers on the floor, I shake my head. Ketchup is dripping down the buttery leather seat, and a few fries are mashed into the carpet from their shoes. Fucking fantastic. I clean up the best I can and drop the bags in the entry hall while the kids run off. Sarah, Kiki, and TJ are chatting in the kitchen.

"There's Uncle Coco!" Sarah's eyes twinkle.

"Sorry Drew threw up." Kiki hugs my neck. "I forgot to tell you he can't eat in the car. Thank you for cleaning him up."

I hand her Drew's beloved blanket, Bankie. "Ye might

want to throw this in the wash."

"Thanks for getting the kids today. TJ was telling us how the other moms had you backed into a corner. I see you made it back in one piece, clothes intact." Sarah squeezes my bicep on her way to the fridge, taking out four juice boxes.

Kiki smiles as she shoves the blanket into a Ziploc. "Yeah, they love a tatted-up man with muscles, especially Grace."

"Ah, yes, well"—I smirk—"as soon as they found out I was the gay dad, they backed off a smidge, but thanks fer the heads-up."

"Ooh, ooh, speaking of gay dads, guess who's on board!" TJ jumps in place.

"TJ," I warn.

"Really? Congrats, you guys! I'm so glad you talked it over." Sarah wraps me in a hug. "I think you'll make an excellent dad."

"Remember, I called dibs on being their godmother." Kiki bops TJ on the nose with her finger before he can push her away. "Connor, I hope you said no to the name Bartie." She snorts and then her eyes bulge. "Shit, I hope that's not an Irish family heirloom name. Oh god, it is, isn't it? Why else would you want such an antiquated name that would scar your child for life? I mean, it's a lovely name—"

"*Kiki.*" TJ motions for her to zip it. She sinks back against the counter, her cheeks red.

"Did you get the film guys to record it?" Sarah asks.

"Wait, ye two've known about this?" I ask, incredulously.

"I mean, we've talked about it…" Kiki's eyes jump to TJ. "Briefly mentioned it this morning…casually in passing, really. Like we high-fived in the hall and I said you guys should be dads. It was seriously not a big production. Not like binders with 'Baby Ryan' bedazzled on them in rhinestones were passed around. Right, Sare?" Kiki gulps her coffee while TJ motions for her to shut up by slicing his finger over his throat.

"You are the worst at this," he hisses.

I try to simmer my temper. I'm annoyed he conversed with them about it before me. "Done ye think we should have talked about it before gabbin' to the girls?"

Sarah tips her head at Kiki. "Let's give these two some privacy."

"We'll be in the family room with the kids." Kiki grabs the juice boxes and they quickly exit the kitchen.

I spin on TJ before he has a chance to disappear. "I can't believe you, Thomas."

"What?" he whines, sitting down at the island.

"I put up with a lot. Lord knows I do, but done ye think we should have discussed this first before telling my sister-in-law that we're goin' to try to adopt? This wasn't even on my radar until an hour ago. She's gonna tell Lex and it will get back to my mom, and you know how crazy she gets."

"Oh, Maggie will be over the moon when we tell her we're going to adopt or hire a surrogate, which is the route I'd like to…" He trails off when his eyes take in my stiff posture and clenched hands. "Of course, you're right. You're absolutely right. I'm so sorry. I'm just excited for us to take the next step. To have a family. I think you'll be an incredible dad and I could dress him in the cutest suspenders and newsboy hat and we'll name him Bartholomew—Bartie, for short."

Heaving a sigh, I pinch my nose in frustration. "TJ, it's more than dressing them in cute clothes, although by yer description, yer already settin' him up to get bullied at school. They aren't something fun for ye to parade around. It's a lifetime commitment. We're raisin' a *human being*, not a French bulldog. And there's no way in hell we're calling our *babóg*, Bartie." I shove my hands in my hair and walk in a circle, tryin' to stay calm. How did this spin out of control so quickly? One minute I'm picking up my niece and nephew, and the next I'm being pigeon-holed into having one of our own. I want kids someday, but not today.

TJ's forlorn expression gives me pause. *Stop thinking about yourself, Connor.* He must really want this. I step over to him and place my hands on his thighs. Wordlessly, I bend down and kiss his pouty lips.

"I love you, Thomas. *Is tusa mo chroí.* You are my heart. But I'm not sure we're ready for this next step yet."

"Yet..." He holds on hopefully to the one word that hasn't killed this crazy dream of his. He threads his fingers with mine. "How can I prove to you we *are* ready? That I want this more than anything in the whole wide world? More than those Louis Vuitton suede boots I cried over in New York. More than the vintage Dior velvet blazer with diamond buttons we saw at auction!"

I press my lips together to keep from smirking, and look up at the ceiling. Heaven knows, I love this man. No one else can drive me to drink one minute, and have me laughing in the next breath.

"We can weather any storm together, Connor. Tell me

what to do and I'll do it. I *really* want this. With you. A family of our own."

I shake my head. TJ won't stop this new obsession until he wears me down. "Well, first, we will not be naming our kid Bartholomew."

"What about Bartie?"

"TJ."

"So Barclay's out, too?" He bites his lip, pleading with his eyes. I close my eyes and rub a spot right over my eyebrow where I feel a headache coming on. "Fine, we won't name him Bartie, Bartholomew, Bennie, or Barclay. What else?" He folds his arms over his chest and leans against the countertop.

I look into his grass-green eyes, so earnest and true. TJ has always reminded me a bit of Peter Pan, the boy who never wanted to grow up. In some ways, it endears me to him because it keeps life fresh and fun, but if I'm honest, it's a lot on me to step up and be the adult a majority of the time. *But isn't that what made me fall in love with him in the first place?* His zest for life makes all the colors in my life pop and fizz.

If I'm going down, there's no one else I'd want by my side, in a blaze of poopy diapers, sticky fingers, and the forever responsibility of another human being.

"Yer goin' to have to get over yer puke aversion. Kids puke…among other gross things," I say gruffly.

He nods. "I mean, I may have to go to therapy and maybe some hypnosis sessions, but I'm willing—"

"And if we do this, we're in it together. Not just me carrying the brunt of it. Ye can't leave me hangin' every time there's a mess to clean up."

He nods again, solemnly. "In this together, until drop-crotch trousers or fishnet joggers come back in style." I raise an eyebrow. He shakes his head. "Trust me, they're never coming back. If they do I hope I'm dead before that happens."

I crack a smile and lean in, brushing another kiss against his lips. "I'm not sayin' yes, but I'm not sayin' no, either. I need some time to wrap my head around this, okay?" TJ looks crestfallen as his gaze falls to the floor. I tip his chin up. "*Moi chroi*, this is not a no, okay? I can see how badly ye want this."

"I think Connor is right, Tammy Jean," Kiki says quietly, tiptoeing into the kitchen with Sarah on her heels.

"Yeah, this isn't a decision that should be taken lightly."

I smile gratefully at the women.

"Besides, it's not like you snap your fingers and everything will fall right into place and you have a baby delivered. It's going to take time," Kiki says gently. "As for *Nashville Next*, they have to know this will be a slow process."

"Kinky, hello? I realize that. You know my motto."

"Don't walk a mile in a stranger's shoes. You might get a foot fungus?" she asks.

"Ew, gross, I never said that. I *said*, don't walk a mile in someone's shoes *unless* they're Louis Vuitton. But no, that's not it."

"When life gives you lemons, squirt them into your enemy's eye and blind them?" Sarah smiles brightly.

"What? Do you two ever listen to me? I said when life gives you lemons, make lemon drop martinis." TJ rolls his eyes, a grin curving his lips. "You guys, come on, you know my motto."

"Never trust someone who smiles all the time because they're probably a serial killer!" Kiki snaps her fingers.

"I did say that, but no—"

"Glitter cures everything!" Sarah shouts, pointing at Kiki like she's a contestant on a game show.

"Always leave a little sparkle in your pocket!" Kiki shouts back.

"Never eat Brussel sprouts before a pool party." Sarah jumps up and down, clapping.

"O to the M to the G! It's when nothing goes right, go left. Seriously, do you *ever* listen to me?"

"I don't get it?" Kiki scrunches her eyebrows. "What the hell does that have to do with what we're talking about? And for the record, I have never heard you say that."

"I don't even remember what we're talking about," Sarah murmurs.

I snort and rub a hand down my face. "I think what he was tryin' to convey is when things don't go yer way, go in a different direction. And I second Kiki. I have never heard ye say that in the five years we've been married. How the feck do ye three Muppets run a business together?"

"Shut up, bitches! I can't hear my TV show," Alexis yells, standing in the hallway with juice dribbling down her chin.

"Oh my god." Kiki covers her face with her hand, quieting her chuckle.

"*Alexis.*" Sarah's cheeks blush a deep crimson. "Where did you learn that word?"

"Uncle TJ said when someone is boddering you, say,

shut up bitches.”

“Sare Bear, I swear, I did not—” TJ holds up his hands in defense.

“You are in so much trouble,” Kiki snorts as she doubles over laughing.

“TJ, did you seriously teach her that?” Sarah screeches. She grabs a towel off the counter.

“*No.* I mean, she might have overheard me at the school. Cracker snacks. She’s got the memory of an elephant! It’s not my fault she’s…gifted.” He looks to me for help, but I’m trying to keep a straight face.

Sarah wipes the juice off her chin as she crouches in front of her. “Alexis, we do not repeat that no-no naughty word, okay?”

“But Mommy, why can’t I say bitches? Uncle TJ says it.”

Kiki’s shoulders shake as she rests her fingers against her closed eyes. “And that, Uncle TJ, is your first lesson in being thrown under the bus by a five-year-old.”

“Zip it over there, Miss Polly Perfect. She probably learned it from Chase. He was shouting it in the school parking lot today.”

“Wait, what?” she asks, quickly sobering.

“And on that note, we’re gonna get a leg up.” I grab TJ’s hand as we quickly try to shuffle out the door.

“Wait until you have one of your own!” Sarah shouts. “And they say bitches in front of the old lady at the grocery store!”

“Already happened today. See you never, skanks!” TJ hollers back as I steer him toward the door.

“Mommy, what’s a skanks?” Alexis asks. Sarah groans.

I pause outside the front door. "TJ?"

"Yes, honey?"

"We still have a lot to talk about, but let's take this slow, okay?"

"Anything for you, my sexy Irishman." He smacks my ass and skips down the steps. Trepidation fills my belly because if I know TJ, he's already got a plan up his sleeve.

Chapter 4

Kiki

TJ's BABY TALK has made the seed I planted in my head a couple months ago start to germinate. I always thought I'd be content with my family of four, but not a day goes by when I don't think about having a third baby. It's turned into a weird private fixation of mine and despite trying, I can't seem to shake it. We need a little girl to balance all the testosterone in this house.

I know I'm a lucky bitch and won the lottery with Tatum. He's not only gorgeous and talented, he's also an amazing dad and husband. I should be satisfied with the three guys in my life, but there's always that little niggling voice in the back of my head wondering, *what if?*

Biting my bottom lip, I stand in the bedroom doorway like a total creeper watching my sexy husband. His tanned skin glows against the white sheets as he lounges bare-chested in black joggers, reading on his phone. He's recently had to get glasses to read the small print and it adds another layer to his attractiveness. Even after six years together, two wild boys, and two very busy schedules that sometimes pull us in opposite directions, the fire still burns strong between us.

I crawl onto our bed, smiling at the memory of when I had to strip off his leather pants one night after a concert. I test the give of the soft cotton material he's wearing and grin. These will be a cinch to take off.

He looks up from his phone and gives me a panty-dropping smile. "Is that black satin nightie for me?"

"What, this old thing?" I wink.

"What are you up to?" he asks suspiciously.

"Who me?"

"You've got that devil-may-care grin on your face."

I pluck his phone from his fingers and toss it on the nightstand. His hands glide up my thighs while I remove his glasses. As much as they make my girlie parts sing, they get in my way. I set them down next to his phone.

"I was thinking"—I thread my finger through his hair and straddle his lap—"about the time you begged me to help you out of your pants."

"There have been many times I've begged you to help me out of my pants."

"I'm talking about the leather ones."

He squints an eye, looking at me like I've lost my marbles. "What leather pants? I don't remember that."

I sit back and scoff. "You are such a liar, Tater Tot."

He furrows his brow and shakes his head. "I swear I have no clue what you're talking about. I've never worn a pair of leather pants." He leans forward and tries to kiss me, but I evade him, putting my hand on his chest, pushing him back against the headboard. He grins at me devilishly, his green eyes dancing. "I like it when you're feisty."

Damn, he's so fine, and normally I'd devour him, but he's lying through his teeth right now and I need him to admit he remembers.

"You seriously don't remember the time you went on stage wearing those hideous black leather pants with the rhinestones on the sides and then called me to come peel them off of you because the sweat had practically glued them to your skin?"

"No, but I should wear leather pants more often if they get you this worked up," he says thoughtfully.

"No, you shouldn't." I sit up on my knees. "What the hell, Tatum? I literally had to cut them off you. How can you not remember? It's the night we kissed and—"

He places his hands on my waist and pulls me flush against his chest, kissing me until I surrender and open my lips to him. His hand trails down my backside and squeezes my ass, pulling me closer. I whimper in his arms, the heat of his chest, the rigid bulge in his pants, and the masculine, woodsy scent of his skin sending my hormones into overdrive. The beat of his heart thrums steadily, while mine feels out of control.

"I remember, Coffee Girl. I was just messing with you," he murmurs against my lips, his husky voice making me want to devour him. "I could never forget our first kiss. You were wearing black leggings with a tank top and a hot-pink bra that drove me wild when I pulled your shirt off."

He pulls my satin nightie up over my breasts and circles my nipple with his tongue before pulling it into his mouth, tugging sweetly until I cry out. He groans as I tug on his hair and grind into him.

"Tater Tot…" I say breathlessly.

"I've got you, babe." He moves to the other breast. A light knock on our bedroom door gives us less than a second warning before it opens.

"Shit, I forgot to lock it." I tug my nightgown back into place. I slide off of Tatum, who grunts when my knee accidentally grazes his erection.

"Mommy? I can't sleep." Drew stands in the doorway with his blankie and sippy cup.

"Okay, bud, I'll walk you back to your room and rub your back until you fall asleep."

"I can't." He stubbornly stands in the doorway. "I had a nightmare."

Tatum sighs and pulls the sheet back on my side of the bed. "Come on, buddy, get…"

Before Tatum can finish the sentence, Drew runs to our bed and takes a flying leap on top of the fluffy down comforter. He snuggles in next to his dad's side and closes his eyes. Tatum looks up at me and chuckles. "Guess we won't be reenacting leather pants night."

"Guess not," I say grumpily, climbing onto my side of the bed. "Oh, I forgot to tell you. Guess who's going to try for a baby?"

"Who?" He puts his reading glasses back on and picks up his phone like we weren't in the throes of passion less than three minutes ago. I glance between him and Drew. This is our new normal these days. If it's not Drew being needy, it's Chase being naughty.

"TJ and Connor are looking into adoption. Although TJ

is really pushing for a surrogate, but I'm not sure Connor is a hundred percent onboard."

"That's cool. Connor will make a great dad."

"So will TJ." I pick up a magazine off my nightstand and flip it open. "Don't you think?"

"TJ?" He pauses. "Yeah, sure."

"You hesitated. Why did you hesitate?" I flip a page and look at him.

"It's just that Connor will have to do a lot of the heavy lifting. TJ will be the fun dad. You know, the Disney dad."

"TJ can be serious when he wants to be."

Tatum throws me a smirk. "Yeah, okay."

"Well, I think they should foster or adopt. It would be so weird to have a pregnant stranger living with you."

"They have to have the surrogate living with them?"

"That's what TJ wants," I say, stroking Oreo who hopped up onto our bed.

"Do they realize how eccentric he can be?"

"Tater Tot…you love TJ."

"I do, but you have to admit he can be a bit…extra at times."

I smile ruefully. "We both know he can be more than extra."

"Exactly."

I bite my bottom lip. "It would be fun if we were pregnant at the same time, don't you think? If you and I tried for a little girl?"

"Kiki, you can't be serious. We're so busy right now. We're going on tour in a couple of months. You were complaining the other day about how you can't keep up with the demand for your wedding dress designs and manage the style blog." He looks down at Drew and pulls the comforter closer to his chin. "Besides, the boys require so much attention right now. I feel like Drew doesn't get enough because of wild-man Chase. Throw in another baby and he'll be completely forgotten."

"We could never forget sweet Drewby."

"You know what I mean."

"But I'm not getting any younger and I don't want our kids to be too far apart. And maybe with a third baby, Chase will mellow out and help with his brother more."

Tatum lifts an eyebrow and gives me a come-the-fuck-on look. "Kiki, we can't even be intimate anymore without one of them interrupting. Case in point." He points his index finger at a passed-out Drew. Oreo looks at Tatum and meows. "See? Even the cat agrees with me, for once."

I toss the magazine to the floor and sigh. "I know life is crazy for all the reasons you said, but there's this burning in my gut. I feel unfulfilled, like something's missing. Our family doesn't feel complete, Tatum. When I hold baby Charleigh, it makes me want a little girl so badly. Sarah says she knows she's done having babies because she's happy to hand Charleigh back to Andie. She doesn't have that urge to have another. But, I do."

He turns on his side and gently wraps his fingers around my hand. "All I ever want is for you to be happy, CG. I'd give you all the babies in the world if I thought we could handle it, but babe, right now, I'm not sure we can. You are an incredible mom, a smokin'-hot wife." He waggles his eyebrows and I can't help smiling. "And an insanely creative businesswoman." He brings my hand to his lips and brushes a kiss over my wrist. My skin pebbles with goosebumps. "If it happens, then it happens, but we don't need to be aligning pregnancies with TJ's surrogate or having a 'let's get pregnant party' with fireworks and sparkle bombs timed to go off when my sperm meets your egg."

"That's creepy, Tater Tot."

"I know. I'm imagining what spins around in TJ's head when he plans shit like this." He leans over Drew and cups my chin. "I love you, Kiki. Forever and always, but let's live in the moment with the wild ones we have under our feet, okay?"

I nod, reminding myself that marriage is about compromise and learning when to push a topic and when to hold back. My problem is that I'm stubborn as hell, and once I get set on an idea, it's hard to turn that ship around. I'll let him think he's won this round for now.

"You're right, Tater Tot. We do have a lot going on."

He gently kisses my lips and I close my eyes, relishing the moment. In his sleep, Drew suddenly punches his fist right into Tatum's jaw.

"Ow, shit," he grunts. "The kid definitely has a right hook." We gaze down at Drew, who looks so angelic with his long eyelashes sweeping over rosy cheeks, his plump lips slightly parted.

I reach up to soothingly stroke Tatum's jaw. "Maybe he'll be an MMA fighter someday."

Tatum looks doubtfully at our second-born. "He'd have to get rid of Bankie first."

"Don't be hating on Bankie. It will be keeping you warm

tonight when he steals all the covers from you."

Tatum sighs and turns off the light. "Goodnight, gorgeous."

"Goodnight, Tater Tot." I stare up at the ceiling, tapping my fingers against my belly. I think about TJ's announcement, and can't wait to see him and Connor with a family of their own. Tatum's right, we're both insanely busy right now. Adding a third would be crazy. But a baby, especially a little girl, would make everything fall into place, right?

Chapter 5

Sarah

CHECKING MY WATCH for the second time in less than five minutes, I turn and grab the keys off the island. "Lex! Come on. We need to leave or we're going to be late."

I grab the emergency call list off the counter and walk down the hall to the playroom where the twins are watching TV with the sitter. "Hey guys, Daddy and I will be back in a bit. Becky is here to babysit, so don't give her any trouble, okay?"

"But Mommy, you said you'd play Barbies with me," Alexis says, stripping the dress off her new doll.

"I bet Becky loves to play Barbies."

Alexa frowns at the sitter. "But she doesn't know how to play like you do."

"I promise I will play when we get back in an hour," I whisper, kissing the top of her head.

"Mommy, don't leave me." Wyatt stands up from the couch and runs over to me.

"Hey bud, it's okay. We won't be gone long. Becky is

loads of fun and she said she'll play Candyland with you." I look over my shoulder and smile at Andie's old babysitter.

Unfortunately, I was in a pinch and needed someone at the last minute. Becky was my last resort, but at least I didn't have to cancel the appointment with Wyatt's therapist. Becky's eyes are glued to her phone, an earbud a permanent fixture in her ear. She blows a bubble and pops it with her tongue.

"But she doesn't want to play with us," Wyatt sulks. "Look, she's on her phone. I don't like her. I want to go with you."

I giggle nervously and look over my shoulder prepared to apologize to Becky, but she doesn't even notice his little tantrum, because Wyatt is right, she's completely engrossed in her phone.

"Jax is right upstairs, bud," I soothe.

"Why can't he watch us?" Wyatt sobs.

"Because Becky is eighteen and responsible...I think." *God, I hope.*

Lex bounds down the back stairs. "Hey, sorry, was on the phone with Tatum. Ready?"

"Yes, I was getting Becky settled with the kids."

"Hi, nice to meet you, Becky." Lex holds his hand out, startling her from her phone.

She stares at his hand and pops a bubble. "I don't, like, touch people's hands I don't know. Who are you?"

"The guy who will be paying you to watch my kids." He pulls back his hand and smiles over at me, perplexed.

"Cool." Becky snaps her gum, brushes past us, and flops down on the couch, ignoring the kids.

"Do ye think there's anyone home?" Lex knocks on the side of his head. I hit his stomach and chuckle, wrenching Wyatt's little fists from my shirt.

"Can you help me with him?"

Lex picks up Wyatt and whispers something in his ear. I quickly make my escape and run to the garage and wait for Lex. It's always hard for me to leave the house without Wyatt having a mini-meltdown.

A few minutes later, Lex slides into the driver's seat and the engine roars to life.

"I'm afraid to ask."

"He'll be fine. I called Jax downstairs to help. He took one look at Becky and informed me he was too old for a stupid babysitter. So, I made him take Wyatt down to the stables to see the new horse. Becky asked who I was again when I walked back into the playroom to say goodbye to Alexis."

"I'm worried about Becky. I mean, I guess it's good she's paying enough attention to people walking in and out of the room, right?"

Lex side-eyes me and it kills any positive vibes I was feeling for her.

"Let's try and make this quick."

"They'll be all right for an hour, Sunshine."

He slides his hand into mine while we ride in silence for a few moments on our way to Wyatt's therapist's office.

"I'm nervous about what Dr. Parker's going to say." I look over at Lex's profile and he clenches his jaw.

"Whatever it is, we'll make the best of it."

"It breaks my heart how much anxiety he has. He's so

little."

"I know, Love. Me too." He squeezes my hand.

We pull into the underground parking garage and take the elevator up to child psychologist, Dr. Sandra Parker's, office. The receptionist shows us into a tastefully decorated room and seats us in front of the desk. Lex and I sit in silence for a few minutes, holding hands. There's a knock, and Dr. Parker strides in.

"Sorry to keep you waiting, Mr. and Mrs. Ryan."

"It's no problem." I smile.

She pulls out a manila folder and opens it to her notes. "You requested this appointment because you want an update on how Wyatt is doing?"

I nod. "Yes, it's been a month and we haven't seen much improvement."

"Well, I don't like to put a time stamp on my patients. Everyone goes at their own pace, but I can assure you he is doing well." She clasps her hands together, her bland smile giving me no sense of relief whatsoever.

Lex shifts in his seat. "We understand everyone is different, Doc, but the preschool is reporting his anxiety seems to be getting worse and his meltdowns are becoming more frequent."

"I see." Dr. Parker adjusts her glasses on the bridge of her nose. She shuffles the papers in the manila file. "Well, Wyatt is doing quite well here. He solves puzzles quickly and when I ask him to color his feelings, they are usually bright and cheerful."

"Color his feelings, what kind of qua—"

I squeeze Lex's hand hard, effectively shutting him up.

"Can we see some of his drawings?"

"I'm afraid I would need Wyatt's permission to do that."

Lex snorts beside me and shakes his head.

"But we're his parents," I insist, leaning forward in my seat.

"I understand, Mrs. Ryan, but if you remember, you signed a contract after my initial evaluation of him. We decided it would be in Wyatt's best interest to keep things confidential."

"But I've changed my mind." I look to Lex and he nods in agreement.

"Wyatt and I have a code of trust. I cannot break that code without his permission. I feel confident Wyatt will share when he's ready."

I arch my neck to see a colorful scribble underneath a paper while Lex distracts her with another question.

"What kind of puzzles is he doing? Can I ask that, or do I need my almost five-year-old's permission for that as well?"

Dr. Parker smiles tightly. "Wyatt enjoys doing cat puzzles."

"Oh, so it's a board puzzle?" I ask. "He loves doing those at home."

Lex holds up his hand, crossing his leg over his knee. "Lemme get this straight, Doc. Wyatt enjoys cat puzzles and colorin'. What the hell are ye doin' for his anxiety?"

"I'm not sure I like your tone, Mr. Ryan. Wyatt and I chat about things while he colors and does the puzzles. They are relaxing, fun activities for him."

"Well, what kind of questions do ye ask a five-year-old with anxiety? Not specifically Wyatt, but a general question for any child."

"A general question I would ask is how is their day going? Or, what activities do they enjoy?"

Lex glances over at me and lifts an eyebrow.

"Does he say what makes him anxious?" I ask, impatient.

"I'm afraid that's between Wyatt and me. Patient/doctor privilege. I would let you know if I was worried he was going to harm himself."

"Harm himself?" Lex sputters. "Doc, he'll be five in a few months. This is utter madness."

"Mr. Ryan, please calm down."

"Nah, I think we're done here. She's away with the fairies, Sarah." He points at Dr. Parker.

"Okay, I think we need to go." I scoot my chair back, tugging on my husband's arm. "Dr. Parker, thank you for your time."

"Of course. I look forward to seeing you both again. Will one of you be dropping off Wyatt next week? Perhaps I can ask him to share a doodle."

"I will, yeah." Lex waves his hand as we head out to the reception area, which translates to Wyatt will not be returning to Dr. Parker's office. "Share a doodle? What the fuck is a doodle? She's about as useless as tits on a bull." he says as we get into the elevator.

"Lex, I'm just as upset as you are, but we need to think about the bigger picture here and that's Wyatt and what is causing his anxiety."

"Coloring, my arse. She's mental if she thinks she's gonna see my son again. How much are we payin' her to give him crayons and watch him put together a fucking cat puzzle?"

"I agree, but I'm not sure where else to turn."

"Sorry, Love, but that 'doctor'"—Lex air-quotes—"is not helpin' our son."

"I'm sorry I signed that agreement. I wasn't thinking at the time that we would need information on how he's doing besides 'he's fine'. I know he's fine, he's my son!"

Lex draws me into a hug and kisses the top of my head. "He's goin' to be okay. We're goin' to be okay."

"I'm so damn frustrated and I feel so helpless. Everyone has a million opinions to offer and I just want Wyatt to feel safe and secure. Is that asking too much?"

"No, Sunshine, it isn't." He glides his fingers through my hair and looks down at me with the most tender expression.

I cry into his shirt. "The one person who I thought could help him refuses to help us. That is so messed up."

"It is." He kisses the top of my head. The elevator doors slide open and we walk to our car with Lex tucking me to his side. "Let me make a few phone calls and see if we can't find another therapist who will share and want to work with us to make Wyatt better."

I nod my head and climb into the car. "Okay."

"I love you, Sunshine. Shilo rum do." He leans over and captures my lips with his. It's our little special saying that means everything will be okay.

"I love you, Lex. Shilo rum do." I smile against his lips. And I believe him, because we've been through some pretty tough storms before and have come through the other side with our hearts pieced back together.

Chapter 6

Connor

I TURN THE key in our high-rise apartment door in The Gulch in downtown Nashville and hear voices in the guest bedroom. Throwing my keys and the mail on our console, I shrug off my wet coat and throw it in the laundry room, my ears attuned to the two male voices chattering animatedly in the back of our apartment. I wasn't expecting anyone here tonight for dinner. Unease pricks the back of my neck as I walk down the hallway. I glance to my left at the empty living room and kitchen and creep to the guest room.

"Oh my god, Jean Paul Pierre Luc, you are everything James described and more." TJ's voice carries out into the hallway. I don't know anyone named Jean Paul Pierre Luc. I hesitate a beat, listening outside the door like a proper wanker. "I like this one, but maybe show me one of yours?"

"With pleasure," a male voice with a horrible fake French accent says.

"Ooh, it's so big. I don't know if it will fit." TJ sounds breathless.

"Monsieur, I assure you, it will fit," Frenchie says in a seductive tone.

What the fuck is going on in there? TJ and I have a strong relationship built on a solid foundation, but even the best marriages can have a niggling of doubt when someone unexpected is in your home speaking in hushed tones about…*big things.*

I close my eyes and take a deep breath right before I knock the door open so fiercely it crashes into the wall. TJ and the French dude scream, while a man with a camera swivels toward me, a guy is holding a boom mic overhead, and another is fiddling with the bright lights set up behind the camera guy. I hold my hand up to shield the blinding light and blink a couple times. *Am I on a bad porno set?*

"What the fuck is happenin' in here?" I bite out, anger turning to confusion. "Who is this sod and why is this feckin' eejit filming?"

TJ holds his hands over his heart. "Jesus, babe, I love when you go all Irish brawny-man on me, but cupcakes and sprinkles, you scared the ever-living bananas out of me! Connor, this is Jean Paul Pierre Luc, designer extraordinaire from the Jean Paul Pierre Luc Collection and that's Cal, Sam, Tina, and Brody from *Nashville Next.* Remember, I said they'd be filming?"

I blink a few more times and scrape my hand through my hair, trying to collect myself. Chagrined, I wave to the camera crew and reach out a hand to the French guy who looks like a washed-up eighties hair-band member trying out for Cirque du Soleil. His sequined black-and-white striped blazer is paired with red, tight leather snakeskin pants and lace-up silver sequined combat boots. A single red silk scarf is knotted around his neck, and he's wearing a hot-pink low-cut tank underneath the blazer. His eye makeup is garish, but somehow completes the look. He's holding a pink bedazzled drill in one hand and a piece of fabric in the other.

"Sorry if I scared ye. I wasn' expectin' anyone to be here. Connor Ryan, TJ's husband," I add, then take a step back.

"Eyes heard zo much about you. Za pleasure is mine, monsieur."

My husband is smiling brilliantly, hanging on every mispronounced syllable of that horrible accent like an eager puppy waiting for a table scrap. Can't he see right through this guy's phony act?

"Right. Um, TJ, can I have a word with ye in the kitchen?"

"Oh, sure. Give me a minute, Jean Paul Pierre Luc?"

"Ez no prue-blem. I'll measure what we de-scuzie, *oui*?"

"*Oui!*" TJ claps his hands and it takes all my self-control not to roll my eyes.

TJ follows me to the kitchen and when we're safely out of Frenchie's earshot, I round on him. "TJ, what the hell is going on? Who is that guy and why is he drilling holes in our guest room?"

He waves his hands in my face. "Shh, he'll hear you. That magnifique extraordinaire is Jean Paul Pierre Luc. He is the hottest designer in Nashville right now."

"*That* guy?" I chuff. "You've got to be joking. Is this something for work?"

"No, silly, he's drawing up plans to transform our guest room into a Las Vegas baby oasis."

It only takes a heartbeat before I see red. "A baby *what*?"

TJ chews his thumbnail. "I mean, the other option was Moroccan camel theme. He had this idea of a camel head spitting water into a fountain. It was a little much, you know? I thought Vegas Oasis had that *je ne sais quoi* appeal to it, don't you think?"

A loud banging comes from the guest room, followed by cursing.

"Jean Paul Pierre Luc, everything okay?" TJ calls out.

"No prue-blem! Zee jeest using my hammer! No prue-blem!" Frenchy shouts. Out of the corner of my eye, I notice Brody, Sam, Tina, and Cal filming us.

"Do ye mind givin' us a moment?"

One of them looks to TJ for confirmation, and I clench my jaw.

"Please, Cal?" TJ clasps his hands in front of him. The men lower their equipment and slink away down the hall. I turn toward TJ and he must see the steam shooting out of my ears because he deflates against the counter. "I can explain."

I cross my arms. "What the hell are ye doin'? We haven't even discussed moving forward with this and ye already have that gobshite designer in here? I don't want to even know how much he's goin' to cost. And why are those guys in our home filmin' us? What happened to privacy? I never said yes to this. It's been three days since we last talked about the whole baby thing. *Three* days!" My voice raises and I remind myself yet again to take a deep, calming breath. "I said I needed time. Ye promised me we were goin' to take this slow."

"Okay, I understand where you're coming from, but *Nashville Next* needs to film and I signed a contract that they would document our journey. They don't want footage of me doing everyday stuff. And Jean Paul Pierre Luc is doing this as a favor to me because I've referred several clients to him. Although truth be told, I think the only reason he took this project on is because he wanted to be on *Nashville Next*."

"How fortunate," I grumble. "TJ, I don't want Jean Paul Poop, whatever the fuck his name is, to design our baby room. We don't even know if we're havin' a baby or adopting an older child. Once again, ye jumped the gun and I'm goin' to be left holdin' the pisser."

"I don't even know what that means, but I swear to you, this will all turn out."

Another crash from the bedroom echoes into the kitchen. "*Merde*! Uh, no prue-blem. All eez okay, *oui*? Zee magnifique! *Très bien*."

TJ blanches while I arch an eyebrow and run a hand over my scruffy jaw. "TJ...we definitely have a prue-blem. I'm usually a pretty easygoing lad, but I've a pain in me arse with this whole situation. I want everyone gone by the time I get out of the shower and then ye and I are goin' to have a proper sit-down and talk."

"*Oui*," TJ squeaks out.

I head down the hall to our bedroom. I glance into the guest room and clench my fists when I see the baseball-sized hole in the wall and that idiot Jean Luc Poop trying to spackle it with fabric and mod podge. "TJ, fix this, now," I bellow as I slam our bedroom door shut.

Chapter 7

Andie

"YOU GUYS, I'VE had it with TJ's crew!" Arms crossed, I lean against Sarah's office door. She and Kiki are starting a new project putting outfits and makeup together for clients when they are on vacation, like they did for me when I flew to Italy on a surprise trip to meet Cam. They proposed the idea on Kiki's blog and it took off like wildfire. "Sorry to interrupt."

"No, it's okay. Come in." Sarah waves me in.

I sink into her couch. "They are out there filming me and asking questions, shining blinding light in my face with their stupid…lights, and I'm over it. Is TJ even around? It's creeping me out."

"That's super creepy," Kiki agrees. "Why are they here filming without TJ?"

"I asked and they said they were waiting for things to happen. I'm literally answering phones and replying to emails. It's unnerving. I got sick yesterday because it was stressing me out. And the worst part? I saw one of them pilfering through the fridge the other day, smelling a container of leftovers."

"Dammit, that's who probably stole my leftover Kung Pao chicken." Kiki goes to the door and shuts it. "Let's get Turd Jam on the phone."

She pulls out her cell and calls TJ, putting him on speakerphone.

"Hey, hey, girlfriend!"

"TJ, where are you? It's loud."

"Shopping for a client. Fab sale over at Haymakers and Co. What's up?"

"Is your film crew with you?"

"No…they should be there. Are they not?"

"Aren't they supposed to be following *your* every move?" I shout over Kiki's shoulder.

"Oh, no, they're set up there to catch any action, like maybe a hunky rhinestone cowboy coming to visit his wife? Or his hot Irish sidekick. Sorry, Andie, Cam is hot, but he's not famous."

"Well newsflash, I told the guys to stay away from work because Lee doesn't want them to be filmed." Kiki winks at me.

"You guys…" TJ whines. "You gave me verbal agreement to let them film you whenever with *whomever*. That includes Tatum Reed and Lex Ryan."

"Yeah, but when it's upsetting Andie and she can't get her work done, then changes need to be made," Sarah says. "I don't think they should be filming here. It's you they're doing the interview about, not us or the guys."

"I completely agree with Sunshine." Kiki nods.

"We'll talk about this later," TJ huffs.

"Actually, Tammy Jean, it's a three to one vote, so…"

"*Fine.* But I will not be forgetting this when I'm rich and famous and you want to come hang out on TJ Ryan's yacht and I'll say, sorry, those tic-tac bitches are not on the list."

"Tic-tac is not a thing." Kiki rolls her eyes.

"Don't roll your eyes at me, Kinky."

"You can't even see me."

"I felt it through the phone," TJ replies and disconnects the call.

"He sounds mad," I say, worrying my lip.

"He'll be fine."

Sarah leans back against her makeup counter. "I'd have thought he would want an entourage following him all over Nashville."

"Yeah, me too," I agree. "Something doesn't quite add up with *Nashville Next.*"

"Oh hey, while I have you both here, I have an idea to help TJ and Connor decide if they're ready for a baby." Kiki rubs her hands together like an evil mastermind. "I've done a little research, and the one I want is pricey, but I think it's going to work."

"Whatever it is, I'm in. Personally, I think TJ is way in over his head and he's dragging poor Connor down with him," Sarah says.

Kiki tells us her idea and Sarah and I agree that it's brilliant. While Kiki and Sarah chat animatedly about the different possibilities, I start to feel queasy. Nausea spreads like fingers around my esophagus, squeezing. "Um…I'm going to go tell the crew guys to leave."

I sprint from Sarah's office and make it to the bathroom

just in time to upend my breakfast into the toilet. The first time I thought it was the stress of being under a microscope, but now I wonder if I'm coming down with the dreaded flu that's been going around.

Chapter 8

Connor

"IT'S PISSIN' CATS and dogs out there." Lex sheds his wet coat and hangs it on an empty chair. "The sky has been pure shite for two days now. Good thing yer closed, people would be spendin' the night in here."

"Yeah, we'd be crowded for sure with the holiday season upon us."

"Christ, I've been up to ninety runnin' all over town today. I'll take a pint of the black stuff."

The bar is closed today, but I came in to do some paperwork. Lex told me he was picking up Sarah from work, so I asked him to stop in for a couple of scoops first. It's been a week since I came home to find Jean Luc Poop measuring for spitting camels, and I'm still in a twist over it. I asked Sarah the other day not to say anything to Lex until I could talk to him. Sometimes you need the advice from yer brother to give ye some perspective.

I wipe down the mahogany wood and place a fresh Guinness in front of my brother, before pulling one for myself. I raise the hatch of the bar and walk around, taking a stool next to Lex.

"What's the craic?" he asks.

"Life is fuckin' grand," I grump.

"What's got your knickers in a twist?" He quickly swipes the foam from his lips.

"TJ wants to have a baby."

"Huh. Does he realize that's anatomically impossible?" Lex grins into his mug. He's always thought he was the funny one.

"You're an eejit." I shake my head and take a sip of beer.

"Okay, sorry, but ye left that one wide open." He chuckles. "Look, you guys are incredible uncles, ye have a strong relationship which is a good foundation for any family. Ye have the patience of a saint—"

"Being an uncle is way different from having one of yer own. We can always give them back to ye when they turn into little monsters."

"Aye, true. But Mum and Da help us loads and you do too. It takes a village. We wouldn't leave ye hangin' in the wind, that's for sure. Didn' ye have this discussion before ye got married?"

"Yeah, but it was down the road. Now, life is chaotic and crazy. Shite, I'm not sure we're ready for a baby. He started dry-heaving the other day when Drew threw up in the car." I push my fingers through my hair and shake my head. "I'm busy with the bar and TJ is...he's..."

"Impulsive, self-centered, pushy, self-obsessed, loud, a little too charismatic, one can short of a six pack—"

I hold up my hand to shut my brother up. "Jesus, Mary,

and Joseph, I married a real wanker, didn't I?"

"Aye, he's no dry-shite, that's for sure." Lex chuckles. "But he's also caring and sweet. The most loyal person I know. And, above all else, he loves *you*, brother. Yer a jammy bastard to have a husband like TJ."

"Aye, I am. And I love him, but that doesn't mean we should have a baby together. At least, not right now. The timin' isn't great."

Lex sighs and sips his beer. "Probably not."

"But once he gets an idea in his head, there's no stoppin' the bastard."

"Nope."

"I won't be able to talk any sense into him," I say miserably.

"Nah. Probably not."

I side-eye my brother. "Yer really fuckin' helpful, ye know? I came home the other night to find some gombeen redesignin' our guest room for a baby room."

Lex arches an eyebrow. "What did ye say?"

"I got mad. He promised me we'd take it slow. Yet here we are, gettin' ready fer a babóg."

"Sure ye know yerself." Lex shrugs and grins. "Give it a lash. Ye never know, it might be the best fuckin' decision ye ever made."

"I don't think we're ready."

"When it comes to babies, yer never ready." He holds up a finger. "And no, I'm not mental. I'm just sayin' there's never a perfect time. Mum always said you were the smart one. You'll figure it out."

I grin and look over at him. "The gobshite is finally

making sense."

"Feck off, ye langer." He bumps my shoulder. "Look, I may not have all the answers, and I certainly don't have it all figured out. I've done a lot of things wrong in me life. If I could untangle that whole mess, I would in a heartbeat…but I made mistakes and I had to learn from them. I learned to forgive myself *for* them. Marrying Sarah was the best damn decision I ever made. She breathed life back into me, and I think TJ has done the same for ye. Was I ready to be a da? Hell no. But I don't regret one second of it. Not with Jax, and not with the twins. Are they easy? Fuck no. Every day brings something new that we have to navigate through. Do I wish somedays I could whisk Sarah off to a tropical beach on a moment's notice and say fuck it to all my responsibilities? Yeah, I do. But when they wrap their wee little hands in mine and say, 'I love you, Da,' it's the best feeling I've ever known. It makes all the hard times bearable."

I rub the spot right between my eyebrows with my thumb. "Shite, I think I might want that too."

Lex nods and takes a sip of his pint. "I know ye do. I see it in yer eyes when yer with mine."

I look down into my half-full beer. "I done have a choice, do I?"

"Probably not."

I glare at him, and he cracks up.

"Ye always have a choice. The question is, are ye gonna choose the right one?" He clasps the back of my neck and shakes it a little. "Welcome to marriage, little brother."

I sit back and chuff. "You must be off your tits. I was born one minute ahead of ye."

Lex shakes his head, then drains his beer. I quickly follow suit. He pounds his glass on the table, finishing his pint seconds before me and wipes his mouth with the back of his hand, a big satisfied smile stretching across his ugly mug.

"I still got it, little brother. Ye better catch up."

"Wind your neck in, ye lickarse." I laugh and pull two more pints from the tap, putting my baby drama to the back of my mind for now and enjoying the company of this *eejit* brother of mine.

Chapter 9

I FOLD MY linen napkin in my lap and pick up my menu, perusing the specials while Kiki giggles over my Jean Paul Pierre Luc story.

"Was Connor mad about the hole he put in your wall?"

I lower my menu. "Kinky, I've never seen him so angry. Like a switch flipped. It brought out all the tingles." I squirm in my seat.

"His yelling made you have to pee?" she asks dubiously. The couple at the table next to us glances over.

"Tingles, not tinkles. Jesus, take the wheel."

"What's your definition of tingles, exactly?" she asks.

"You know, the shivers…goosebumps. It was a total turn-on. He was like an Irish dark-haired Thor pacing the bedroom, all shirtless, angry, and dripping wet from his shower. It was so hot."

"I don't think I've ever heard Connor raise his voice or use the word 'tingles'."

"He didn't!" I snap in irritation.

"So, he didn't raise his voice when he used the word tingles when he tinkled?"

"You're annoying me."

"I know." She sits back with a smug smile.

"Can we please move past the word 'tingles'?"

"I'll try my best." She bites her lip, lifting her menu.

"Anyhoo, it was a whole new side to him I've never seen before." I grip my menu tight. "So hot and distracting. I have no clue what we were fighting about because all I wanted to do was role-play Thor. I even gave him a kitchen mallet while he was lecturing me, but he wasn't in the mood for my bollycocks."

"Stop right there. Whatever cocks and balls you want to talk about, you can keep to yourself. I don't need specifics."

"Well then, you'll be happy to know nothing happened. He went to bed mad, even after I tied myself naked to my chair with my tie."

"That's disturbing." She snaps her menu shut. "I hope you didn't get all tingly and tinkle on yourself."

"You've lost your best friend card. Are you happy now?"

Kiki takes a sip of water, regarding me carefully over the rim of her glass. "All joking aside, maybe this is a sign you two aren't ready for this journey yet. Clearly, you're not on the same page."

"Kinky, please don't be such a Debbie downer and wah-wah all over my child-bearing dream. God, it's like a sauna in here, don't you think?"

"Maybe you're going through the change."

"I swear, if I sweat in this silk shirt, I'm going to get pit stains and die." I check under my armpits, but thankfully

I'm in the clear.

Kiki wrinkles her nose while looking to see if anyone is watching us. "Stop smelling your pits in public, please. Someone will probably take a picture of us and it will be tabloid fodder. The reason I asked you to lunch today was because I wanted to talk to you about a couple things. The first is *Nashville Next*."

"What about them?"

"Are you sure their intentions are good? I mean, they haven't been filming you much, and the other day you said they're looking for action. You're fabulous and all, but something seems off."

"I mean, they want our story...but I might have stretched the importance of it a bit. We aren't the main focus. They're tired of filming me ordering coffee and sweatin' to Britney at the gym."

"What do you mean you're not the main focus? I thought they were following your baby journey. Who's supposed to be the star of this little exposé?"

"I might have told a little fib and pitched it as a story about Tatum and Lex and how we all work together, and that Lex's brother and I are trying to have a baby. Kind of like a fun little sitcom reality show. Like *Friends*, but kind of, not really. Don't be mad."

"Like *Friends*, but kind of not really? What the fuck, TJ!"

"I knooow, but when I got a call back from the producer, I was so excited. He kept asking questions about Tatum, Lex, Will, and Matt. I don't even know what he was asking, I just said sure, where do I sign?"

"TJ, you realize you're going to have to call them and tell

them the truth, right?"

"But Kiki, couldn't Tatum—"

"No," she says firmly. "He can't. TJ, you have to get these things passed by his publicist and manager. Hell, probably even by the record label. You can't sign him and the guys up for something without their knowledge."

"I mean, I did kind of get Tatum's permission a few months ago when I said, 'Wouldn't it be fun to be on a reality show?' and he said, 'Yeah.' So, I'm not totally out in left field here, right?"

Kiki groans. "TJ, you're on another planet. It's not going to happen. I'm happy for you if they want your and Connor's story, but I can guarantee Lex and Tatum will not be doing an interview or any kind of filming with *Nashville Next*."

"Kiki, I signed a contract."

"Well, maybe you should have consulted everyone first."

"Fine. I know you're right, I just got so excited when they called," I say glumly.

Kiki gets out of her seat and wraps her arms around me, kissing my cheek. "I know your intentions were meant to be good, but I don't trust *Nashville Next* not to throw all of us under the bus. They're known for digging up dirt. I'm sorry to kill your *Nashville Next* dream, but trust me when I say, I'm looking out for everyone's best interests, okay? I love you."

"Love you, too." I pout, stirring my straw around in my drink. "What's the other thing you wanted to talk about?"

"So, I invited you to lunch today not to talk about your pits or your tinkle problem or even *Nashville Next*, but because I wanted you to meet Gloria. She should be here any minute."

"Ooh, this is exciting. I love meeting new people. Is she a client?"

"No."

"Are we hiring her? Is she a designer? No, wait, a long-lost sister of Tatum's. Wouldn't that be so crazy?"

"TJ, no—"

"Is she your new nanny? Your new assistant? I'm so glad you decided on hiring someone because, no offense, but you look super tired and rundown. Like raggedy-ragged."

"Did you know that when someone starts a sentence with 'no offense', it's ninety-nine percent of the time quite offensive?" Kiki growls. "But thanks a fucking lot—"

"So that's a no on the assistant? That's a shame. Oh! I know. You guys went with my idea of hiring a barista for the studio, so I don't have to go get coffee every three hours. I'm so excited!" I clap my hands. "It's a brilliant idea if I say so myself. Thank you, Kinky. This totally is a mood changer for me after you gutted my heart with *Nashville Next*."

"She's not a fucking barista!" The couple next to us look over and scowl. Kiki leans in and lowers her voice. "Can I get a word in? *Jesus*. Maybe you need to cut back to two cups a day."

"I could never function on two cups. You might as well put my jammies on and put me to bed. Goodnight, Irene. Two cups…that's poppycock." Her piercing glare would turn most people into a withering crisp. I sigh and motion for her to continue. "Fine, tell me, who is this mysterious Gloria person?"

"Gloria is a social worker. I found her online. She works in the foster care system and specializes in helping those in the LGBTQ community."

"Nope. We decided we weren't going that route. Remember poor little Gino?"

"It can't hurt to see what she has to say about their program." Kiki looks up. "I think this is her. Be nice."

"Hi. Mrs. Reed?" An attractive African-American woman wearing a navy suit approaches our table.

"Oh yes, hi! Gloria?" Kiki scoots her chair back and stands to shake the woman's hand. "Please have a seat here." She pulls out her chair and motions for her to sit. "TJ, this is Gloria Rooney from Child Services. I called her because I thought it might be a good idea to talk to someone in case you and Connor decide to go the foster care route," Kiki says carefully. She mouths to me, *Be nice*, when Gloria's back is turned.

Gloria sets down her shoulder bag next to her chair. "So, I don't normally do this…meet at a restaurant, but Mrs. Reed thought it might be easier for you to meet in public."

"I bet she did." I sniff. "I'm so sorry to waste your time, Gloria, fabulous name by the way, but I don't think my husband and I would like to be foster parents. We're looking to adopt a baby."

Kiki kicks me under the table right in the shin, causing my eyes to water. *What the hell?*

"TJ, it wouldn't hurt to have Gloria explain a little about how the program works."

"Oh, I know how it works."

Kiki sighs. "He watched the Mark Wahlberg movie

about fostering."

"I'm afraid Hollywood doesn't always get it right. I'm not going to sugarcoat it, being a foster parent—a caring parent—is difficult."

"But, Gloria, what if I get attached to little Gino and he gets taken away? I'm not sure I could handle it."

Gloria looks at Kiki, who in turn rolls her eyes. "His imaginary foster kid is named Gino," Kiki explains.

"I see. Well, that certainly can and does happen. Sometimes an extended family member becomes aware of the situation and decides they want to raise the baby. Often, the grandparents step in. We believe in doing our best to keep the family together. In most cases, these children are not coming from stable homes. A lot of times the babies are born with drugs in their system and you're dealing with a screaming infant whose little body is being weaned off the drugs. You and Connor must understand that."

"Which is why I don't think fostering is for us. I'm sorry to waste your time." I straighten my silverware next to my plate while Gloria leans down to pull something out of her bag.

Kiki kicks me under the table in the same spot on my shin, and I vow to never let her borrow from my Hermès silk scarf collection ever again. I straighten up in my chair and grimace at my best friend, who's giving me some weird crazy eyes like she's telepathically trying to convey something. I widen my eyes in return and shrug. *This isn't an episode of Lassie, hon. No comprendo.*

She picks up her butter knife and squeezes it in her clenched fist like she's about to throw it across the table, straight into my heart. I place a hand over my chest and scrunch my brows. *Do it, sister, and I'll tell Tater Tot it was you who broke his favorite guitar, not Chase.* She lifts an eyebrow and drops the knife when Gloria straightens in her chair with a pamphlet.

"Here, TJ, this helps explain a little more about becoming a foster parent. You can share this with your husband. In case you change your minds."

I nimbly take the pamphlet from her outstretched hand.

"Gloria, tell me, if TJ and Connor have a change of heart, what is the next step for them?" Kiki asks sweetly while grinding her high heel into my foot. Aside from the blinding pain, I'm questioning our friendship and wondering if she should be committed.

There's no question. She should be. I shove her foot off and try to kick her, but I miss and stub my toe on the center table leg instead.

"Great question, Mrs. Reed. They will need to take our classes and we'll have to do a home visit and background checks, of course. Once they get approved, it's only a matter of time before a baby or child becomes available."

The server approaches our table and takes our order. After he leaves, Kiki focuses her attention on Gloria. "But it's not a guarantee the baby will stay with you?"

"I'm afraid not. Sometimes you can have the baby for a week, sometimes two days. Sometimes it's a year before the mom cleans herself up and the child is placed back with her."

"Even though she was on the D.R.U.G.S.?" I whisper.

"Yes," Gloria whispers back. "As long as she's clean and putting in the work, the judge always tries to reunite the child with their biological mother."

"But what if you've become attached to the baby?" I frown.

"It happens, I'm afraid. But we're looking for the best-case scenario for the child. A lot of foster parents jump back in, helping their loss by taking in another child."

"But what if we're the best-case scenario for little Gino?"

Gloria smiles genuinely. "I have no doubt you would be. I can put in a good word for you, but ultimately, it's the judge's decision."

"Well, then we're screwed. You know Tennessee doesn't protect LBGTQ rights. It's difficult for gays to become parents."

"What? TJ, that's not true." Kiki frowns.

"TJ is correct, I'm afraid. Tennessee is one of the states that allows tax-paying agencies to discriminate against LGBTQ in the name of religion. There is a chance a social worker or judge can deny you because you're gay."

"What? That's insane," Kiki says. "TJ and Connor would be the most loving, stable parents compared to where they might end up. I've heard some horror stories about foster parents only housing kids for the money or being sexually and verbally abused."

Gloria holds up her hands. "I know. We vet all of our foster families, but sometimes they fall through the cracks and the children suffer. It was a tough pill for the LGBTQ community to swallow. We *just* got the Supreme Court to allow gay marriage in all fifty states. That was a huge historic push for equality, but it didn't protect their rights for fostering or adoption. I'm not going to sugarcoat it, TJ. You and Connor are in for an uphill battle. Tennessee is listed as the sixth-most conservative state in the country. We've come a long way, but not far enough. There are still a lot of people who don't want equal rights. But that's why I'm here, so I can advocate for your rights to adopt or foster children. I'm on *your* side."

Gloria looks down at the chicken salad the server places in front of her. "Thank you, this looks delicious."

"Their chicken salad is to-die-for, great choice," I murmur, stirring my ketchup with a French fry. I'm distraught over the news that adopting and fostering may not be as easy as we thought.

We dig into our food and eat in tenable silence before Gloria sets her fork down and pulls out a folder and notebook from her bag. "Here's some more in-depth information for when you and Connor are ready. My card is attached."

"If we didn't want to go through all this heartbreak and trouble, then we should go through a surrogate. Is that what you're telling me?" I ask Gloria, giving Kiki an I-told-you-so look.

"Being a foster parent can be one of the hardest jobs out there, but also one of the most rewarding. You're saving a child's life." She presses her napkin daintily to her lips. "TJ, why don't you tell me why you and Connor want to start a family?"

I put down my cheeseburger. "I've always loved the idea of having kids of my own, of having a big family one day, but it didn't seem possible for an eccentric gay man in his thirties. And then I met Connor and saw him with his nephew…something inside me knew we had to have a family of our own. That we deserved it.”

“Has it been a difficult process for you so far?”

“Well, we just started. But, yes, we’ve had some surrogates turn us away because we were gay.”

“I’m sorry to hear that, but I’m not surprised,” Gloria says.

“Oh no, you didn’t tell me that.” Kiki covers my hand with hers. “This is so damn unfair.”

“I started my research after you had Drew. Remember when I was your doula?”

“I could never forget,” she deadpans. Gloria suppresses a smile.

“Well, right after Drew was born, I signed up with a surrogate agency, to see where it might lead, but nothing came of it. They asked what I was looking for in a surrogate and I said I wanted someone with shiny hair that loves to binge-watch *Emily in Paris* with me when Connor has to work late. Turns out that was not a checked box in my favor. I’m sorry, but if this woman is going to be living with us for nine months, she can’t be lounging on our couch in ratty sweatpants, eating my husband’s Greek yogurts and complaining how she never has time to wash her hair or change her underwear. Am I right?”

“Oh jeez,” Kiki mumbles.

Gloria chuckles. “I see your point, but TJ, are you sure you’re not lonely? Sounds to me like you’re more in need of companionship than a baby.”

“TJ doesn’t like to be alone, that’s for sure,” Kiki chimes in. I give her a look that says she needs to chime her way on out. She shrugs. "What? It's true."

"Are you and your husband from Nashville?"

"No ma'am. Connor is from Ireland and I was raised by my Nana Rose in Albuquerque. After college, I moved to California and Nana moved to Florida to a retirement center."

"Are you close to Nana Rose?"

"The closest. She's amazing. My parents died in a car accident when I was younger and my nana took me in."

"I'm so sorry." Gloria gives me a sympathetic smile. "Family is important. Do you ever imagine what would have happened to you if it weren't for Nana Rose?"

"No, never. Nana Rose rescued me when I had no one left. I don't like to think about what could have happened if she hadn't taken me in. Whenever I was sad, she used to load me in the car, roll all the windows down, and speed down the highway. She'd turn the volume up and play her favorite tape cassette, Laura Branigan's Greatest Hits. The song "Gloria" would come on first and we'd stick our heads out the window and belt out the lyrics. It made me feel like I was flying in the wind. Like I was invincible." I smile wistfully.

"That sounds like a wonderful memory."

Leaning forward, I hum the opening notes of the song, 'Gloria.' I nod my head and point when Gloria laughs and shakes hers. "Was it something that they said, are the voices in your head…"

"Calling Gloria!" Kiki joins me. We look at Gloria expectantly, and she dissolves into a fit of giggles.

I'm waiting for everyone in the restaurant to join in, so I can get up and do a dance routine while shouting "Gloria," but it doesn't happen. Instead, a few people glance our way and then resume their conversations. In my mind, it would have been magnificent, like a dance mob where we take over the restaurant, our hands raised in song.

"Can't say I've ever been serenaded before." Gloria breaks into my daydream.

"What? Oh, well, when you've got a great song with your name, it has to be belted out in a crowded restaurant."

"I like you, TJ."

"I mean, Glore, how can you not?" I ask, causing Kiki to snort water up her nose.

"You've got pizazz and spunk. That's refreshing." Gloria smiles, jotting down a few things in her notebook. She tucks it back into her satchel after we're done eating. "Call me if you decide to be a foster parent. You and Connor deserve to have the same rights as everyone else. I promise you won't regret it."

I stuff the brochure and information packet she gave me into my messenger bag. I doubt I'll ever call Gloria, but it was lovely meeting her. "Gloria, Gloria, calling Gloria," I sing her name and she giggles, gathering her stuff.

"Mrs. Reed, a pleasure. Thank you for lunch. It sure beats the cottage cheese and apple I brought to work with me today."

"You're welcome. It was nice meeting you too, Gloria."

"TJ, good luck on your journey."

"Thank you, Gloria." We wave goodbye and wait for the check.

"Dammit, I should have had *Nashville Next* here to film." I wipe my mouth with my napkin and toss it over my plate. "That serenade would have been a hit."

Kiki rolls her eyes and shoves a forkful of salad into her mouth. "You're welcome by the way," she says around a mouthful of food.

I sigh. "Kinky, I appreciate you, but how many times do we have to discuss not talking with your mouth full of food? It's *très* unattractive."

"I meant, you're welcome introducing you to Gloria."

"I know and I'm grateful you're in my corner, but I still think the surrogate route is best for us."

"Can I ask you something that will probably make your hair angry?"

"As if that's stopped you before?"

"Are you lonely? Is that what this is all about? You want a distraction for nine months with someone to watch Netflix and paint each other's toenails?"

I scoff. "That's redunculous. Are you preggers?"

"We're not talking about me."

"OMG, you're prego!" I jump up.

"I am not pregnant, you idiot. Sit down before someone gossips to the tabloids. Tatum is feeling a little traumatized after having the boys. He's not sure he's ready for another. But that's not the point. We're talking about Y.O.U., as uncomfortable as it's making you right now, which is strangely peculiar since you love talking about yourself. I mean, Sarah, Andie, and I have been busy with work and our families. I can't remember the last time the four of us went out."

"One hundred and forty-two days ago, twelve hours, and thirteen minutes." I stir my iced tea with my straw. "But I'm not counting or anything. Look, I get it. You guys have families and you're busy."

Kiki pouts her lips, her eyes softening. "I'm sorry, TJ. We need to do something asap. But is that really what's going on here? You're bored and lonely? You guys could always get a pet."

"Kiki, you know I totes adores you—"

"But?"

"But, you're wrong. I want a family. I want what you guys have."

"You didn't mention Connor…does he want it?"

"Of course he does."

She lays her fork down and looks at me with her know-it-all, smug, I'll-embarrass-you-if-you-don't-listen, eyes. "TJ, you can't keep doing this stuff behind Connor's back. If you're in this together, then you're going to have to *do* this together. And I'm not so sure Connor wants to do surrogacy, which is why I set this meeting up."

"He does, Kiki. He's totes on board. We're doing interviews next week…*together*. Look, I know I should involve Connor more, but he won't give me a decision and time is a ticking. You heard Gloria. We're climbing an uphill battle and if I have to steamroll over Connor to get up that proverbial hill, then hell or high water, sister."

"You're doing it all wrong, Tammy Jean."

"Thanks for the four-one-one, Kinksadoodle," I bite out. "But I've got this, okay? Okay. Should we order dessert? At least a cappuccino. OMG, that rhymes with Gino." I run my index finger from the corner of my eye down my cheek, like I'm crying.

She frowns, placing her napkin next to her plate. "Let's say Connor *does* want a baby. Pushing him in the wrong direction will only make him push back. He's freaking Irish, for fuck's sake. Do you know how stubborn they can be?"

"Duh, I'm married to the man."

"I know Connor wants to know that he has choices. You *are* steamrolling right over him." She lays her credit card down on the bill while I pretend to study the dessert menu. "Listen to your bestie for the restie, Teej. You need to *woo* Connor. Prove to him you can handle whatever comes your way and that you're in this together. He'll come around."

"And if he doesn't?"

"Then you're going to have to cross that bridge when you get to it. Come up with an alternative plan that will make you both happy."

"And how do you propose I *woo* Connor into wanting a baby, Dr. Phil?"

"I thought you'd never ask." She claps her hands, procuring a large box from under the table. I stare at it, perplexed I hadn't noticed it before. "Open it. It was my idea and I must admit a brilliant one. It's from the three of us." She nods to the white box with the blue satin ribbon. Opening the top, I dig through the matching blue tissue and gasp.

"Is this what I think it is?"

"Yep. The Baby Pro 2000. It records all of your baby's cries, sleep times, feedings, diaper changes, car seat time, and other stuff." She arches her neck and points to the instruction manual I've dug out of the box. "We'll know if you're feeding the baby because it goes to the app on our phones. But not yours. This is pure trial for you and Connor."

"Can I change its onesie? This shade of blue is hideous. Like a sad scrap of hospital scrubs."

"It tracks outfit changes as well, so yes. Unfortunately, the company preprogrammed a name. I'm not sure if you can change it or not." She rips the instruction manual out of my hands.

"What's his name?"

"BB-2."

"He's named after a *Star Wars* droid? What the hell, Kiki? I can't name my kid BB-2."

"The *Star Wars* droid was BB-8. We think it's kind of cute. It's short for Baby Blue model 2."

"I'm supposed to call my baby, Baby Blue? That's horrific."

She gives me her stop-being-a-dumbass look. "It's not a real baby. This is a trial to show Connor you guys are ready for this. *Comprende?*"

"Fine. Come on, Benji, let's take you shopping for some appropriate clothes."

"Benji?" Kiki grins.

"I shall call him Benjamin Blueberry."

"Because that's not gay or anything."

I smile. "It's perfect, thank you. Connor is gonna love it."

"Come on, let's go shopping. You'll need diapers, formula, and a car seat. Remember, follow the instructions and you'll be fine."

The bitch is lucky I forgive easily, because this just might work.

Chapter 10

Sarah

"JAX, I'M LEAVING for an appointment! Your dad's down at the barn," I shout up the stairs. He doesn't respond, so I take a few steps up and call again. "Jax, can you hear me? Boys?" I bite my fingernail. He told me this morning he was going to be studying for a chemistry test in his room with his friend Sam after school. I didn't see him when they got home, but I know they're up there from the music playing. He's been so lackadaisical about his grades lately that I was thrilled to hear he had a study buddy and they were taking this test seriously.

I check my watch and groan. I'm going to be late for my appointment if I don't leave in a few minutes. I spring up the stairs toward Jax's room. He's fifteen now, almost sixteen, and he's been a good kid with a few lasting issues with his mom. I can't blame him. Lex's ex, Alana, has always been manipulative and selfish, and his dad was never in the picture. It's a wonder Jax turned out to be such a great kid.

"Jax?" I want to be the cool parent and not barge in, but I'm late, which calls for Cool Mom to take a back seat. I turn the knob and swing the door open. My mouth drops open and my eyes widen. "Oh my god, oh my god, I—oh god."

"Mom, get the fuck out!"

But I can't. I stand there, frozen, my hand glued to the doorknob. Sam must be short for Samantha. It's a pretty name for the attractive teenage girl currently lying naked under my equally buck-naked teenage son.

"Mom," Jax shouts again, spurring me into action.

"Shit, I'm…" I turn on my heel and slam the door shut.

I pause in the hallway, not sure which direction to turn. Lex…I need Lex for this one.

"Jax, you and Sam need to get dressed and be downstairs in the office in ten. No, five!" My shouting voice sounds steady, but I'm shaking like a leaf. He can't ejaculate in five minutes, can he? The thought of him ejaculating is too much for my brain to handle. Why does the word 'ejaculate' keep spinning around in my head? *Gross, stop thinking about him doing that, Sarah!*

I'm not a prude by any stretch of the imagination, and I've seen my share of people doing whatever they please on tour, but seeing your teenage son in the act is something I wish I could burn from my retinas. *Please, God, tell me he's using protection.*

Lex is down at the stables, so I type out a text telling him to get his ass up here pronto. I call my appointment and cancel, and settle the twins in the playroom with their favorite show and some snacks.

"Sunshine? What happened? What's wrong?" Lex shucks off his cowboy boots at the back door before jogging into the kitchen.

"Everyone is okay," I say tentatively. Lex visibly relaxes, his shoulders lowering as he heaves out a sigh.

"Shite, ye had me running like a wild man up here. Weren't you supposed to be leaving for an appointment? Do ye need me to watch the twins?"

I hold up my finger. "Jax is studying chemistry upstairs with his friend, Sam."

"Yeah, so?" He shrugs, putting his hands on his hips. "You called me up from the stables to let me know he was studying?"

"Did you know Sam is short for Samantha?" I huff, flinging my arms out.

"I can't say I did, but what's the big deal?"

"I caught them studying biology instead of chemistry…horizontal in his bed."

Lex scrunches his brows and a split-second later his eyes widen. "Shite."

"Yeah, shite. And I walked in on them."

Lex covers his mouth with his hand and silently shakes. I hit him with the dish towel. "It's not funny! I'm scarred for life."

"Awe, Sunshine, you'll survive." He pulls me into his arms and kisses my lips. "Mom walked in on me once and chased the girl out with her broom all the way down to the pier. The lass was so scared she jumped naked into the water. I was thirteen and it was my teenage babysitter…" He chuckles and shakes his head.

I roll my eyes. "Thanks for the good-ol'-days visit down memory lane, but I didn't chase her out. I stood there like a pervert staring at them. I couldn't move." Lex's body shakes again with laughter. I lean away from him, pressing my hand to his chest to push him away. "It was humiliating. I can't believe he was having sex in our house with the kids downstairs. What if Alexis walked in on them? Imagine the endless amount of questions she would ask. Or Wyatt? He would have started crying for sure. Jesus, the least he could have done was lock his door."

"Okay, okay, shh. I'll talk with him, Sunshine." He buries his nose into my neck.

"Yeah, you will, because they're waiting in the office right now."

"Now?" He frowns. "I was hopin' ye and I could sneak back to our room and—"

"Lex Finlay Ryan, get your ass in there right now."

Lex drops his arms. "Fecking teenagers."

"Have you talked to him about using protection?"

"Yes, Love. I've had every talk under the sun with him."

"Apparently you need to have a repeat course on sex-ed."

We walk toward his office and open the double doors. Jax and Sam are fully dressed, sitting in the two chairs in front of Lex's desk. Samantha looks over her shoulder and her cheeks bloom crimson.

"Fuck, Jax," she mutters. "Your dad is home? I am officially dead."

Jax doesn't answer her, choosing to stare intently at a spot on the floor. His knee bounces manically up and down. Lex sits down in his chair while I lean against the wall. He smiles at Samantha, who immediately looks down at the same spot Jax is so interested in.

"What's the craic?"

Samantha looks from Lex to Jax, her lips parting. "Um, Mr. Ryan sir, we weren't smoking crack."

"It's an Irish expression," Jax whispers. "He's asking what's the story."

Samantha looks thoroughly confused, and I have to bite my lip to keep from smiling. Irish slang has been challenging to learn for this Tennessee girl, especially when Lex and Connor go back and forth. I'm completely lost when the whole family gets together.

"I heard you two were found in a compromising situation. Ye've made a right bags of this, Jax."

"Da," Jax groans, his face flushing.

"Mr. and Mrs. Ryan, I can explain—" Sam starts, but Lex holds up his hand.

"No need to explain. We're all adults here, are we not? And as adults, I assume you've been tested for STDs and you were practicing safe sex?"

"I, uh…" Samantha looks at Jax with wide eyes. "*Are you clean?*" she hisses.

"Ah, lass, that should've been a question before ye got naked with my son. Does he have a gammy penis?" Lex picks up a pen and holds it up, inspecting it like it's a model of a penis.

Samantha looks horrified. "What's a gammy penis?" she asks Jax.

"Da, stop. You're embarrassing me." Jax shifts in his seat and I have to hold myself together to keep from giggling.

"It means 'wonky'. Was it weird or is our Jax here a well-endowed stallion?"

"Da!" Jax barks, standing up. "Stop, please."

Lex laughs and sits back in his chair, flipping the pen between his fingers. "Sit down, boyo, I'm only messing with ye. But in all seriousness, when ye have sex in my house with yer mot under *my* roof, I need to make sure ye covered yer bases. Did ye use protection?"

"Yes," he grouses, sitting back down. "She's not my mot, we're chemistry partners."

"Ah, I see." Lex looks at Jax thoughtfully. "Well, yer mum and I can't stop ye from havin' sex with future Colleens, but ye need to be mindful of yer family. One of the twins could have busted in on ye."

"Shite," Jax whispers.

"Yeah, shite."

"Um, what's a mot and who's Colleen?" Samantha interrupts.

"Nothing, it means a girl," Jax grumbles.

The door to the office opens and Alexis walks in. "Mommy, the show ended. Hi, Daddy."

"Alexis, what have we told you about knocking?" I look pointedly at Jax, who shrinks in his seat.

"Hey, Mouse. Give us one more minute and we'll be done here, 'kay?"

"Okay, Jose." Alexis looks at Samantha curiously and then at Jax. "Jax, your skanks is pretty. Later, bitches." She blinks and then walks out like she didn't just light a bag of shit on fire and throw it in the middle of the room.

I slide my hand down my face and groan. Lex gives me a pointed look. "Where the hell did she pick that up from?"

"One guess." I fold my arms over my chest. *I'm going to fucking kill Uncle TJ.*

"Um, Mr. Ryan? Can I get your autograph?"

"I think we're past autographs, Samantha," I say before Lex can dig in his desk drawer for paper. The nerve of this girl.

Jax gets up, grumbling, and stomps out of the office. Samantha grabs her backpack off the floor. "It was, um, nice to meet you. I'm, uh, sorry about our…er, study session." She dashes out the door.

Closing my eyes, I pinch the bridge of my nose. "We're screwed."

"Yup." Lex drops the pen and leans back in his chair. "We've got a teenager."

"A sexually active one. I'm so not prepared for this."

He reaches out his arms, coaxing me toward him. He pulls me onto his lap. "Ah, Sunshine. He's just like me at that age."

"Is that supposed to make me feel better? Because it doesn't. And I can't stop Alexis from talking like she's Cardi B. And Wyatt's in therapy. What are we doing wrong, Lex? Do I need to cut back on work and be more present here? Maybe we shouldn't all go on tour with you this summer."

"Shh, Love. It's going to be okay." He kisses my neck and I relax against him. "You and I have weathered worse than this. Yer comin' on tour with me. Shiloh Rum Do, Sunshine."

"Shiloh Rum Do."

"Mommy, Wyatt is crying!" Alexis yells from the other room. "Shut up, bitches, I can't hear the show."

"Jesus, Mary, and Joseph, she's got a mouth on her. Mom will wash her mouth out with soap if she hears that."

I roll my head back and forth against his chest. "She's like a parrot picking up all the bad words."

Lex smiles. "I've got this. Go take a hot bath and relax."

I nod, relenting, because suddenly I feel exhausted. When did life get so complicated?

Chapter 11

Connor

I ARRIVE HOME from work around midnight and walk into a crime scene. Pausing in the living room archway, I take in my surroundings. It looks like a bomb went off in here. TJ is passed out on our sectional, with Kiki's youngest, Drew, draped across his chest, snoring. Colorful marker is all over the side of TJ's face, down his arms, and there's paint in his hair.

I hold my fist to my mouth and try not to laugh. Pizza boxes and plates with half-eaten crusts are strewn across the coffee table, juice boxes are toppled over, leaking sticky liquid down the side of the table, and there's popcorn all over the couch and floor. A massive blanket fort is set up in front of the television. I step over and lift a blanket to discover Kiki's eldest hellion, Chase, curled up under a blanket, hugging a realistic-looking baby, also covered in marker. Something moves beside him and I jump back. *Is that a cat?*

I walk back over and nudge TJ while I pick up the remote and flip off the movie they were watching.

"I swear, Officer, he was in my care the whole time," TJ mumbles in his sleep.

"TJ." I shake his shoulder.

"Gladys, don't hang up," he yelps, sitting straight up. Drew slides down next to him like a sack of potatoes.

"Babe, it's me. I'm home."

TJ blinks rapidly and covers his hand with his chest while I gently pick up Drew and walk him down to the guest room. I tuck him into the bed and check his breathing because he hasn't made a peep with the transition. He surprises me by suddenly rolling over, his eyes fluttering open. I make a shushing sound and he grabs his blankie, sticks his thumb in his mouth, and closes his eyes. Lights out.

"I must have crashed." TJ startles me. Standing in the doorway, he runs a hand over his hair, grimacing as he pulls popcorn out of it.

"I didn' know we were havin' the boys over for a sleepover."

"I didn't realize you were working so late."

"I texted you. Mac called in sick, so I had to stay." I kiss him before sliding past, heading toward the living room.

"Ah, well, that explains it. Chase hid my phone, and my watch died. You should have emailed me."

"Emailed you?" I laugh. "My bad. Next time I'll send a text, call, email, and let the post office know." I pick up the pizza boxes and set them on the counter. "Funny thing, I swear I saw a cat in the tent with Chase, but it's not Oreo or the spazzy white one."

TJ nibbles on his thumbnail. "Don't be mad."

"TJ." I hang my head and shake it before grabbing a wet rag to clean up the spilled juice.

"You said we should get a puppy, but they're a lot of work."

I pause in my cleaning and look up. "That didn't equate to getting a cat."

TJ holds his hands up. "But a cat is easy. And I know you're not allergic because we've been around Kiki's cats, and I thought it would be a good start in our baby plan. The boys and I went to the Humane Society this afternoon. Chase wanted to name him Mr. Poop, which Drew thought was hysterical, but I said we should wait for you to help pick out a name. Please don't let it be Mr. Poop. Can you imagine Nana Rose knitting a poop emoji on a sweater for him? Not to mention, she's a girl."

"Hmph," I grumble while I clean up the popcorn. TJ fluffs the pillows and cautiously looks over at me. I straighten up and fold my arms over my chest. "Ye know, a cat is not comparable to adopting a baby."

"I *know*, but I wanted to show you I can take care of a living creature." He plops himself down on the couch, his eyes suddenly widening. "Crap, where's Benjamin Blueberry? Shit, shit, shit." He flips a couch cushion and then kneels on the floor to look underneath.

"Is Benjamin Blueberry the cat?"

"Uh, not exactly."

I run my fingers through my hair. "Christ, what other animal did ye bring home?"

"He's a fake doll-baby the girls gave us to practice with,

but apparently, he's wandered off. Benji? Where are you?"

"Uh, Love, I don't think the doll is goin' to answer ye back, and if it does, I want it the fuck out of me house."

"Benjamin Blueberry?" TJ claps his hands, searching the room. "It's time for bed."

"Is Benjamin Blueberry wearing a Gucci onesie? If so, he's sleeping with Chase."

TJ rushes over to the fort Chase is sleeping in and peers inside. Placing a hand on his chest, he sits back. "Oh, thank God. If I had lost two in one night…"

"What do ye mean, lost two in a night?" I move a pizza box off a chair. "And why are ye covered in marker?"

"This?" TJ looks at his arm. "Well, it all started when we were having a dance party and the 'I Like You' video with Doja Cat came on and Chase told me I couldn't pull off a face tattoo like Post Malone, and I said the hell I can't." TJ snaps his finger in an arch. "But then it got a little out of control. Drew got in on the action and colored all over my arms. I think I look pretty fly for a white guy if I do say so myself."

"Please don't ever say that phrase again."

"Then we played hide-and-seek. Chase got bored after two rounds though, and we forgot about Drew, who was hiding in the laundry room for an hour, so that was fun having a panic attack when I suddenly remembered he was missing and couldn't find him. God bless Gladys at nine-one-one. She's the real hero of the story for helping me breathe into a paper sack over FaceTime. After that, we ordered pizza and built a fort. I love those two, but Jesus, they're demanding."

"Wait a minute. Ye didn't realize Drew was missing for an *hour*?"

"I mean, he's so damn quiet and Chase is a nonstop attention-seeking chatterbox that requires endless amounts of patience. Benji kept crying and needing a diaper change. I thought I was going to lose my mind. I didn't even realize Drew was missing. Again, thank God for Gladys, who talked me off the ledge and told me to canvas every room in the apartment. Poor little Drew-bear was sitting in the laundry room closet sucking his thumb with Bankie. Oh my god, do you think I've scarred him for life?"

"He'll be fine. Sounds like ye had quite a night on yer own." I sit down next to him and take his hand in mine, looking around at the war-torn living room. Even though the house is a complete mess, it's kind of nice coming home to tuck little ones into their beds. And it's nice to see TJ all grumpy and tired with food in his hair, trying, because I asked him to.

The calico cat crawls out from the fort and walks over to us, jumping up on the couch next to TJ. She sits and stares at me with an owlish expression. I reach out and let her smell my hand. "I think we should name the cat Bartie. That way, when we have a baby, there's no chance in hell our kid will get stuck with that name."

"Thank God you're saying okay to the cat because I couldn't return her to a life behind bars…wait, did you say *when* we have a baby? Not if, but when? Does that mean down the road in ten years or…?"

He looks up at me hopefully and my heart swells. "*Mo chroi*, I think I'm ready. Let's do it."

TJ pulls me into a strangling hug, scaring Bartie off the couch. He screams silently into my chest and squeezes my biceps.

"Are those screams of joy?"

"Yes! I don't want to wake up Chase. He's like a Chihuahua on crack."

After a moment, I untangle myself from him and look into his grass-green eyes. "There are goin' to be some rules, though."

"Yes, yes, whatever you want."

"I need to be a part of the decision-making. No more Jean Luc Poop or tellin' the girls things before we discuss them, or bringin' home pets from the Humane Society. If we're goin' to do this, we're goin' to do it together."

"Totes agree. One hundred million bazillion percent."

"I am open to adoption or surrogacy, but I think we should start with adoption first."

"Yes, totally fine." He nods his head like a bobblehead doll. "We can practice in the meantime with Benji."

I give him a tired smile. "And last, I want ye to know how much I love ye, and there's no one else I'd rather be doin' this with. *Go síoraí, mo chroí.*"

TJ sighs and brings my hand to his heart. "Forever, my heart. I love you too, my sexy Irishman."

I touch my lips to his and close my eyes, the chaos in the air stilling when I breathe in his scent. I groan as he pulls away from me.

"Come on, let's go to bed. I'm exhausted," TJ sulks. "Kiki's kids take every ounce of energy and brainpower from you and crush it in their little hands like miniature villains plotting to take over the world. It's a special talent Chase has. I love them, but they're a lot."

"And yet look, ye survived. I'm proud of ye, babe." I stand up and extend my hand to help him up. "Ye think Chase is okay out here for the night?"

"Are you kidding me? That kid could survive sleeping on a bed of nails. Just *don't* wake him."

"What about Benjamin Blueberry?"

"For once, the demonic baby isn't crying, so let's leave him sleeping with Chase."

I smile and lean in, touching my lips to his again. I murmur, "I can't believe we're going to do this."

"You won't regret it." TJ's teeth graze my neck, causing me to shiver. "I'll call the lawyers tomorrow. I know we can't do anything tonight, but maybe tomorrow night can we circle back to how hot you look when you're all growly angry with your shirt off?"

I chuckle. "I'm not holding a mallet while we have sex, Love."

TJ trails down the hall after me. "Not during sex, no. That would give me serial killer stalker vibes. But what if you held it—"

"Nope."

"But it makes me all tingly," he whines.

"It makes ye want to take a piss?" I turn and wait for him in our doorway, lifting an eyebrow.

"What? No. Have you been talking to that bratty ex-bestie of mine?" He marches past me and I grin, closing the door. If only he knew how much Kiki and I talk.

Chapter 12

Andie

CHECKING MY WATCH, I finish loading the photos from this morning's shoot onto my computer. Charleigh will be waking up from her nap soon and I'll have to get Enzo from preschool. After that, I won't have time to edit the photos until after everyone goes to bed. I'm so tired lately, I wonder if I need to cut back on the photography jobs, or tell Sarah, Kiki, and TJ that I need to cut my hours at work. The thought makes me nauseous. They're the reason my photography business is so successful. The reason I met the love of my life, Cam, and the reason I'm still living in Nashville. I owe them everything.

Nausea rolls in my belly. I rush to the bathroom and upend the contents of my stomach into the toilet. I sit back on my heels and flush it down. Jesus, this flu is lasting forever. My phone dings with a text from my best friend, Mandy.

Mandy: *I got the go-ahead for a girls' weekend! Are you free next weekend?*

Me: *Sure*

Mandy: *I can hear the enthusiasm bursting in your voice.*

Me: *Sorry, I'm not feeling well. I just threw up.*

My phone rings and I groan, knowing Mandy will call back every thirty seconds if I don't pick up.

"You can still come this weekend," I tell her. "It's probably stress. Or a stomach bug."

"You've been complaining about being nauseous for three weeks," Mandy says all-knowingly. "Denial ain't just a river in Egypt, my friend."

"What are you talking about?"

"Andie, you're pregnant. Auntie Mandy knows these things. She also knows your ovulation schedule, the fact that you never throw up, and that you and Cam hump like sex-starved island dogs, any time of the day, anywhere."

"First of all, you're insane. Second, how do you know my ovulation schedule?"

"TJ and I had a tracker from when you were pregnant with Charleigh. He had to because he was your doula."

"And you have it because…?"

"Because as your best friend and godmother to Enzo and Charleigh, it's my duty to know when Forbes baby number three is on the way."

"Well, you're going to be disappointed. I'm not preggers. I never got sick with Enzo or Charleigh. Cam has been out of town a lot and I had my period…" Shit, when was my last period? "It doesn't matter. I'm on the Pill. I'm done having babies."

"Oh hello, Mrs. Curtis from seventh grade sex-ed class?

I'd like to buy a 'you can get pregnant on birth control' for five hundred, please."

I roll my eyes even though Mandy can't see me. "You're wrong. Stress can make you vomit. Or I have that nasty flu going around. I'm exhausted."

"Another symptom of pregnancy. According to your ovulation app, you were ovulating last month on the week of the eighth. Did you and Cam happen to shebang the orangutang? Tug the bug? Get jiggy with the piggy?"

"Oh my god, please stop." My best friend is certifiable. I think back to the week of the eighth. "Cam was in town…"

"I knew it! Go take a test. Bless it, I'd peel out of this driveway faster than Deacon can say Bass Pro Shop sale, but Michael has a math test tomorrow I need to help him study for and Hunter has baseball tryouts after school on Wednes-day—"

"Mandy, it's okay. You're not missing anything because I'm *not* pregnant."

"Go! Take it! Call me back in fifteen. Never mind, don't bother. Setting my timer now. And you know what will happen if you don't answer. Now go," she barks, causing me to jump.

"Fine," I groan and hang up on her. I check Charleigh's monitor and see her stirring in her crib. Charleigh will be eighteen months next week. There's no way I can be pregnant. Cam and I agreed two is enough with our busy lives. He will shit a brick if I am.

Oh god, what will I tell the others? TJ? He'll be so upset. I pull out a pregnancy stick I have left over from when we were trying with Charleigh and pee on it, placing it on my bathroom sink. Charleigh cries from her room.

Heading back downstairs with Charleigh on my hip, I walk down the hall toward our bedroom. I pick up the stick and my stomach drops. Two pink lines. Shit. My phone rings.

"It's been fifteen minutes, what's the verdict?" Mandy asks before I can say a word.

"I'm pregnant," I say miserably.

"Why do you sound upset? This is something to be celebrated!"

"Mandy, Cam and I literally *just* had a conversation about how busy we are and having two kids is enough. I was thinking about how I might have to cut back on my photography. And what about our trip to Greece we've planned for the next book this summer? That's not going to happen now."

"Andie, it's December. You'll be what? Seven months in July? No problem."

"How am I going to tell TJ?"

"He'll be over the moon."

I place a fussy Charleigh in her high chair and give her some sliced bananas. "He and Connor are trying to find a surrogate. They want to have a family."

"Oh, that's exciting! I promise, he'll be ecstatic for you. Okay, well, that confirms it! I'm coming for sure next Friday. Can't wait to celebrate!"

"Mandy, I don't...Mandy?" I look down at my cell, but the call has disconnected. My phone pings and I expect it to be my best friend blowing up my phone with a list of baby names or an article on having baby number three, but it's from Kiki and Sarah.

> **Kiki:** *Emergency meeting tomorrow morning before TJ gets in. Check the BB-2 app.*

I open up the app the three of us installed to track BB-2. It covers the baby's movements, feedings, sleep cycles, and diaper changes. There's also a little camera installed in the left eye that takes short videos. There are only three videos, so I pull up the first clip. It's Chase holding the baby. He holds it up to a calico cat and pets the cat with BB-2's head. The cat swats at BB-2 and the clip ends. The second clip is a gray blur, like fabric out of focus, and the doll-baby crying. I pull up the last clip. It's the sky with a tree and there's a coffee cup. The video shakes and the coffee cup falls on BB-2 before the doll falls. The video goes haywire and blacks out.

> **Me:** *I watched the videos. I'm pretty sure BB-2 has second-degree burns and flew off a moving car.*
>
> **Kiki:** *Jesus. I haven't watched the videos. I just saw the car seat time and wigged.*
>
> **Sarah:** *Poor BB-2. I hope it's still in one piece. We have to say something you guys. This is wrong.*
>
> **Kiki:** *We'll confront him in the morning.*

I sigh and place my forehead on the cool table as Charleigh babbles from her seat. I'm going to have to keep this pregnancy under wraps for now. It will kill TJ when we tell him he failed BB-2. I can't add insult to injury by announcing I'm pregnant.

Chapter 13

THE ELEVATOR DOORS slide open. I check my reflection one more time, noting the faded marker which still hasn't washed off from this past weekend when the boys stayed over. Luckily, I don't have to meet with any clients for the next few days since I'll be helping Kiki working in-house on some wedding dress design ideas and then it's Christmas break.

Andie waves at me before picking up her phone. "He's here," she says and promptly hangs up the receiver. She peers at me. "Good morning, TJ. What's on your face?"

"Slay the day, Shorts." I throw my jacket and satchel on her desk like Miranda from *The Devil Wears Prada*. Kiki and Sarah walk out of their offices, frowning. "Ladies, looking snatched today. What's the tea?" I sit in the window seat and cross my legs. "FML, that reminds me of coffee. NGL, I could use a gallon of the chipmunk buzz."

"Tammy Jean, stop with the teen lingo crap, already." Kiki folds her arms over her chest. "We have a bone to pick with you. Where's BB-2?"

"You mean Benjamin Blueberry? Kiki, that is an excellent question." I pretend to ponder while I pick a piece of lint off my pant leg. "Define the definition of *where* exactly. Do you mean like *Where in the World is Carmen Sandiego* or *Where's Waldo?*"

"TJ," Sarah cries, "did you lose the baby?"

"Take a chill pill, Sare Bear. He's safe-ish…"

"What the hell does safe-ish mean? Oh my god, he's at Neiman's, isn't he? Probably stuffed under a sales rack," Kiki says, throwing her arms in the air. "I knew we should have put a tracker on him."

"TJ, that baby was expensive. It's not something we picked up at Target in the toy section. You can't just leave it somewhere."

I rub my temples and groan. "Sare Bear, I love you, but I don't appreciate you whining this early in the morning before I've had the appropriate amount of caffeine."

The elevator dings and Connor steps off. "Love, you forgot the doll in the car seat. He was cryin' again. I think yer supposed to do something. Oh hey, everyone. Sorry to drop and run, but I have to set up for a brunch we're hostin' downstairs today for a tech company."

"Thanks, C-Pub." I wink.

"C-Pub?" Kiki laughs.

"That's his millennial name."

"I've never heard of a millennial name. That's not a thing." Kinky smirks.

"It's the rage on TikTok. You're just jelly you don't have a cool name like C-Pub."

"I don't answer to it." Connor ducks his head, handing

me the baby.

"What's a millennial name?" Sarah asks.

"It's your first initial with something you do after it. So, Connor works at a pub, so he's C-Pub."

"Why wouldn't you just call him C-Bar?"

"Because, Kinky, that doesn't sound as good. Hello, amateur hour. Andie would be A-Cam for Andie and camera."

"So I'd be S-Makeup?"

"No, Sare Bear, you would be S-Shine. Sounds better."

"What would I be?" Kiki asks. "K-Dress? Ooh! What about K-Bestie?"

"More like K-desperado."

"What? I'm not desperate." Kiki slumps down next to Sarah. "You know what, I don't care. Millennial names are dumb. It's not even trending on TikTok. You probably made it up."

"Whatevs, K-Hater."

"Hey guys, can we get back on track?" Andie raises her eyebrow.

Connor waves goodbye. I toss the baby on the bench beside me, causing the three of them to gasp. "What?"

Andie frowns. "TJ, you can't fling the baby around like it's a doll."

"Newsflash, Shorts, it *is* a doll." I roll my eyes. "You guys are acting like I'm Michael Jackson and just dangled Blanket over the balcony."

"What the hell happened to BB-2?" Kiki stands and grabs the doll.

"Why is one eye shut?" Sarah screeches. "And why does

he have marker all over his skin?"

"Calm-a-mentos and chill. Sare Bear, again, can we take that screech about five octaves down? Thanks, chica." I stand up from the window seat and check my watch. "Look, I'd love to discuss baby Benjamin Blueberry BB-whatever, but I have a mocha frappe calling my name right now and I need caffeine like nobody's business, so if we can shelve this, that would be great."

I turn and shudder when I catch a glance of Kiki holding Benji in the morning light. Good god, he's frightening. He looks like Big Baby from *Toy Story 3*.

"Sit your happy ass back down, mister." Kiki points a finger at the window ledge.

Andie clears her throat. "According to our BB-2 baby app, your baby has been crying incessantly—"

"Gurrl, you don't have to tell me. He won't shut up. I've had a migraine all weekend from the crying. It's totes ridic. My only salvation is the car seat. He stops crying. Absolutely loves it."

"Are you telling us you lock BB-2 in his car seat and leave him there?" Sarah asks, her eyes bugging out.

"You say that like it's a bad thing." The three of them share a look. "Oh, come on, you guys, I'm kidding. *It's a doll.* I wouldn't do that to a real baby, obvi."

"TJ, have you fed him and changed his diaper?"

"Well, duh, Kinks. Look at his super cute Burberry outfit. He even has a matching hat and booties. I went a little crazy at that baby store in Franklin. I got him the cutest matching baby trench coat, too."

"Oh my god." Andie sighs. "TJ, this wasn't for you to

play dress up. This was a chance to feel what it's like to have a real, live baby. If this is any indication of how you would take care of one, then I'm sorry, friend, but you may not be ready for this."

"Don't y'all think you're being a wee bit dramatic?"

"Your baby has permanent marker on his forehead that strangely matches your own. Why do you have marker on your forehead?" Sarah shakes her head, waving a hand in the air. "You know what, never mind. I was going to donate this to Jax's high school, but I can't give them this. Look at his eye! It doesn't stay open anymore. Like he's perpetually winking. It's creepy."

"Thank you." I throw my hands in the air, grateful they're finally catching on. "He *is* creepy. He cries and pees and if I throw him on the couch, some kind of annoying alarm goes off. And don't get me started on the greenish-brown goo that comes out of his butt. Like what sick person came up with the design of this thing? I was at Haymakers the other day meeting a client and he wouldn't stop crying. Turns out he was upside down in the Baby Bjorn I was wearing. It was *trés* awkward when the client pointed it out." I take a deep breath and try to find my inner chi. "I didn't want to say anything, y'all, but Benji is really cramping my style."

"TJ? Why is his arm duct-taped to his shoulder?" Kiki has undressed him on Andie's desk.

"We had a little incident with the car door." I laugh nervously. "Yikes. Who knew it could take off an arm? Totally nutcray." Kiki gives me a look that could melt one of Madame Tussaud's wax statues. I fold my arms over my chest and sit back down. "At least I taped it back on."

"According to the app, you had him in the car seat for a total of eighteen hours on Sunday. He's dehydrated. He needed a diaper change twenty-four hours ago and hasn't eaten in two days." Andie reads from her phone, arching an eyebrow. "*Two days*, TJ?"

"TJ, what the fuck?" Kiki shouts. "You and Connor were supposed to be practicing. Now I have to turn you into Child Services."

Standing up, I huff and grab the Baby Bjorn out of my messenger bag Andie unceremoniously shoved off her desk. I snatch Benji from them and tuck him into the baby pouch. "Happy?"

"Uh, TJ? He's upside down." Sarah points at my chest.

"Pimento cheese on rice cakes," I bite out, unbuckling the Bjorn and ram Benji right side up, yanking his legs through the holes. "You guys, I've got this. Give me a few more days to show you I can make Benji my bitch."

"Did he just say he was going to make his doll-baby his bitch?" Andie asks.

"Thank God *Nashville Next* isn't here filming this shit," Kiki mutters.

"Fine, a few more days, Tammy Jean," Sarah says sternly. "Prove to us you're ready for this."

"And what happens if Benji doesn't cooperate?" I ask, covering my bases in case Benji Blue goes exorcist on me.

"Then we go to Connor and let him know our findings."

I gasp. "You wouldn't dare."

"We would," Sarah says with an evil little smile. The other two nod their heads in agreement. "Pretend BB-2 is a real baby and his life depends on you.”

“Fine. I’m off to the *café con leche*.” Benji emits an ear-piercing wail, causing all of us to flinch. “See?” I whisper, covering his mouth. “He’s possessed.”

“Maybe he’s the colicky prototype,” Andie says thoughtfully.

“Count on you bitches to get me the colicky BB-2 model,” I grump, stuffing a bottle in his mouth before hitting the elevator button.

“Three days, Turd Jam!” Kiki shouts.

“In the bag, bitches,” I call over my shoulder. As soon as the elevator doors close, I slump against the wall and groan. The next three days are going to be hell on earth with this little psycho Chucky doll.

“Lord, I don’t ask for much from you, but *please* give me the strength for things I can’t handle, like closing his arm and head in the car door and getting violently attacked by Bartie the cat. Also, please show Connor and the girls I *am* ready for this. And for the love of all who are holy, please let those Versace leather pants be on sale next week at Neiman’s. Amen.”

Chapter 14

Connor

WATCHING A FRAZZLED TJ tryin' to change the screaming doll's diapers is probably the highlight of my day.

"Can you help instead of sitting there all smug, like you'd do a better job?"

I hold my hands up in surrender. "Sorry, Love, but I'm under strict orders not to help ye with Benji."

"Those sadists. Why are these diapers so big?" He reaches for the duct tape on the counter and winds it around the top of the diaper and the baby.

"Uh, Love? Pretty sure yer not supposed to tape the baby's skin. It's very delicate, ye know?"

"This isn't a *real* baby!" he hisses, shoving a bottle into the baby's mouth. Benji immediately stops crying. "Sweet Jesus, silence has never sounded so good." He leaves Benji lying on the counter and collapses against the couch cushions.

"Thomas, ye can't leave the baby lying on the counter unattended."

TJ scowls at me before pulling himself off the couch. He snatches Benji and the bottle off the counter and sits back down in a huff. Benji's muffled cries and an alarm ring in the air and TJ's face crumples. "I think this thing is defective. Why is he always crying?"

"Well, maybe ye shouldn' wedge him between the pillow like that." I point to poor Benji facedown against a throw pillow.

"Ugh, it's not hard to sit up, Benji." He tries to straighten Benji's legs into a sitting position, but the doll flops over. The alarm continues to beep and I have to turn away from him to keep from laughing.

"Connor, this isn't funny."

"It's hilarious, Love." I smirk. "Done be mad at me. I'm an innocent bystander."

"I'm not," he snaps. "Ugh, how many days has it been?"

"Since ye told the girls you've got this baby thing in the bag?"

"You mean the three evil witches. It's been at least a month."

"It's been a day."

"Nooo," he cries, flopping back against the cushions, holding Benji to his front. Seeing him with a baby on his chest, even if it is a psychotic doll, warms my heart.

"Look, I know yer tryin'. And I love ye for it. So, Benji isn't the best baby in the entire world—"

"He's Satan's spawn."

"Okay, well, that's a little harsh, but yer doin' good, getting his feedings in and nappies changed. I'm proud of ye, Love."

"Even though I drove away with him on the hood of the car the other day?"

I nod. "Ye stopped when ye noticed, didn't ye?"

"Only because my Frappuccino was there, too."

"Well"—I clap my hands together—"baby steps. I know yer gonna be the best dad. Kiki's boys adore ye, and so do Lex's kids. Yer always up for a fun time."

"His eye fell out yesterday when I turned him over." TJ grimaces, smoothing a finger over the Band-Aid holding the eyeball in place.

I reach into my back pocket and hold out a baby-blue sequined eyepatch. "Which is why I picked up this little gem on the way home today."

"Oh my god, I love it!" Squealing, he puts the eyepatch over Benji's eye. "Where did you get a bedazzled eyepatch?"

"Surprisingly, there's a weird fetish for pirates at the Leather and Lace store over off Broadway."

"Oh Benjamin Blueberry, did you see what Daddy got you? I guess it's hard to see with one eye. He got you an eyepatch from an adult sex store. He's the best dad in the entire world." TJ sobs, tossing Benji to the side and covering his face with his hands.

I freeze for a moment, unsure of what to do. I think I've seen TJ cry once in the five years we've been married. Husbandly instincts kicking in, I slide from my chair over to the couch next to him and put my arm around him. He turns into my chest, grabs my shirt, and unleashes a torrent of tears. I stroke his back and murmur soothing Gaelic terms of endearment until he quiets. "Tell me what's wrong, *moi chroí.*"

TJ leans back and wipes his face. He blows his nose with Benji's onesie that was lying on the coffee table. "You're such a loving, caring, and responsible dad, and I'm a pathetic loser."

"Love, that's not true—"

"No, it is true, and you know it. How am I going to be a dad if I can't even keep Benji together in one piece?"

I'm silent for a moment as I gather my thoughts. "Being a good da doesn't always mean yer on top of everything. A good parent is loving, which ye are. A good parent wants their child to succeed. And if they fail, they're gonna help them pick up the pieces and keep going. Ye may not be the most…in-control da, but yer gonna be the fiercest cheerleader our child can count on. TJ, you are the heart and soul of this marriage and I expect ye to be the same as a parent. So what if our kid has to wear an eyepatch and duct tape. It gives him character."

TJ blows his nose again. "You think so?"

"I know so."

"If I'm the heart and soul, what does that make you?"

"Me?" I smile. "I make sure all the moving parts stay together."

"No, you're the glue that keeps us together. I'm so lucky to have you, babe." TJ kisses my lips. I melt against him.

"I'm the lucky chancer in this bit, Love. I don't care if our kid has nontraditional parents. As long as he or she is a happy baby, then I'm good."

TJ smiles and wipes his cheeks with his hands. "I'm good, too. I'm sorry I broke down. Benjamin Blueberry made me lose my shit."

"I've heard kids can do that to ye." I smile and rub his back.

"Do you think we'll love our baby unconditionally?"

"What do ye mean?" I ask.

"I'm worried because I don't feel any kind of connection with Benji Blue. At first, it was fun buying him clothes and stuff, but now when I look at him, I feel…nothing. Well, that's not true. He makes me irritable, which makes me feel bad, and then I want to cry because I have like zero connection with this voodoo Chucky doll. My point is, I'm more in love with Bartie the cat than Benji Blue. What if this happens when we get the real baby?"

"Babe, it's a doll. I'd be worried if ye did feel a connection with him." I pick Benji off the couch and hold him up in front of us. His blue eyepatch catches the light, looking like a mini disco ball over his eye. He's wearing more duct tape than clothes, and the marker scribbled all over his arms gives him a worn appearance. There are tire marks from when he fell off the car yesterday. My mom would have heart palpitations if she saw this damn doll.

I can't help the deep rumble in my chest from bubbling to the surface. My shoulders shake, mirth consuming me. Moisture glazes my corneas and when I turn to look at TJ, whose brows are pinched together in concern, I laugh harder.

"You've made a right bags of this shite, to be sure. This doll is fucking banjaxed."

"Oh, come on. Is he that bad?" As if on cue, Benji emits a quivering cry that sounds like he's underwater or his batteries are on the brink of dying. "That can't be good."

We both laugh until we can't breathe. I set Benji on a

blanket and turn to TJ. "I promise we can do this, Love. Our baby will not end up like poor Benji Blue."

"I know you said you wanted to go the adoption route first, but it could be years until we get a baby," TJ reminds me. "Would you consider talking to some surrogates after the holidays?"

I take a deep breath. "Are ye sure that's the path we should take?"

He nods enthusiastically. "We need to get the ball rolling."

I take his hand. "Okay, Love. I know ye want this to happen now, but we've got plenty of time. Promise me ye won't jump all-in without consultin' me first."

"I promise." TJ squeezes my hand, and with his other, he crosses his heart. He plants another, firm kiss on my lips.

I wrap baby Benji in a blanket and pray we're making the right decision.

Chapter 15

Cam

FINALLY, AFTER AN exhausting week in California meeting with the franchise owners of The Social Hour, I'm home. I take off my overcoat and hang it on the coatrack in our front hallway. Enzo runs to meet me and my heart beats double-time. I love this little guy so much.

"Daddy!" He leaps into my arms. Andie comes around the corner from the kitchen with baby Charleigh on her hip, babbling and banging her rattle against her arm. Andie looks as weary as I feel. Guilt pricks me in the gut for being gone. I lift Enzo into the air and squeeze him tight.

"How's my Superman?"

"It's Spiderman!"

"Oh, my bad, Spidey. Catch any bad guys today with your Spidey senses?"

Enzo grins and shakes his head.

"You didn't? You might want to go check the house in case you missed one."

He squirms and squeals in my arms as I tickle him under

his ribs. I set him down and he runs down the hall. "Come on, Vader! We have bad guys to catch!" Our dog Vader gallops after him. I smile at Andie.

"Hey gorgeous, how are my girls?"

"We're good. Tired, but good." Leaning in, she kisses my lips. Charleigh whacks her rattle on the side of my head. She gives me a big gummy smile and I return it, kissing her head.

If you had told me six years ago, I'd be a dad to two kids, married to the most beautiful woman in the world, I would have laughed and served you another beer. My business was my baby, and nothing was going to get in between us. But then I met Andie and Enzo, and my whole world turned upside down. She showed me not only could I have it all if I wanted it, but that perhaps my priorities were shifting.

I sold the West Coast bars two years ago but still fly to California every quarter to meet with my lawyers and make sure the properties I own are being maintained. It's also a chance for me to visit my parents and make sure my older sister Brooke is looking after them.

I have two Social Hour locations thriving in Nashville that I run with Connor, and I'm looking to open a third here soon. Unfortunately, that means life is about to get crazy busy.

"I'm tired too. It was a long flight. I've missed you guys."

"How are your parents and Brooke?" Andie turns to head back into the kitchen and I trail behind her, loosening my tie. Vader picks up a toy and follows behind me, squeaking the stuffed squirrel.

"Brooke is still Brooke, even though her life is falling apart. She and the boys have moved in with Mom and Dad."

"What? Where's Graham?"

"Rehab." I frown.

"Oh no. How's your sister handling it?" Andie asks as she puts Charleigh in her high chair, scattering fruit on her tray.

"I guess Brooke threatened him with divorce and gave him an ultimatum."

"Wow, I'm kind of surprised she brought up divorce. Your sister seems like the type to keep the illusion going no matter the cost of what the other person is going through." She wipes her hands on her leggings. "Sorry, that wasn't very nice."

I pull a beer out of the fridge and sit down at the kitchen table. "No, that's pretty accurate. I would have never found out the truth if Dad hadn't told me. Brooke wants everyone to believe he's on assignment in Europe and she and the kids are living with Mom and Dad because they're getting their house renovated. But the truth is, they had to sell their house. Graham had a lot of debt and insurance wouldn't pay for the luxury rehab center he insisted upon."

"Yikes. What comes around goes around."

Charleigh begins to fuss, banging her rattle on the tray. Andie takes a frozen teether out and hands it to her. I pop one of Charleigh's blueberries in my mouth and make a silly face, causing her to squeal with delight. She kicks her legs out and throws a handful on the floor which Vader quickly cleans up. I pick up the teether and she grabs it from my hands, shoving it into her mouth.

"Brooke will never learn. I doubt Graham will either. I feel bad for my nephews, but at least they have Mom and

Dad as a safety net. Anyway, enough about her. Tell me what I've missed this past week."

Andie picks up the salad tongs and tosses the lettuce. "Oh, um, well…let's see. Charleigh is teething, Enzo made a new friend at preschool, I'm pregnant, and Mandy's coming for a girls' weekend. She'll be here tomorrow." She turns and stirs the sauce on the stove.

Did she say what I think she said?

"Andie, can you repeat that last part?"

"Mandy coming for the weekend?" She looks over her shoulder, her eyes softening with something akin to sympathy. "I know it will be a lot since you've been gone for a week, but I promised her—"

"No." I shake my head, interrupting her, and slowly set down my beer. "The part about you being pregnant?"

She bites her bottom lip. "Six weeks along. I know it's not the greatest timing and I—"

I jump out of my chair and gather her in my arms, kissing her full lips. She breaks the kiss and searches my eyes. "You're not mad?"

"Mad? Are you kidding me? I'm over the moon! This is the best Christmas gift you could have given me. I wish the kids were in bed right now so I could make love to you and show you how fucking happy you make me." Placing my hand over her stomach, I lean in and kiss her again.

"Cam…" She pulls back. "It's horrible timing. You're about to open a new location. Mandy wants me to travel to Greece when I'm seven months pregnant to start our next book. I had some awful client of Kiki's scream at me today because she couldn't get in with her for a wedding dress fitting and it was my fault because I forgot to schedule her after I was sick, and I had to turn down four photography jobs this week because my whole world is imploding and…I can't breathe." Tears leak from her eyes.

"Hey, hey, don't cry," I soothe, swiping my thumbs across her cheeks. "Deep breaths, Andie."

"I'm feeling so overwhelmed and I'm nauseous every morning. I haven't told Kiki or Sarah yet, because I know they're going to be upset I'll be going on maternity leave. And TJ. Oh god, I don't even know how to bring it up to him. He and Connor are going to hire a surrogate, but he's terrible with Benji and I'm not so sure it's a good idea…" she blubbers.

I steer her over to the chair next to Charleigh, who is happily smacking her teether on her tray.

"Wait, the sauce…" Andie cries.

I stir it once and turn off the burner. Pulling a chair in front of her, I sit down and take her hands. "Baby, slow down. I can talk to Kiki if you want. I know for a fact they will be ecstatic. As for TJ and Connor, I wouldn't be too worried about them. I'm not sure who Benji is, but TJ and Connor are terrific with our kids, right?" She nods. "Connor has mentioned TJ wants to start a family, but he said it could be years before anything happens. I asked him recently if he could handle overseeing the two Nashville locations while I open the Franklin bar and he said it wouldn't be a problem. He'll have his hands full."

She squeezes my hands. "It's the worst possible timing, you know?"

"Babe, there's never a good time. That's why it's called a

surprise. We'll handle it like we do everything else. One day at a time. But I will tell you this. The sooner you tell Kiki, Sarah, and TJ, the better you'll feel and they can strategize how to cover for you when you're gone. Maybe even take some things off your plate in the meantime. And if it's getting too much to work for them, you need to let them know."

"But I owe them for so much."

"Andie." I lean in and wipe her cheeks dry. "Honey, you don't owe them anything. That's not how they operate. They love you and want you to be happy."

"I don't want to leave them, I love the three of them so much, but I don't think I have the energy to work full-time anymore." Andie looks over at Charleigh, giving her a watery smile.

I stand up, taking Charleigh out of her high chair. "I'll go bathe her before we eat. Talk to them, babe." I lean down and kiss her. "I love you and I love this baby growing inside you. We will be okay, I promise."

She nods, and I head down the hallway toward the bathroom with Charleigh babbling. I put on a brave face for Andie because I can see how tired and upset she is, but she's right. The timing of this pregnancy isn't the greatest. *I hope I can keep my promise.*

Chapter 16

IT'S BEEN TWO weeks since Connor agreed to interview potential surrogates and I've been on my best behavior not to rock the boat, but now that the holidays are over, I'm getting antsy, afraid we've already wasted time. Benjamin Blueberry was returned to the girls a few days ago, and I feel like I finally have my life back. No more screaming at random times, no more throwing up putrid water on my Versace silk shirts, and blessedly, no more diaper changes with ill-fitting Huggies. Kiki told me she wanted to tell Gloria, but as my bestie, she decided she'd rather hold it over my head until she needed a favor.

Today we are sitting down with prospective surrogates and I'm about to jump out of my skin. I'm so excited. The four lattes I've had this morning probably aren't helping.

We've been on this Zoom call for five minutes and I can tell Connor likes Amy. I'm not as impressed. She lacks the spunk and go-getter attitude I'm looking for in the woman who will be carrying our baby for nine months. I called our lawyers to get the ball rolling on the adoption process but was disheartened to find out Gloria was right. It could take years. We've been put on a list and were told to get our lookbook together for potential moms. Connor and I agreed it can't hurt to interview the surrogates I found, feel them out and see if it's a more viable option than adoption. Which is why we are currently listening to Amy from Seattle drone on about her mind-numbing tech job. I zoned out a few minutes ago.

Adjusting my tortoise-shell anti-blue-light glasses, I cross my leg over my knee and glance at my watch. "Sorry to interrupt, but I have a few pertinent questions before we have to move on to our next appointment."

"Oh, sure." Amy smiles, but it doesn't make me feel happy. It annoys me. "Do you like sparkles?"

Connor heaves a sigh next to me. "Here we go."

"Do I like sparkles? Um, I guess?" Her eyes flick to Connor. "I'm not sure what you mean."

"It's a yes-or-no question. Pretty straightforward," I reply.

"I, uh…"

"What TJ is asking is if you mind having someone blow glitter in your face." Connor peers at me and raises an eyebrow in that sexy Irish way of his, making me want to throw him down on this table. Unfortunately, Amy's annoying voice immediately crushes my fantasy.

"Oh, uh, no, definitely not. I would not enjoy that."

"Hmm." I draw a big X next to her name and the words 'hates glitter'. "Tell me, Amy, how much coffee do you consume on a daily basis?"

"Oh, I don't drink coffee." She smiles like that's going to win her points. It doesn't.

What psychopath doesn't drink coffee? "You're telling me you live in Seattle and don't drink coffee? That should be illegal."

"Oh my god," Connor murmurs, rubbing his forehead. That's his tell when he's exasperated with me, but I don't care. The woman carrying my child has to be simpatico with me. I try to picture myself on the couch next to Amy, both of us wearing avocado vitamin C masks while we toss popcorn into each other's mouths, watching *Bridgerton* and swooning over Regé-Jean Page's butt. Amy looks like she'd be more interested in doing taxes than chilling with me.

"I'm an herbal tea drinker." Amy shrugs. She adjusts her glasses. "Besides, it's not good to have caffeine during pregnancy."

"She's probably a hippie," I whisper loudly to Connor, who groans. Bartie jumps up on the desk and meows. I pick him up and hold him to my chest. "One last question and then I think we can call it a day. What do you think of the name Bartholomew?"

"Wasn't he an Apostle?"

"Uh, I'm not sure." I look over at Connor and he shrugs.

Amy types something on her computer. "Yep, he was."

"Okay, well that's not why I was asking. I'm curious to know what you think of the name?" Lord Jesus, I'm trying to hold it together, but I'm seconds away from hanging up on her.

"Oh lass, don't mess this up," Connor mutters under his breath.

"I mean, it's uh, a little old-fashioned, if I'm being honest."

"Well, what name do you like if the baby is a boy?"

"I don't think that's up to me."

"Oh my god, Amy, can you just play along? What name would you choose if the baby were a boy?"

"Ooh-kay. I've always liked the name Lucas."

I shake my head and shudder. "Yeah, no, I can't. It reminds me of locusts, those annoying gross bugs that make a lot of noise and leave their empty shells everywhere in the summertime."

I can feel Connor glaring at me.

"Is that a cat? I'm highly allergic to cats."

Drawing a big X, I write, 'kills cats'. I slam my notebook shut and Connor slumps back in his chair, defeated-like.

"It was nice to meet you, Amy. We'll let you know what we decide." I click off the session as she's about to open her mouth. "Ugh, she was *awful*. Thank God we could Zoom live with her. Applicants are so different on paper, don't you think?"

"TJ, you can't judge a person's character by whether they like sparkles, the name Bartie, and if they prefer vacationing in St. Tropez or the Swiss Alps. It's not realistic. And what were all the weird questions about coffee?"

"She's a cat killer, Connor."

"She said she's allergic to cats."

"Same diff. She can't be hating our firstborn, Bartie." I lovingly scratch under Bartie's chin. "And can you believe she wanted to call the baby Locust? Our baby would come out with buggy eyes."

"Jesus, I feel shattered." Connor rubs his forehead. "Yer being ridiculous."

"What do you want me to ask? What's your favorite color? It's probably brown. She looks like a brown-is-my-favorite-color kind of girl. She totally lost me when she said Harry Styles had horrible fashion sense. Come on, I can't let that woman carry our baby for nine months with deep-seated aggression like that toward Harry. And who lives in Seattle and doesn't drink coffee? That's like living in Nashville and hating country music."

"Lots of people live in Nashville and don't like country music."

My eyes go round. "Well, that's just blasphemous."

Connor arches an eyebrow. "Didn't you used to tell me you hated country music?"

I kiss Bartie on the head and put him down on the floor.

"It's grown on me."

Connor gets up and goes to the fridge, bringing back two flavored seltzers. "I don't think I can survive hearing ye two bicker for the next nine months, anyway. Who's our next interview with?"

"Penny from Van Nuys."

"Ah, the rollerblading Colleen." Connor shuffles the bios on the desk in front of us. "Where did ye find these applicants?"

"1-800-knock-me-up," I deadpan. He side-eyes me as I click the mouse. "I'm kidding. You'd be surprised. There's an entire network of surrogates on TikTok."

"That's seriously frightening," he grumbles. "I can't tell if yer joking or not."

"I think Penny's going to be the one. I can feel it all the way down in my bikini briefs." I click on our Zoom link and wait for Penny to join.

"Love, I don't want ye to get yer hopes up if she's not. It's a long shot findin' someone that will be perfect for us—"

"Hiya, hiya!" Penny's picture pops open, her red curly hair taking up most of the screen. "Sorry I'm a little late. Couldn't get the darn computer working."

"Ooh, love her bubbly, upbeat vibe," I whisper to Connor, who ignores me. "Hi Penny, I'm TJ and this is my husband, Connor."

"Sweet! Nice to meet you."

"Penny, why done ye tell us a wee bit about yerself?"

"Ooh, love your accent. Are you British? No wait, Australian." She laughs and I can feel Connor stiffen next to me before clearing his throat.

"Irish."

"Cool, cool." She fumbles with her laptop, adjusting the picture. "Something about myself…sure, yeah. I'm a thirty-six-year-old personal trainer in Van Nuys. I've been a surrogate four times and love the whole process."

"What do ye love about it?" Connor asks.

"Oh my gosh, I love being pregnant. I love helping others conceive their dream baby. I know this sounds crazy, but the process of giving birth is so surreal and spiritual. It's this weird fascination of bringing another human life into this world, you know?"

"If your friends could use one word to describe you, what would it be?" I ask.

"Oh, easy. They would say I'm a free spirit."

"That's two words," Connor whispers.

"Do you have any children of your own?" I ask, nodding my head while I scribble down the words *surreal, spiritual,* and *free spirit.* Amy said her friends would have called her responsible. *Bor-ing.* I also have noted red hair and an upbeat attitude. Connor glances down at my notebook and rolls his eyes.

"No, I'm single. But honestly, I don't want the responsibility of children. I'm happy to carry them to term and hand them off to the parents." She smiles. "They are all yours to stay up with all night long."

"Ye said ye would be open to movin' here?" Connor asks. "What about yer job?"

"Oh, I guess I should have clarified. I'm in between gigs at the moment, so the timing couldn't be more perfect. I'm anxious to move to a new city and try something different. Born and raised here, but if I'm being honest, it's gotten a little stale. I'm ready for adventure!"

"Yes, Penny, I love it!" I cry out, punching the air with my fist. "What do you think of sparkles?"

"Ooh, I love sparkly *everything.* Look! My shorts are sparkly." She stands up and shows us the booty shorts she's wearing. "Sparkles Delight was my stage name back in my college days."

"Er, what do ye mean, yer stage name?" Connor asks.

"Oh my god, do you sing?" I ask, about to pee in my pants with excitement. I can imagine Penny and me singing karaoke duets wearing matching sparkly outfits. Connor places a hand on my bouncing knee.

"Oh, no, I can't carry a tune. I was a dancer and then a

roller derby queen after I dropped out of college. It wasn't for me."

"A woman of many talents." I nod my head and try to dial back my excitement when Connor pinches my side.

"Do ye have any questions for us?" Connor asks in his serious business voice.

"Yes. How soon could I move in with you?"

"Right away!" I nod enthusiastically. "We want to get the ball rolling."

Penny smiles brightly, her shoulders relaxing. "That's great."

"Penny, yay or nay to Harry Styles?"

"I *love* Harry. How could you not? I'm dying to go to a concert."

"Me too!" I squeal.

Connor nudges my leg with his. "Okay, Penny, it was nice to meet you. We still have a few more interviews to go—"

I gasp, cutting him off. "Babe, Penny is it. She's perfect for us. We do not need to look further."

"TJ…" Connor's brows knit together.

I hold up my finger. "Penny, one more question. What do you think of the name Bartholomew?"

"Ooh, I think it's cute. You could call him Bartie for short or Lo-mew."

"Oh. My. God." I press my hand to my heart. "I love Lo-mew. It's like we are long-lost twins finally reunited."

"Oh, Jesus," Connor mutters. "Penny, we are very interested, but we still have a few more interviews. We'll be in touch by tomorrow. It was lovely to meet ye."

"You too. Um, is he okay?" she asks, pointing to her screen. I'm a blubbering mess as I grab a few tissues from the desk to blot my eyes.

"I'm perfect, Penny. I love you." My words garble in my throat.

"Oh, for fuck's sake." Connor clicks the Zoom call off and bites out, "Really?"

"Come on, you know she's perfect." I sniffle and then blow my nose. "She's carried four times, so she's a seasoned baby carrier, like a UPS truck. She likes to be pregnant. She loves sparkles and it was kismet that she called our future baby, Bartie. It's like the universe is pointing all the arrows at Penny. Can't you picture me lounging on the couch with her while we paint each other's toenails and asking, *Penny for your thoughts*? It's so perfect."

"No, I can't. Stop acting the maggot. Ye can't be serious, Thomas? She's jobless, has no prospects in her hometown, was an exotic dancer and roller derby queen. And honestly, I'm a little concerned about why she wants to move in with us right away. Ye think she's capable of carrying our child?"

"Connor Ryan, shame on you. Now look who's being judgmental. Penny fits in with us way more than stuffy, herbal tea-drinking, cat-killer, Amy. And I know my Nana Rose would adore Penny. She's passionate, fiery, eager—"

"Yeah, yeah, yeah, and she likes sparkles. I know." He stands up and plows his fingers through his hair. "I'm…concerned."

"About what?"

"About all of this!" He paces the kitchen. "The lawyer said it could take years for a private adoption. You want

Sparkles Delight to be our host mom…it doesn't feel right."

Sal coughs and I turn. He raises his hand in apology. I completely forgot *Nashville Next* was behind us filming.

Connor glares at the film crew. "And for the love of God, can we please have a little privacy once in a fuckin' while 'round here?" He grabs his jacket and storms out the front door.

I look at the camera crew helplessly and shrug. "I don't know what got his knickers in a twist. I thought Sparkles Delight was perfect, didn't you guys?"

Chapter 17

Connor

I'M USUALLY A pretty go-with-the-flow lad. It's hard to ruffle my feathers, but this whole baby thing has me on edge. I know I agreed to start a family with TJ, but I feel like I'm on a runaway train bulldozing its way right into a mountain with TJ at the helm. I imagined this process taking years. TJ is ready to have this stranger come live with us next week! My chest feels tight and my skin is itchy. Pulling out my cell, I call Lex.

"What's the craic?" he answers.

"Minus craic. I need something to take the edge off. You and the boys free for a couple pints?"

"Yeah, we've just finished up at the studio. Hold on. Oye, Connor wants to get off his tits. Ye eejits in? Yeah, we're all in. Meet us at The Tavern."

"See ye in ten, and Lex? Thanks a million."

"See ye in ten."

I'm just finishing ordering an Uber when my phone dings with an incoming text.

TJ: *Are you okay? What happened? Are you upset about the film crew?*

My initial instinct is to ignore him. Obviously I'm not okay, and it pisses me off that he doesn't understand why. I can't believe he told Penny yes. We were supposed to make this decision together. I have major reservations about her, but Thomas did what he always does. He jumped without looking. He literally took that circle of trust between us and snapped it in two. I'm so mad I can't think straight. I put my phone in my back pocket and walk down toward the coffee shop. The coffee shop TJ and I go to every morning together before work.

"Fucking hell." I pull my cell back out and pace outside the shop. As much as my blood is boiling, I don't want him to worry.

Me: *I need some space to clear my head. I'm on my way to meet up with the boys and will be home later.*

I turn my cell off and shove it into my back pocket when my Uber pulls up to the curb. Ten minutes later the driver drops me off in front of The Tavern. It's an old hole-in-the-wall establishment the band frequents because no one knows who they are or cares.

Lex, Tatum, Matt, and Will are at a table in the back with a round of beers in front of them. I sit down and Lex claps me on the shoulder.

"Life grand, brother?"

"Feckin' ragin'," I say, lifting my beer. "Slainte."

"Slainte." The guys lift their beers.

"Rough day, Connor?" Tatum asks.

"Rough week." I drink half the pint and set it down.

Tatum arches an eyebrow and chuckles. "Trouble in paradise?"

"This whole baby thing has gotten out of hand."

"Baby? Awe, congrats man." Will holds out a fist and waits for me to bump it. I reluctantly press my knuckles to his.

"Maybe. We're in the process of interviewing surrogates TJ found from God-knows-where and it's a fucking nightmare," I say.

"Well, your first mistake was putting TJ in charge." Tatum chuckles. Lex clinks his beer bottle with his.

"Aye, I think yer right." I frown, looking down at my pint.

"See? That's why I'll never settle down. Marriage is a buzzkill," Matt says, tipping his beer back.

"No, the reason you don't settle down is that no woman in her right mind would date you long-term." Tatum smirks.

"Hey, I'm grateful. Less baggage to carry around."

"Dude," Will scoffs.

"What? Look how miserable Connor looks right now. It's not my fault you three settled down with one person for the rest of your lives. And sugar bear, here"—Matt wrestles Will into a headlock—"is next because he thinks Torie's hung the moon. No, thank you. Give me a hot piece of ass with no strings attached any day of the week."

Lex shakes his head. "Stop being a fucking eejit and let's help my brother figure out his problems."

I shake my head and chuckle. "Actually, I appreciate Matt's honesty."

"You mean bullshit," Tatum interjects.

"I always knew Connor was the smarter brother." Matt gives my brother a shit-eating grin.

"Another round." Tatum signals the server. "Tell us what happened and maybe we can help."

I sigh and scoot my empty beer glass away from me. "Where do I start?"

"Start at the beginning," Will says.

"We looked into adoption, but our lawyer said it could be years. Guess not too many people are too keen on givin' up their baby to two gay men. So we've been interviewing these women from all over the country to be a surrogate. TJ's gone looney over this geebag who I wouldn' want to carry my child and he hates the one I liked. It's like he's gone pure barmy. He's hired some gobdaw designer named Jean Luc Poop who wants to turn our guest room into a Las Vegas brothel. He wants a bedazzled unicorn in our family photos, and to pretend Enzo and Charleigh are our kids so we look like we have experience. He came home with a stray cat to prove to me he can handle kids, but he can't even stomach throw-up, much less clean the litter box. The girls gave us a live doll and TJ left it on the rooftop of the Jeep and accidentally ran over it. He has a film crew following us around twenty-four-seven and some woman named Sparkles Delight is going to be living with us and I feckin' done know how to handle it all. I'm in bits, do ye know like?"

Four blank faces stare back at me. My brother chuckles into his fist while Tatum leans back in his chair and shakes his head. "Fuck the beer. This calls for whiskey."

"I'm on it." Will heads to the bar to get the liquor.

"Done get the cheap stuff. Put it on Tatum's tab," Lex calls over his shoulder.

Tatum punches him in the arm. "You're lucky it's for your brother."

Will brings back a tray of whiskeys and we all take a shot.

"Damn, that burns." Matt scrunches his face.

"Don't be a pussy, Ingles," Tatum says. "So, Connor. What's a Sparkles Delight?"

"The name of the surrogate TJ wants to use. That was her dancer and roller derby name."

"What kind of dancer?" Matt waggles his eyebrows.

"Take a guess, ye fuckin' cabbage." Lex passes out another round of shots.

"Pretty sure she wasn' a ballerina," I agree with Lex before downing another shot.

"Well, what do you want to do? Adopt or go the way of surrogacy?" Will asks.

"I dunno anymore, youknowwhatImean?" I sigh. "I want TJ to be happy, but at what cost to my sanity?"

"I get it," Tatum says. "Kiki wants to have another, but we're going through a rough patch with the two boys, and both our schedules are so slammed I barely see them as it is. Chase is a wild man and honestly a lot to handle. And Drew gets pushed to the wayside by his brother. He's like a sponge, soaking up all the extra attention we can give him when Chase isn't around. Kiki really wants a girl, but the boys dictate our lives right now. I don't think Kiki and I have slept alone in our bed for the past two weeks. Even with all the help we have, they're a lot of work. At what point do you say enough is enough?"

"Aye, Sarah and I are up to our ears in psychologists and therapy to figure out why Wyatt is always cryin' and when Alexis isn't driving us up the wall with all her questions, then we have to worry about her sayin' inappropriate things. Not to mention having a sexually active teenager in the house. Sarah walked in on Jax having sex the other day with some Colleen in his room. Christ, at fifteen, I wasn't a saint, but at least I had my guitar to focus on. We never had to deal with social media and crap like Snapchat and Be Real where dick pics and tit shots are an everyday occurrence. It's not easy raising kids in today's world. It's a feckin' full-time job."

Matt holds his fist out to Lex.

"What the fuck is that for?"

"Dude, congrats to Jax." Matt laughs and punches his fist toward Lex.

"Get the fuck out of here, eejit." Lex pushes his hand away.

"Shit, what did you say to Jax?" Will asks.

"What could I say?" Lex shrugs. "I told him to wrap it and make sure his door is locked next time."

"Damn, is this what I have to look forward to?" Tatum looks mildly panicked.

Lex laughs and clasps his shoulder, gently shaking it. "Dude, you are in so much trouble with Chase."

I take a sip of beer and shake my head. "Enough is enough."

"Jesus, you dickwads sound like grumpy old men. This is why you should get divorced and be single like me." Matt sits back and grins, putting his hands behind his head. "No problems or headaches here in Matt-ville, just easy-breezy living."

"Shut up, ye tosser," Lex says while Tatum throws a wadded-up napkin at his face. The server brings over two more rounds of whiskey.

"You might want to bring us a bottle and leave it at the table." Tatum smiles charmingly at her.

"Shite, I'm gonna be pissed after this," I grumble.

"Nothing like a little whiskey therapy." Lex clasps my neck and shakes it. "Ye can stay the night at my place if ye need to."

"You started without me?" Cam walks up to our table, shrugging out of his coat, and pulls up a chair.

"Cam!" We all lift our beers. My business partner and one of my best friends, Cameron Forbes, is the genuine real deal. He's smart, successful, and has an incredible family. He's a jammy chancer if there ever was one. And even though we're not related by blood, he feels like a second brother to me.

Tatum thumps his brother-in-law on the back and hands him a shot. "Cam, you better catch up. We've got sparkles and unicorns and baby-mama problems to solve."

"If TJ's involved, you won't be solving shit." He smirks and lifts the shot to his lips. "Here's to those who wish us well…"

"All the rest can go to hell!" we shout, taking a shot with him. He downs the shot and lifts the second one, pouring it down his throat in quick succession. He winces and slides the empty glass toward the others on the table.

"Aye!" we roar. Will pounds the table with his fist. The

server comes by and drops off another round of beers and a bottle of their finest whiskey. My vision blurs as I try to read the label, so I give up and return my attention to the guys.

"Cheers to Connor for becoming a dad, because you know hell or high water, TJ is going to make it happen." Cam claps me on the back.

"Cheers!" The guys pound the table again.

"Shite," I mutter and down another shot. "Promise me one thing."

"What's that, brother?" Lex sways next to me.

"Done let TJ name the baby Lo-mew."

"Did you say Low-mule?" Tatum laughs hysterically.

"Why am I suddenly craving lo mein noodles?" Will asks.

"Not even over my dead, fucking lifeless body will I let my nephew be named Mule," Lex growls.

Cam shakes his head and laughs while Will and Matt argue over what Chinese place has the best lo mein. We clink our glasses again, and my world tilts on its axis. I laugh hard at a joke Cam makes and the whiskey washes away my angst over this whole baby thing.

THE SUNLIGHT STREAMING through the blinds makes my head pulse. Rolling over in bed away from the light, I groan. My tongue sticks to the roof of my mouth and feels double in size than a normal tongue should. I try to peel my crusted eyes open. All I want to do is stumble to the bathroom for a piss, drink a large tumbler of ice water, and down some Tylenol so I can hide back under the covers for the rest of the day.

"Well, it's 'bout time yer up. I was goin' to have Da come in and use the cowbell on ye." My mum bustles around the room picking up my clothes. I guess staying in bed is a pipe dream.

"Mum? What are ye doin' here?"

"I should be askin' ye the same, sure ye know. Yer brother and ye stumbled yer arses over here in the wee hours of the mornin' and insisted we take ye in. Lex said ye were moanin' and groanin' about needin' yer mum." She sits down on the side of my bed and brushes the hair off my forehead. "Why are ye here, *a stóirín*?"

"TJ and I had a minor squabble, so the guys took me out drinking. I don't remember much from last night."

"Ah, so did the whiskey do it? Solve yer problems?"

"No, Mum, you know it didn'. It just gave me the gawks."

She chuckles. "Of course, it didn't. Well, right on with yerself. I have a cuppa for ye when yer ready. Lex has already gone home."

"Thanks, Mum." I swing my legs over the side of the bed. Plowing my fingers through my hair, I hold my head for a minute, letting the blood settle. My phone on the nightstand flashes two missed calls from TJ. Fuck, I never called him last night.

"Are you okay?" he asks, picking up as soon as the call connects.

"Aye, sorry, Love. Got a little fluthered last night. I don't know why, but Lex brought me to my parents' condo to sleep it off."

"I was so worried when you didn't come home last night. I called Cam and he said you were with your brother. Do you need me to come get you?"

"I'm sorry." I rub my forehead with my fingers. "No, I'm fine. I'm gonna hang here with them for a bit and then I'll catch an Uber home."

"Okay. Call me if you change your mind and need a ride."

"Will do." I sound hollow. "TJ?"

"Yeah?"

I pause. I want to say I'm sorry that I stormed out, that I caused him to worry last night, but the words won't come.

"See ye in a few," I mumble and disconnect the call.

After splashing my face with cold water and brushing my teeth, I walk into the kitchen to find my mum at her secretary writing notes. "Where's Da?"

"Ah, he went to the coffee shop 'round the corner to meet with his crew."

Since my parents spend half their time in the States now, Da has made friends with other retirees who spend their mornings at the coffee shop gabbing like old hens. They sold their landscaping business when they decided to split their time between here and our home in Kinsale, Ireland, but Mum continues to help with their bookkeeping.

I pour myself some tea from the kettle and settle in at the kitchen table.

"I made some scrambled eggs and rashers. Would ye like some?"

"Sounds grand, Mum."

She places a loaded plate down in front of me and takes a seat. Her hands wrap around a ceramic mug that TJ got her for her birthday. It reads *Sassy Irish Lassie* on it.

"So why done ye tell me why yer sorry arse is sittin' at me table without yer fella by yer side, hm?"

"It's complicated."

She eyes me for a beat. "Try me."

"TJ wants to start a family."

"Well!" she crows. "I think that's a grand idea, done ye know. Yer so good with yer niece and nephews."

"I'm not sure we're ready. In true TJ fashion, it's turned into a circus."

Maggie sits back and takes a sip of her tea. "Why done ye think yer ready?"

"Because we're both busy. TJ has his job, and I'm always at the pub. Cam's talking about opening a third location for The Social Hour in Franklin. When do we have time for kids?"

"Aye, I see." She takes a sip of tea, sets the mug down, and taps the wood table with her fingernail while I shovel eggs into my mouth. "Did I ever tell ye the story of when I found out I was pregnant with ye and yer brother?"

I open my mouth to tell her I've heard it a thousand times, but she plows right over me.

"Eat yer rashers before they get cold, now. I remember it like it was yesterday. I went to the midwife in the village and she confirmed I was haven' two, done ye know. Yer father and I had thrown all our savings into the business and didn't have a pot to piss in. I was scared and so was yer da. We weren't tryin' for ye, but there ye were. Two more mouths to feed and yer da was working from sunup to past down most nights. I thought our world was goin' to crash down around us."

She pauses and takes a sip of tea.

"I never knew this version, Mum."

"Aye, because we never told it to ye. We never wanted ye to think ye weren't wanted because ye were, but the timing was awful. Nothin' was goin' right with the business and we were in a new place with no help from family. I told Finn we should pack up and head back home. He'd work at the local grocer and I would do the books for my da. We fought about it daily, done ye know. Almost ended our marriage over it, the way we were strugglin'. I prayed and prayed to God to show us the way. We either had to give up on our dream or stay and possibly lose everything."

"So, what happened?" I ask.

"The good Lord answered, right he did. He gave us the most beautiful twin boys. I took one look at ye and I said to Finn, 'We're gonna make this work, hell or high water.' We would have been miserable if we had moved back home. Hell, we were miserable where we were, but we were a team, he and I. Buildin' a life for our little family of four. I loved yer da very much, sure ye know. So, we made it work." She winks. "My point is, there's never a perfect time to start a family. Yer never ready for what God throws yer way, but if He's chosen ye to be a da, then ye run with it."

"He hasn't chosen me yet, Mum."

"Ah, *moi chroi*, but He will. And when He does, I can't imagine more lovin' or givin' parents than ye and TJ."

"But TJ *is* running with this and I'm worried it's in the wrong direction."

She covers my hand and squeezes. "When ye love someone like ye love TJ, it's a special kind of love. One that lasts. Ye can't control every situation that comes yer way. Let him run. Let him make mistakes and be there for him when he does. Life is about pivoting, is it not? Now is not the time to head in the opposite direction." She squeezes my hand again and smiles fondly. "I love yer brother, but ye were always the sensible one. Don't let him ply ye with whiskey every time ye and TJ take a wrong turn." She scoots her chair back. "Now get a leg up. I'll drop ye off at home on my way to Zumba."

"Since when do you do Zumba?"

"Since yer da and I started taking a class together."

"Da does Zumba?"

"Keeps us feelin' young," she shouts from the hall closet. "The sex is amazin' after."

"Jesus. I think my breakfast just came back up," I grumble. "TMI, Mum."

"What does TMI mean?"

"It means done ever discuss yer and Da's sexual relationship out loud again."

"Oh, Connor." She bustles back in, laughing. "Done be such a prude."

I stand up and hold the door open for her. "Thanks for breakfast and the talk."

"Always, *moi chroi*." She pats my chest where my heart resides, and I lean down to kiss her cheek.

I close the door and text TJ.

Me: *Mum's dropping me off. Be home soon… I'm ready to*

run with you.

TJ: *Oh babe, sorry to disappoint, but I'm not much of a runner. You know I don't like to sweat. But I can skip beside you, or throw in a cartwheel. Maybe I can ride a golf cart beside you with pom-poms. I'll definitely cheer you on.*

Me: *I was being metaphorical.*

Typical TJ. I snort, erase the text, and start again.

Me: *Sounds good, Love. See you soon.*

Chapter 18

I'VE JUST HUNG up the phone with Penny when Connor walks in. Don't get me wrong, the man is always a walking specimen of perfection, but this morning, he's looking a little rough around the edges.

Without a word, I pour him a cup of his favorite tea while he settles onto the barstool at our granite kitchen island.

"Thanks, Love." His voice is gravelly and deep. It makes me shiver. "Where's the camera crew?"

"They're not filming today. Not much going on." I shrug and lean against the counter. "So, I know you got a little upset yesterday and I realize I was going ninety down a one-way street, blindfolded. I'm sorry."

Connor nods. "I'm sorry I left abruptly. I needed to clear my head and I've come to the conclusion, with a little help from my mum, that it's okay to let you take the lead. And even though I want to be part of the decision-making, I need to trust that you've got this."

I blow out the breath I was holding. "Connor, I would never want to go in a direction you're uncomfortable with. We're in this together. Partners for lifey, wifey. And at the end of the day, if we're not on the same page, it won't work."

Connor smiles, gently covering his hand with mine. "So, what's the plan? Are we going to get Jean Luc Poop to redecorate the guest room for Penny?"

I chuckle. "It's Jean Paul Pierre Luc, Connor. But sadly, no. He's booked until summer now."

"Oh, Love, I'm sorry I ruined your plans with him."

I wave a hand in the air between us. "It's okay. His latest inspiration was to spray-paint the carpet and walls in graffiti and call it New York gangster. I wasn't sure I was down for that. It would have sent the wrong message to impressionable baby Low-mew. I mean, can you imagine? He'd be wearing a bandana around his head with his jeans around his knees and his Huggies hanging out, doing gangster signs to signal he needed a bottle of milk. And which side do you pick? Bloods or Crips? What if we chose wrong and the other gang breaks into our apartment and vandalizes?"

Connor wipes his hand across his mouth, trying to hide his grin. "I can't imagine that happenin'."

"But I did call Penny back and tell her we needed some time to talk it over. She said she'd be ready when we were. And I also called my new bestie, Gloria. Kiki introduced me to her. She's the social worker who's been assigned to us and she's coming over in a few to do a meet and greet and to check our home to make sure it's suitable for foster care."

"I thought you didn't want to do foster care?"

"It's not my *top* choice, but I don't want to leave any

stone unturned," I say.

Connor stands up and stretches, then comes around the island and wraps me in a hug. "I think it's good to get the ball rollin' with Gloria. I'm gettin' in the shower because I smell manky. If ye want Penny to carry our baby, then call her and let her know."

"Really?"

"I'm in yer corner, TJ. We're doin' this together, yeah?"

I squeeze him hard and let go. "You do smell mangy. Go shower."

Connor chuckles. "It's *manky*, not mangy."

"Same diff." I sniff. "Manky, ranky, mangy… Hurry up, Gloria will be here soon." Anticipation rolls around in my belly like pop rockets and Coke. We're doing this! I pick up my cell and call Penny.

"Hello?"

"Penn, it's TJ. I know I *just* got off the phone with you, but I talked to Connor and we're ready to move forward."

"Woo hoo," she shouts. I love her fervor.

"How soon can you move here?" I ask.

"Book my flight, Mama is ready!"

"Okay, send me your info and I'll have a moving service come to your place and pack everything up to be shipped here."

"Oh my gosh, TJ, that is so kind of you guys."

"We're in this together, right?" I squeal in delight.

"Absolutely. Emailing you all the details now."

I hang up with Penny and sit back. No one can wipe the perma-smile off my face. Connor and I are going to be dads! It's a dream I've always wanted but never thought could come true for someone like me. An oddball gay kid from Albuquerque, New Mexico. Now look at me. I'm living the dream of owning a successful business with my three best girlfriends, married to the sexiest man alive, living in a city I'm crazy about, and we're about to become dads. It doesn't get better than this.

I've already cleaned up the condo, but I light a citrus candle and make sure all the throw pillows are fluffed. I ponder canceling Gloria's visit since I got the green light from Connor to call Penny, but she's due to be here in five minutes and that would be rude. Besides, I like her, so there's no harm in having her come by for a chat.

The doorbell rings precisely at two p.m. Gloria is a stickler for being on time.

"Connor, she's here," I shout down the hall.

"I'm coming." He exits the bedroom looking freshly shaven and clean. Mmm, god he's tasty like a Little Debbie's zebra cake.

I turn and open the front door. "Gloria!" I sing and air-kiss her cheeks. "How's my girl?"

"TJ, good to see you again." She giggles and squeezes my arm.

"I'd like you to meet my husband, Connor."

"It's nice to meet ye, Gloria." Connor shakes her hand.

"Oh, TJ gushed about how handsome you were, but your accent tipped the scales for me." She laughs and shrugs out of her coat, handing it to me. "I can't believe I said that to a client."

"Oh, Gloria, no shame here. He is the total package." I wink at Connor and his cheeks pink up. He's so adorable.

"Can I get you a bev? I've got spring and sparkling water, wine, beer, coffee, tea, *me*!"

Gloria falls into a fit of giggles. I love making her laugh.

"TJ, you are something else. I'll have a coffee if it's not too much trouble."

"Trouble is my middle name." I wink at her.

"I don't doubt that." She beams.

"You and Connor can chat and then we'll give you a tour of the place."

"Sounds delightful." She smooths her black slacks as she sits down in a chair in the living room. She opens her satchel and pulls out a file. "Connor, tell me a little about yourself."

I busy myself in the kitchen trying to catch pieces of what they're saying, but the darn coffee machine is too loud. I make Gloria's coffee and bring it into the living room to find the pair smiling and giggling over Connor's baby book. I set the coffee on the table next to her.

"Wasn't he adorbs?"

"Still is, TJ." She scrunches her nose adorably and I give her a high-five. Connor squirms in his seat. He slams the book shut and stands.

"Well, that's enough pictures and compliments about me. Would ye like a tour, Gloria?"

Gloria stands and picks up her coffee. "I'd love one."

I point out the guest bathroom and laundry room, Connor's office, and our bedroom, saving the second bedroom for last. "And this would be the baby's room." I swing the door open and cringe at the basic gray walls, the black furniture from my single days in California, and the muted carpeting. "It's not decorated how I'd want it, but this is all new for us. We use it as a storage room for right now. But of course, we'd get it ready for a baby. It has an ensuite bathroom with a tub."

Gloria peeks into the bathroom. "And don't forget to baby-proof it."

"Of course, yes," I quickly say.

"And what's with the fabric glued on the wall for?" She steps up to the wall where Jean Paul Pierre Luc threw his hammer through the drywall and then hastily tried to paste fabric over the hole as if we wouldn't notice.

"Oh, that." I laugh. "Unfortunate accident with a designer. It will be repaired properly."

She nods and turns. "Well, your home is beautiful and very tidy. I noticed you have a cat? There's a litterbox in the laundry room."

"Ah, yes, Bartie, our Tortie. She loves kids, but she's hiding under our bed right now. Is that a point against us?"

Gloria hums. "I think it's important for children to be around animals. I believe it teaches them to be responsible and kind. It also shows me that you are caring. Do you own your place or are you renting?"

"We own it," Connor says.

"But we're thinking about buying a house," I say hastily, panicking that being in a high-rise might be a point against us.

Connor turns to me, arching an eyebrow. "We are?"

"Well, something on the table for discussion. We can't live in a condo forever with little ones, can we, Gloria?"

"Lots of people do it every day in New York." She smiles. "I will make a note in your file. Let's sit down so we can go over a few things."

We return to the living room and I sit next to Connor, who slings his arm across the back of the couch. His fingers are a featherlight touch against my neck, grounding me. I didn't realize how nervous I was to have Gloria in our home. It feels like we have a detective interrogating us with a magnifying glass looking over every inch of our lives.

"I want Connor to be aware that with social services, we can call you at any time, day or night, to help us with a baby or child in need. It could be on a Monday at ten a.m. or in the middle of the night. Usually, the circumstances aren't great."

I blanch, and Gloria nods.

"It's sad, but it's reality. Are you both prepared for that?"

Connor looks over at me, and we nod. "I'm used to workin' late hours and bein' up early."

"Remind me, you're a bartender?"

"I co-own The Social Hour bar. And yes, I do bartend on occasion when we're short-staffed."

"Does that happen a lot? Having to work late nights?"

"Sometimes. But I've got a great staff. They are like family, so we try to help each other out when we can."

Gloria looks at Connor thoughtfully. "We have a saying at my job I think you're familiar with."

"What's that?" Connor smiles at me. I squeeze his leg reassuringly.

"*Last call.* It means we're calling in one of our foster families because the shit has hit the fan—excuse my language. It means you're my last hope."

"That's a much different version than a bar's last call," I

tease. "Don't worry, Gloria, we are prepared to be on call twenty-four-seven."

"Good. Often we use you as a temporary placement until a family member can step up. I need you to be aware of that scenario as well. It's easy to get attached to the babies."

Connor clears his throat and leans forward. "What if we wish to foster an older child?"

"Well, that most certainly is a possibility and a better scenario for keeping the child long-term if it's a good fit, but I will warn you, these children have been through a lot emotionally. Some of them are drug babies and have cognitive issues. Some of them have witnessed things no child should ever have to see. Some of them are shut down and hard to reach, even in the most loving homes. These are the children who get lost in the system. They aren't wanted by anyone, and it affects them mentally and emotionally. I'm not trying to scare you. I just want you to be aware, okay?"

"Yes." We nod.

"Great. I will enroll you in the weekly classes. I understand, Connor, you work a lot of nights, so TJ, you will still need to come on your own."

"Do I get to see you, Gloria?"

"Of course." She smiles.

"Well, then it's a no-brainer."

Gloria stands to leave, swinging her satchel over her shoulder. She hands Connor the same folder she gave me at lunch. "My card is in here if you have any questions. You can call me anytime. Connor, it was a pleasure meeting you. Thank you both for inviting me into your home and for wanting to become a part of the foster community."

"Thank ye for yer time, Gloria," Connor says. We stand in the doorway and wave. Once she's safely on the elevator and I've blown her at least a hundred air-kisses, we return to the apartment.

"So this foster thing might not be such a bad idea—"

"I called Penny and we're packing up her apartment and booking her a flight," I squeal. Connor's smile falls, and my stomach drops. "Shit, too fast? Too soon? You gave me the green light."

Connor sits down on the sofa and closes his eyes. "Aye, yer right, I did…Penny it is, then."

I sit next to him and place my hand on his thigh. "Babe, I know you're concerned about her, but her enthusiasm trumps my worries. She's so excited to be doing this with us."

Connor smiles, but it doesn't quite reach his eyes. He places his hand over mine. "Then I'm excited too, Love. I guess we need to research where to have the procedure done and we'll have to pick out a donor egg, set her up with a doctor, and get the guest room ready."

"Already done. Well, I contacted the clinic for IVF treatment. I have an appointment set up for you in a few weeks at the spank bank."

"A spank bank?" Connor's eyebrows adorably draw together.

I shove his leg and whisper, "The sperm bank. We need your swimmer for the egg."

"Ah, right. I forgot we agreed I was donating that part."

"All this talk has made me sleepy. Let's stay in, order food, and watch a movie since you have to work every night this week. Oh, and make sure you have next Sunday off because that's when I'm booking Penny's flight. Eeek! I'm so happy." I clap my hands and jump off the couch. "Pizza, Chinese. Indian?"

"Anything but Chinese," Connor says testily.

"Crab Rangoon isn't calling your name tonight? I thought it would be cute to get fortune cookies and save them in our baby book. A memento from the night we hired Penny."

"I don't feel like lo mein," he grumbles, roughly opening the fridge door and grabbing sparkling water.

"Okay, kind of random, but I'm gonna go with it. Indian it is." I smile brightly and dial the number to our favorite Indian restaurant. It's all coming together, finally.

Chapter 19

Lex

SARAH LAUGHS, HER golden hair catching in the afternoon sunlight while we take a ride through the fields before dinner. It's something we agreed to do once a week, no matter how busy our schedules get. Wednesdays are for family. My heart beats steadily as I maneuver my horse over to hers. I'm the luckiest chancer in the world. No matter how chaotic life gets, my Sunshine always is by my side chasing the storm clouds away.

"Sunshine, have I ever told ye how beautiful ye are?"

"Every day, Lex." She smiles, her cheeks turning rosy. I love that I can still make her blush.

"And I'll say it until the day I die."

"Mommy, why does Daddy call you Sunshine?" Alexis asks, looking up at her mom in that sweet curious way she has about her. Christ, my heart is full right now.

"Because, Mouse…there ain't no sunshine when she's gone," I sing, causing Wyatt and Alexis to giggle. "When I first met your mum, she was the most upbeat ray of sunshine. Her smile was addicting. When you were around her, life just got better, like you were warmed by the sun.”

“I believe your words were ‘sunshine on crack’.” Sarah laughs.

“Aye, my little sunshine on crack. Shilo rum do, Love.”

“Shilo rum do, Lex,” she whispers, meeting me halfway and kissing my lips.

“Barf,” Jax mutters on his horse behind us. I look over my shoulder at him and scowl.

“You know, Jax, women like it when you give them compliments.” Sarah winks at me.

“Mama, what’s a complo-ment?” Alexis asks. She’s wedged in the saddle in front of Sarah, while Wyatt rides with me. They’re almost ready to ride on their own, but for now, I love moments like this when we’re all together.

“A compliment is saying something nice about a person. Daddy called me beautiful.”

“Because you are bootiful.” She smiles up at Sarah and my heart sings.

“So are you.” Sarah kisses the top of her head.

“Can we talk about something else?” Jax groans behind us. He’s such a surly teenager. It makes me chuckle, remembering how I used to be. My parents knew nothing, girls were everything, and my guitar was life.

“Sure. Let’s talk about what happened last week.”

“Lex…” Sarah frowns, pointing down at Alexis.

“We’ll make it PG,” I say.

My horse snorts and Wyatt tenses. “S’okay, buddy. He’s only sniffing the air.”

Wyatt reminds me of the new skittish horse we recently

brought in. She was neglected and abused and scared of her own shadow. Jax and our trainer have been working with her, and the new therapist thought it might be good to have Wyatt help as well. I've also been teaching him how to play the guitar, which seems to relax him.

"We don't need to rehash it for the millionth time," Jax bites out.

"I think rehashing is good. It makes you remember why it was such a bad idea."

Jax grunts. "She was my study partner."

"Really?" I peer over at Sarah, who gives me a warning glance. I zero in on the blanket and basket of snacks we brought with us. "Do you have *picnics* with all your study partners?"

"What are you talking about?" Jax asks, bewildered.

"I'm just sayin' if yer going to invite someone on a *picnic*, ye should at the very least show respect for them. Picnics shouldn' be in the car or in the jacks—"

"Or while your mom is ten feet away," Sarah chimes in.

"Well, I'd rather he have a picnic in his bedroom than some strange place. Also, not every girl should be invited to your *picnic*. You should have feelings for them."

"Da," Jax groans, catching on. "You're mental. It's not like I planned to have a 'picnic'. It just happened."

"Mommy, why are Daddy and Jax having picnics without us?" Alexis asks.

"I want to picnic," Wyatt says.

"They're not having picnics, baby. It's just talking." Sarah looks at me, exasperated.

"All I'm saying is, if yer going to have *picnics*, make sure no one is taking pictures of the desserts to post later on social media. And remember to keep yer salami wrapped. Oh, and keep your picnic basket locked if ye do have a picnic in yer room."

"Da, this is so stupid."

"Let me ask you this. Are ye a picnic virgin? Have ye had other picnics before?"

"Lex," Sarah warns.

"Da, I'm not discussing this right now."

"I'm curious." I shrug. "I started having picnics at yer age, ye know."

"I'm not having picnics!"

"Jax, it's totally normal to have picnics. I'm just sayin' be smart about it, bud."

"The only reason she wanted to have sex is because you're my da!" Jax yells. He kicks the side of his horse and gallops on ahead of us, back to the stable.

"Shite," I grumble.

Sighing, Sarah shoots me a glare. "Picnics, Lex? Really?"

"I was only teasin' him."

"You need to go talk to him. Hand me over Wyatt."

"You can't ride with both of them."

"I'll walk the horse and they can ride."

Sarah swings a leg over her horse and steps down. I place Wyatt on her horse behind Alexis. "Hold on to yer sister."

"Mama, can we go on a picnic?" Wyatt asks.

"Mama? What's sex?" I hear Alexis ask and Sarah groans as I steer my horse in Jax's direction. She's going to kill me later.

After a few minutes, I catch up to him back at the stable.

He's untacking his horse when I swing off my Appaloosa and tie him up.

"Jax, I'm sorry—"

"Do you know how hard it is being the kid of someone famous?" He clenches his jaw, unbuckling the girth.

"No, I don't." I look at the ground and shake my head. "But I have an idea."

"It sucks. Everyone wants a piece of you."

"That, I am familiar with." I smile ruefully. "So is your Uncle Tatum. And it does suck."

"I can't trust anyone because I wonder who wants to be my friend because they like me or if they're using me because I'm Lex Ryan's kid." He hauls the saddle off and carries it into the barn. I follow him, not sure what to say.

"Jax, I'm sorry, bud. I never thought my fame would be a hindrance to ye."

He walks by me like he didn't even hear me and grabs the saddle blanket off his horse. "When Samantha asked to come over and 'study' and maybe meet my famous da, I thought, why the hell not? If she's willing to throw herself at me, why shouldn't I cash in on your fame?"

"Oye, that's a wicked line to be walkin' there, boy." I follow him back into the tack room. "First of all, women are to be respected, got it? I've had me fair share of picnics before I met yer mum, but I always respected the woman, ye know what I mean?"

"Yes, sir."

"I know ye think I don't know what yer goin' through, but I've been in yer shoes." *God, if only he knew the truth about the hell his biological mother put me through.* I stand with my hands on the doorjamb, blocking his way out. He reluctantly leans against a wall. "There are users and there are givers in this world. The users leech yer happiness. They don't care what happens to ye, they're in it for themselves, along for the glorious ride. Then there are people like Sarah and yer Uncle Connor. They are the givers. They love ye even when they've seen ye at yer worst. No matter what, they are there for ye. The givers are who ye need to look for in the crowd."

"How do I know if someone is a giver or a user?"

"Lemme ask ye this. Did Sam make ye feel good?"

He scuffs the floor with his boot. "No, Da. I felt like I was being used. Like she didn't give a shit about me."

I nod. "Come here."

He pushes away from the wall, and I throw an arm around his shoulders, steering him back outside. He's almost as tall as me and lanky. His black hair falls into his eyes. He reminds me so much of me and Connor at this age.

We walk out to the paddock and I point to Sarah in the distance, walking Alexis and Wyatt on her horse. "See yer beautiful mum and yer sister and brother? They will always have yer back. No matter how angry ye make us, or what embarrassin' situation ye get caught in, we will be here for ye. Same with yer Uncle Connor and Uncle TJ. Yer friends Trip and Mason? The ones you've been friends with since seventh grade? They're yer givers, too. You'll know how to find us, bud. Most of the time, we're standin' right in front of ye, quietly holdin' out a hand to help ye up."

Jax nods quickly and swallows, his cheeks flushed. "I'm sorry, Da."

"Nothing to be sorry about, Jax. It's called growin' up."

We wait for Sarah to walk the younger ones in, and I exhale a shaky breath, moving my hand to Jax's back. I love this family so fiercely.

"Daddy! Mommy said we can have a picnic tonight on the covered porch and watch the sunset," Alexis crows from atop the horse.

"Did she now?" I waggle my eyebrows at Sarah. She rolls her eyes, but she can't hide her bemused smile.

I look at Jax, and he grins, shaking his head. "Twisted."

I clap him on the back, feeling like a million bucks. I think I just survived my first teenage crisis. Da will be so proud.

Chapter 20

Connor

THE SOUND OF drills and sawing behind the closed door has the hair on the back of my neck bristling. "TJ?"

"Back here," he calls, poking his towel-turbaned head around our bedroom door. "Getting dressed."

I stalk down the hallway. "I thought we weren't remodeling the guest room?"

"Did I say that? I don't believe I said that." Taking the towel off, he runs product through his hair. "I said I won't be using Jean Paul Pierre Luc. But luckily, his cousin, Fontaine, was available." He looks over at me while I pace. "But don't worry, he isn't nearly as eccentric as JPPL."

I stop pacing. "His name is *Fontaine*?"

"I know, totes adorbs, right? I think it means 'fountain' in French. Anyhoo, Fontaine is in construction and is building bookshelves for us. I wanted it to be a sweet surprise when you came home tonight, but he's taking longer than expected." He holds up a hand. "Don't worry, I promise we'll pick out the rest of the nursery stuff together. We have plenty of time." He washes the gel off his hands and kisses my cheek. "Ready to go pick up our baby mama from the airport?"

My eyes soften at the excitement in TJ's voice. "Ready as I'll ever be. Do ye think it's safe to leave Fontaine here alone?"

"Totes safe. Let's tell him we're leaving." He looks down at his watch. "Sam and the crew guys are meeting us downstairs. I hope that's okay. I wanted them to film us meeting her for the first time."

"Whatever ye want, Love." I squeeze his hand. TJ has been a lot more cognizant of the film crew being in our personal space. They haven't been around much, so I assume he said something to them.

TJ knocks on the guestroom door before opening it. "Fontaine? Fontaine!" he shouts and the drill turns off. "We're leaving. You'll be done in two hours?"

"Yeah, no problem," a deep Boston accent responds. I arch my neck trying to get a look at this guy because I can't picture that voice matching the name Fontaine or being cousins with Jean Luc Poop. He's facing the wall, wearing a plain white t-shirt, a manly no-nonsense toolbelt, Levi's, and steel-toed boots. His head is bald and shiny, like Mr. Clean.

"Hi, I'm Connor," I pipe up. Fontaine peers over his shoulder at me and frowns, then returns to his work. Grunting, he snaps his measuring tape up against the wall. He takes a yellow pencil from behind his ear and marks the measurement. "It was nice to meet ye," I say. We close the door and I raise my eyebrows at TJ. "Are ye sure that guy is related to the other designer?"

"Who, Fontaine and JPPL? Of course, silly. First cousins. Moms were both from Pare-ee. You can see the similarity when they smile."

"Fontaine smiles?" I joke as we grab our coats and the car keys. TJ picks up a large posterboard covered in bright fluorescent marker and glitter. "What is that?"

"Oh, I made a sign to hold up at baggage claim so she knows who we are."

"I'm pretty sure you can see that sign from space." I chuckle. "Besides, she's seen us on the video chat."

"I know, I...I want her to feel special. This is a big moment for us. We're about to meet our baby mama, Connor." He sniffs.

"Awe, Love, are ye gettin' emotional on me?"

"Yes," TJ blubbers. I hug him as we ride the elevator down and greet Sam, Brody, and the other crew members from *Nashville Next* in the parking garage. They follow us in their car to the airport. TJ's knee doesn't stop bouncing the entire way there.

"Ye nervous, Love?"

"A little. You?"

"Yeah, but eager too."

TJ leans over to smack a kiss on my cheek. "In this forever."

"Forever, *mo chroí*."

We park and head to baggage claim with the *Nashville Next* crew trailing behind us. TJ checks his phone. "Okay, her plane landed ten minutes ago, so she should be on her way down if she's not already here." He holds the sign up, craning his neck to see above the crowd.

I check to see which baggage claim is assigned to the Los Angeles flight number. "Let's head to carousel six."

TJ holds his sign up like a little kid. "Ooh, is that her? That redhead over there."

I turn to see who he's pointing at, but when the redhead turns around, we both deflate. "Definitely not her. Why don't ye try callin' her? I'll hold yer sign."

TJ nods, handing it over to me. "Make sure you hold it high so she can see it, babe." He dials her number. "It's going straight to voicemail. Must still be on airplane mode."

We stand and wait for another ten minutes with TJ calling her several more times. Everyone from her flight has come and gone. My heart sinks as I look over at TJ's crestfallen expression. His glitter sign, long forgotten, lying on the floor.

"Love? I done think she's coming."

"There must be a mistake. She may have missed her flight. Or maybe she's here, but she's stuck on the plane? Perhaps she's helping an elderly woman to her gate or she's trapped in line at the women's bathroom. You know how women like to pee right after they get off a plane. Maybe—"

"Love, she's not coming." I place my hands on his forearms and squeeze to get his attention.

"But she has to come, Connor. I sent her a plane ticket and money to move her stuff here."

I close my eyes. "How much money did ye send her?"

"Enough to cover the movers and whatever else she needed, about five thousand. You don't think she spent the money on something else, do you? She was so anxious to move here…"

I rub my forehead as I desperately try to stave off the growing headache. "She duped us, Love. Come on, let's go home." I glance back at the camera crew, shaking my head, and fold my arm around TJ.

"I don't understand. We talked every day. You should have heard the excitement in her voice. It was genuine, I know it was." Tears trickle down TJ's cheek and I want to punch my hand into the tiled wall and roar at the night sky about how unfair this is, but mostly I want to hold him and tell him we'll be okay and we can try again. But I know that's not true. This kind of betrayal stings and leaves you jaded.

TJ dials her phone once again when we get back into the car. The Bluetooth picks up and puts the call on speaker. "Babe, maybe we should let it go—"

"Hello?" Penny answers.

"Penny? It's TJ." His voice cracks with excitement. "Where are you? We came to the airport to pick you up, but couldn't find you. We're still here. Are you here? Are you lost?"

"Oh, shit. TJ, I totally forgot. Sorry, I...I'm not coming."

Seconds slip past. TJ's mouth dramatically hinges open. I shift in my seat and squeeze the steering wheel until my knuckles turn white.

"But why?" he says finally. "What do you mean you're not coming?"

"Funny thing..." Her laugh sounds tinny. "I um, got back together with my boyfriend about a month and a half ago."

"Okay, and?" TJ waves his hand impatiently.

"And, I'm pregnant. I tested this morning and sure enough, two pink lines popped up. Isn't that crazy?" Her enthusiasm swallows the silence in the car.

"But you don't want kids."

"I mean, I didn't *plan* for it to happen, but here we are," she chirps.

"Here we are," TJ echoes. "So, you're having a baby, just not ours?"

"I know, wild, right? Shows you what can happen when you're not taking birth control."

"Condoms, Penny. Have you ever heard of condoms?" TJ's cheeks turn splotchy.

"You sound upset."

I blow out a humorless chuckle and shake my head in disbelief. How can she sound so cavalier about this?

"I'm beyond upset," TJ barks. "We had a deal. You signed a contract."

"Well, I don't know what you want me to do. I'm pregnant."

"You said that already."

"Penny, what about the money TJ sent ye for movin'?" I ask.

"Oh, well, of course, I'll send it back. Of course. Look, I need to go, but we can chat more later, okay?" Penny disconnects the call before we can utter another word.

"I don't think I'm going to get my money back," TJ says despondently. He gazes out the window at the passing scenery.

"No, Love, I done think so."

"I'm in total disbelief, babe. I mean…who would have

predicted this? Who would have thought Penny would betray us like this?"

I want to stick my head out the window and shout, *Me! I predicted it!* Instead, I press my lips together and keep my eyes on the road. Glancing over at TJ, I grab his hand and squeeze it, feeling sad for my man's tender heart. I'm so pissed at Penny for hurting him and making him look foolish. "No one could have predicted she would get pregnant with her own baby."

"Didn't she say she was single?" His voice cracks, going an octave higher than normal. "She said, and I quote, *'My life is stale here. I'm looking for adventure'.*"

I nod. "Something like that."

"God, I'm so embarrassed, Con. I've been running around town telling everyone I know we're having a baby by surrogate. Jace and Greg from the gym were so jelly and wanted to know what agency we were using. I told them she was the most amazing surrogate from the University of Life Beginnings—"

"Wait, is that a real agency?"

"No, Penny and I made it up. Ugh, now I have to tell them it fell through and see their smug little smiles on their arrogant, stupid faces."

"Ye don't have to tell them shit."

"I'm chicken fucking little, Connor. I even told the lady bagging my groceries at Whole Foods. How am I going to hold my head high around town?"

"Who cares what everyone thinks? We'll tell them it didn' work out. They don't need to know the details, right? It's our business, no one else's."

TJ looks over and squeezes my hand back. "You're right, babe. No one needs to know."

His phone rings over Bluetooth. "Ooh, maybe it's Penny and this was all a huge mistake and she's on the next flight. Hello? Penny?"

The Bluetooth takes a few seconds to connect. "Hello, TJ?" a man says.

His face falls. "This is TJ."

"Hey, it's Jordan Marks with *Nashville Next*. We spoke a couple weeks ago."

"Yes, Jordan, hi." TJ turns to me and whispers, "He's their producer."

"Listen, TJ, I have some bad news."

I hold my breath and listen while Jordan rubs salt into the raw wound Penny sliced open.

Chapter 21

I FLOP MYSELF into the chair by the Nespresso machine.

Andie looks up from her desk. "TJ, are you okay?"

"No." I sigh dramatically.

"Did they run out of sprinkles at the coffee shop?"

I shake my head.

"Did they have a horrible sale at Neiman's?" She lowers her voice and whispers dramatically, "Did Tyrese snub you again?"

I wave my hand. "I know you called for a meeting this morning, but I have some bad news. Can you call the girls out here? I'm too weak to get up."

Andie gasps, holding her hand over her throat. "Tell me Nana Rose is okay?"

"She's fine, Shorts. Please hurry, I can't hold on much longer."

"TJ, I swear to God, if this is like the time they canceled your Netflix subscription by accident and we all thought someone died, I will personally kill you in your sleep."

"Who's killing who?" Kiki asks, coming out of her office.

Andie rolls her eyes and points at me with her pen. "Something's wrong with TJ. He's not himself."

"What's wrong, Tammy Jean? Was Marco not there to make your morning coffee?"

"I'm too depressed to drink coffee today," I say.

"Oh, this is bad," Kiki murmurs to Andie. "Sarah? Get out here! We have an emergency."

"What's wrong?" Sarah rushes out.

"TJ, tell us what's wrong," Kiki says, taking a seat.

I hug the magazine I've been holding to my chest. "You know how we were supposed to meet Penny, our surrogate, yesterday?"

All three nod.

"The one with the rollerblades?" I sob.

Sarah hands me a tissue. "Yes, we know," she says. "You've got her picture up in the office kitchen. How did it go?" Her eyes dart to Andie and then Kiki.

"It didn't. She never showed up," I choke out.

"Oh my god, why not?" Sarah asks.

"Because she's pregnant with her boyfriend's baby."

"Awe, TJ, I'm so sorry." Andie gently pats my back.

"I knew she was a bad egg from the get-go," Kiki says. "Man, that sucks, Teej. I'm really sorry."

"And to top it off, she stole the money I sent for her to move here. *And* I wasted money on a plane ticket she never intended to use."

"Wait, she knew she was pregnant when you booked her flight?" Andie asks.

"I don't think so, but who knows? She's a con artist and

I'm the dupe."

Sarah rushes over, wrapping me in a hug. "Oh TJ, you're not a dupe. No one could have predicted she would do this. I mean, you guys spoke daily."

"Me," Kiki says, holding her hand up in the air. "I predicted it. Connor wasn't thrilled about her, either."

"Kiki, you're not helping." Sarah frowns while she strokes my back. I sit back and theatrically blow my nose.

"But that's not the worst of it." I sniffle. "*Nashville Next* called yesterday and said they're dropping the story."

"Can they do that?" Andie asks indignantly.

"Page four, clause fifteen," I monotonously recite the memorized email I received this morning. "*Nashville Next* has the right to end the contract without reason or warning. They said our story wasn't moving along fast enough and they'd wasted enough production time. Basically he said I overpromised and underdelivered."

"Oh, Tammy Jean, I know how badly you wanted to be on there." Kiki walks over and wraps her arms around me.

"And you want to know what the cherry on the fucking sundae is?"

"Oh god, there's more?" Andie's eyebrows raise to her hairline.

I hold out the magazine. Kiki snatches it from me and gasps. "No."

"Yes. Sonja King is having a baby."

"Wait, why does that name sound familiar?" Andie asks.

"She's the reality star that loves to hate us, yet she keeps coming back for us to do her hair and makeup," Sarah says. "She always comes in with her best friend, Amanda."

"Oh, the one who ate cheese balls with her gum." Andie nods. "I remember her."

Kiki flips through the magazine, with Sarah looking over her shoulder. "Sonja King announced she's three months pregnant with Simon Brown's baby, her new beau she met four months ago on the reality show, *Love Lost and Found.* Look for *People Magazine*'s photo spread of her nursery designed by legendary Nashville designer, Jean Paul Pierre Luc, in our next issue. She's also set for a live interview with Josie Janson from *Nashville Next.* Oh no, this is bad."

"The worst! She not only stole my baby news, but she took my nursery designer and my reality show on top of it." I stomp my foot, jealousy trumping my despair.

"Technically, she didn't steal your news since you don't have a baby... You know what? I'll keep my lips zipped." Andie shrinks back into her chair after noticing Kiki shaking her head vigorously.

"You guys, my life is over, *finito*, ruined."

"TJ, no, it isn't. Everyone will forget about Sonja by tomorrow," Sarah soothes. "And Connor told us you weren't using Jean Paul, so what does it matter?"

"Sare Bear, no one will forget Sonja. This is just the beginning. Her social media accounts will remind fans daily with baby updates and JPPL room pics. I'm sure E! News and TMZ will report about it. Short's is right, I have nothing. Nothing to live for."

"TJ, I didn't mean it like that. You have so much to live for..." She looks helplessly at Kiki and Sarah.

"Relax, Shorts. I'm not going to *endanger* myself. Cheese Louise in clam sauce. I love myself and Connor, and you three bitches too much. Oh, and caramel macchiatos, I could never give those up. And Tatum's butt in his Levi's, and Cam's muscular shoulders…"

"TJ, focus." Sarah snaps her fingers, bringing me back to my doom and gloom.

"You know what? *Nashville Next* sucks. They don't know a good thing when it's right in front of them. Screw them. We're going to go bigger. Brighter!" Kiki tosses the magazine in the trash. "Sonja King can eat a dick."

"Kinky, I appreciate the support, but it's over. Connor and I lost the only baby prospect and now *Nashville Next* Pete Davidsoned us. What's the point of any of it?"

"Pete Davidsoned?" Andie wonders.

"Yeah, you know the SNL guy who jumps from one relationship to the next and tattoos everyone on his arm? It was so tradge when Ariana dumped him and then he went running to Kim K, but seriously everyone could see that was a cover for both of them, probs set up by her mom. And then she dumped him and everyone was like whoa, let's take a breather Pete and Kim, and be on your own, but he was like I'm jumpin' right back in—"

"I'm sorry I asked," Andie says, massaging her temples.

"Wait, so you're not going to adopt or foster because *Nashville Next* pulled the plug?" Sarah asks.

I shrug. "I don't feel as passionate about it as I did before."

"But TJ, you *really* wanted a family. That doesn't have to change," Kiki reasons. "You can hire another surrogate."

"You guys don't understand." I pout. "There was no one else like Penny. I'd never have that cat killer, Amy, carrying my child, or the Mountain Dew lady. Penny was my last hope."

The three of them share a look.

"You know what you need?" Kiki says.

"To hide under my covers for the rest of eternity?"

"You need a girls' night out. Tonight."

"Yes!" Sarah shouts.

Andie smiles. "Mandy's coming into town tonight. She'll want to get her dance on."

"I'm never dancing again."

"TJ, remember what you said to me when I was down in the dumps over Cam?"

"That he's too pretty to want someone in ratty sweats with no makeup and greasy hair like you?"

"Uh, no. At least I don't think so. Did you say that?" Her brows furrow before she shakes her head. "Whatever, it doesn't matter. You told me life is too short not to get your dance on and I needed to get out of my tragic sweatpants. It worked, didn't it?"

"I think I need to go home and water my fern." I shrug. "Can't you bitches let me wallow?"

"You don't own any plants, Taco Juice, and no we can't. We'll arrange for the guys to watch the kiddos. Go get a coffee and take the rest of the day off. We'll pick you up at seven."

I reach for the magazine in the trash, but she moves it out of reach with her heel. "Nuh-uh. You don't need to obsess over this article all afternoon. Sonja is a Tic Tac, now go." Kiki pushes me toward the elevator.

"But I don't want to go out," I whine. The elevator

doors open and Kiki waits for me to walk into the carriage.

"Thomas Jean, go home, take a nap, shower, and put your big-boy boxers on—"

"You mean the ones that say 'big boy' on the crotch?"

"That's disturbing but sure, whatever floats your boat. You, sir, are going out on the town."

"You guyssss," I whine.

"We got you!" Sarah shouts. "Oh shoot, Andie, didn't you want to tell us something?"

"Oh, um, just that Mandy was coming. See you soon, TJ!" she waves at me as the doors close.

MY STOMACH ROLLS as I get tossed out of my seat and land against the window as Mandy takes a corner on two wheels while Eminem shouts *'my name is'* from the speakers. Kiki and Sarah grip their armrests as she skids to a stop in front of the club.

"Jesus, Mandy, where's the fire?" Andie scolds.

"You guys get out and I'll find a spot!" Mandy shouts over the music.

"Thanks for the whiplash," I grumble, getting out of the van.

Music thumps in the club, but I'm not feeling it. I'm so dejected. We grab a table in the back and order drinks. Normally I'd be out on the dance floor already, but all I want to do is curl up in a ball and be miserable. *Will I ever want to dance again?*

Kiki leans into Sarah and says, "I'm worried about him."

Nodding, Sarah mouths, *Me too.*

"Hello? I'm right in front of you."

"Fine. We're worried about you. Sue me." Kiki hops off her chair. "I'll be back."

Sighing, I take a sip of my cocktail, but it tastes like watered-down vodka and Juicy Fruit gum. I push my drink away.

"Hey, TJ! Looking fresh tonight!" Rachel, a sales assistant from The White Dove Boutique, passes our table and touches my silver sequined blazer.

"Gracias, Rachel." I limply wave my hand and look away, hoping she gets the hint and moves along. She chats with Andie for a minute then waves goodbye. I spy Kiki talking to the DJ spinning on the second floor. She wanted to go to a karaoke bar, which I normally would love, but I told them I couldn't handle being under the spotlight with adoring fans tonight.

"You going to dance, TJ?" Sarah asks.

"Sare Bear, I can't. I feel like Britney when she cut off her Insta account comments after everyone was trolling her and her fans wanted to send her a wellness check. I just want to go home, put on bad outfits, and dance to the music in my head."

Sarah tosses Andie a look. "I hate seeing you so gloomy, TJ," Andie says. "We feel helpless. What can we do?"

"*Nada*, Shorts." Sighing, I stir my cocktail with my straw.

Mandy slides up to our table and drops off a drink for herself and another for Andie. "I am going to get my dance on!" She spins herself out onto the dance floor as the song "Players" by Coi Leray blasts over the sound system.

"Oh jeez, Mandy is such a dance freak," Andie says. "TJ, please go save her?"

"She looks happy, twerking by herself."

Mandy points to our table and does some weird pulling-a-rope pantomime, while shouting, "Girls are players too!"

Kiki bounces back to our table. "TJ, this next song is for you and guaranteed to cheer you up."

Mandy pulls herself back to our table and takes a long sip of her cocktail, fanning herself with the cocktail napkin. "It is hotter than a naked coochie sunnin' on the patio in August. Egg-fryin' hot, you know what I mean? Y'all, I could fry an egg on my coochie right now, it's hotter than the devil's armpits."

"Mandy!" Andie rubs a hand down her face. "We get it."

"That paints quite a picture, Mandy." Kiki laughs.

Saweetie's "Best Friend" plays over the sound system.

"Oh my gawd, I love this song!" Mandy yells at the top of her lungs like Oprah, shaking her hands in the air. She dances at the table while the girls clap and take turns singing the lyrics. Kiki knows I blast this song every time it plays on the radio, and I love them for trying to cheer me up by singing it, but even this can't lift me out of my funk.

"I've got to go home," I cry, jumping up from the table. My throat tightens and my clothes feel suffocating. The chatter and music are too loud and the walls of the club seem to be closing in on me. I have to get out of here or I might puke. The girls look at me, their eyes wide and mouths open. "I appreciate all of you, but I can't tonight. I'm sorry."

"TJ, wait." Kiki scrambles out of her chair, almost falling flat on her face.

I need to get out of this club, out of this city. I can't stay here and wallow or I'll lose my mind.

"Where are you going?" Kiki shouts.

Anywhere but here. I need to go hide, where I can lick my wounds and heal. Where my husband and friends won't give me pitiful looks and whisper in front of me. I need a place for my sad heart to land. I need my nana.

"I'm going to go see Nana Rose. I'll call y'all when I get back." I hadn't planned to go see her, but as soon as the words leave my lips, I know it's what I need to help heal my heart. I push through the crowd, out into the street to call an Uber. Then, I text Nana.

Me: Nana, I'm coming to visit.

Nana: Ooh delightful, honey. When?

Me: I'm catching the first flight out tomorrow.

Nana: Just you?

Me: Yes, Connor and I are fine. I need to see you.

Nana: Oh dear, this sounds serious. I'll cancel my poker tournament tomorrow. See you soon.

Me: Thanks Nana.

Nana: Don't be a fiddle fart and thank me. That's what nanas are for.

Chapter 22

MOST PEOPLE GRADUALLY change over the years. It's a natural part of growing older. Their looks become weathered, their bodies shrink a few inches, and their minds turn fuzzy. My Nana Rose is the exception. She may have shrunk a few inches, and acquired a few more laugh lines, but she's the same old free spirit, spitfire she was thirty years ago.

Nana lives in a large retirement community in West Palm Beach, Florida. The brochures show lush green golf courses and quaint little bungalows nestled near the beaches with stunning sunsets. You can go shelling in the mornings, crafting at lunchtime, tennis in the afternoons, or ocean swims in the evenings. Even I want to move here.

What the brochure doesn't show you is a bunch of eighty-year-olds zipping around in their golf carts and having sex in the dunes like they're eighteen again.

After the sex scandal of '09, where there was a big chlamydia outbreak, Breezy Palms Retirement Resort was not taking any chances. They now proudly display condom jars at the front desk and in every bathroom in the facility. The thought of Nana having sex makes me want to drive my car into the ocean. No, thank you. But, I have to admit, she is happy here and has a busier social calendar than I do.

I pull up to Nana's single-story, twelve-hundred-square-foot cottage home nestled in between palm trees, hot-pink bougainvillea, and birds of paradise. It's painted a pale blue with white shutters. It's quaint and charming, located right on the beach. I couldn't have asked for a more beautiful place for my Nana to live, and it brings me comfort being so far from her.

The front door almost collapses on its hinges as the five-foot-three hellfire I lovingly call Nana Rose comes bursting out the door. "He's here," she cries out, throwing her arms up above her head. She pulls me into a tight squeeze, then quickly releases me, squinting her eyes. She's wearing a neon-yellow leotard paired with a neon-pink sweatshirt cut to hang off one shoulder, from her *Flash Dance* days, no doubt. Her purple leg warmers cover up her spindly legs and she's wearing white Reebok high-tops. Her box-dyed orange hair is cut to her chin with pixie sparkle strands sprinkled in. Connor always said she reminds him of that little old lady who sings the hip-hop hippity-hop song from the movie, *The Wedding Singer*.

"Nana, were you on your way to aerobics class?"

"Oh, well, if you consider couples' intimate yoga aerobics, then yes. Henry asked me to be his partner." She waggles her eyebrows and I block the mental image of Nana doing downward dog over some crotchety old guy named Henry. "But never mind that. Let me get a look at you!

You've grown."

"Nana, I stopped growing in the ninth grade."

"You're parting your hair differently."

"Nope. It's the same."

She taps her fingertips to her lips, then snaps her fingers. "You're gay and coming out of the closet."

"Ha-ha, Nana. I never had to come out of the closet because you already knew."

She squeezes my biceps and giggles. "I knew the moment you begged me to crochet you a yellow vest with the white daisies and big purple buttons like the one I had."

"I loved that vest."

"All right, well, I can't figure out what's different, so let's get inside before this horrid sunshine burns you to a crisp with your red hair and delicate skin. You certainly don't want to add more freckles to that collection."

I roll my eyes when she turns to walk up her front path. "I barely have any freckles because you used to put zinc oxide on my face and a big bucket hat on my head whenever we went out. No wonder I was such a dorky kid."

"You were adorable. Remember when you begged me to perm your hair when you had the mullet in eighth grade?"

"Nana, we don't talk about those dark days. I'm still mad you gave Kiki a picture."

She peers at me over her shoulder and pauses. Her smile falters as she waits for me. "I know what's changed, Thomas Jean. You're sad. Oh, my heart." She rubs her hand in a comforting circle on my back. "I've got the margarita machine out for Margarita Mondays. How about I whip us up a batch and you can tell me all about it?"

"But Nana, it's eleven thirty."

"So?"

"And it's Saturday, not Monday."

"Who made you the margarita police? My house, my rules. If you don't like it, you can go stay at the hotel down the road."

I smile at the memory of her saying that phrase when I first went to live with her. "Okay, if you insist." I drop my bag in her guest room and gaze longingly at the bed. I'd give anything to crawl under the cool cotton sheets and sleep for days.

The sound of ice crunching and Nana humming from the kitchen snaps my attention.

Walking over to the sliding-glass doors in her kitchen, I push on the handle and take a deep breath of the salty air. The ocean breeze gently blows on my skin and ruffles my hair. "You're so lucky to be living in your dream house, Nana."

Nana was a dance instructor in Albuquerque when my grandfather passed away from a heart attack, leaving her with a sizable inheritance. Grandpa was the love of her life and left a big hole in her heart that I helped fill when I came to live with her a year later. Losing her husband and then her only child a year later had to be painful for Nana, but she never let me see it.

"I am very fortunate and count my blessings every day. Now come over here, have a seat, and tell me what happened. You said you and Connor are fine. Did you and Kiki get into a spat?"

"No." I sip the tart, icy liquid. The salt-rimmed glass

cuts the tang of the tequila. "Ooh, this is delish. You always make the best lime margaritas, Nana."

"I'll make mango ones while you're here. Jerry loves them."

"Who is Jerry?" I raise an eyebrow. "I thought you said his name was Henry?"

"Now, Thomas, don't change the subject." She sets out a bowl of chips and salsa. "Continue."

"Well, you know how Connor and I agreed to start the baby process?"

"Yes," she says cautiously, taking the seat across from me at the table.

"We agreed to hire a surrogate because adoption could take ages. We found the most amazing woman named Penny. She loved rollerblading in her bikini, she loved sparkles and life..."

"She sounds wonderful." Nana's eyes glitter with interest.

"She bailed on us, Nana. I paid for her to move to Nashville, bought her a plane ticket, and she never showed up. Said she was suddenly pregnant with her boyfriend's baby."

"That rollerblading floozy."

"I was so thrilled to finally have found a surrogate who I could bond with and she ends up being a lying, baby-making, sparkle-loving—"

"Harlot," Nana finishes before taking a sip of her margarita. "You know, Thomas, there are other surrogates out there. There's also adoption."

"Penny broke my heart, Nana. I'm not sure I can get over her betrayal to try again. Besides, it's harder for two gay men to adopt than a heterosexual couple. It could take us ages."

"What's the rush? You came to me when I was fifty. I did okay, didn't I?"

"You did amazing." I smile and reach for her hand. "And I'm forever grateful."

"I know you are, honey." She gently squeezes. "TJ, as you know, I'm a big believer in living life to the fullest. We can't wait around and hope for something to land in our laps. We have to make it happen."

"But Nana…"

"Don't you banana me, mister." She wags her finger, trying to sound stern, but her nose crinkles and she giggles. "Remember how I always used to say that to you?"

I nod, nostalgia making my eyes prick with tears. "I remember. 'Don't banana me' and then you'd call me Mr. Pouty Pout Poutamus when I'd stomp my feet. It would make me so mad."

"You were quite ornery."

"Still am." I crunch on a chip and sigh. "Kiki and the girls don't think I'm taking this seriously."

"Why would they think that?"

"Because they gave me this possessed scary doll as a test run for having a baby and I didn't take care of it."

"Hmm, and why didn't you take care of it?"

"Because it wasn't real. I want the real thing, Nana, not some weird doll."

"I see. Well, I think they were trying to help you, honey. Sometimes you can be a bit self-absorbed."

I drop the chip and stare at Nana. "I can't believe you just called me selfish. That hurts."

"It's my fault, Thomas. I was too easy on you growing up. Treated you like you were the star of the show and lavished you with attention. Sometimes, you get blinded by what you want and you can be a real…prima ballerina to those around you."

I open my mouth and shut it. Nana's delivery may have been dismal, but she's right. I have been self-centered. The girls were only trying to help and I ran their doll over with my car—accidentally, of course. And Connor…poor Connor. I've treated him so badly by not listening to what he wanted.

Nana raises an eyebrow, as if she could read my thoughts, and covers my hand with hers. "I'm truly sorry the Sparkle Queen didn't work out. And I'm sorry I called you self-absorbed."

"No, you're right. I have been. I've been awful to the girls and to Connor. And now, I'm…lost. I don't know which direction to turn."

"Thomas, I raised you to be an independent, free thinker. That love always wins. And when life gets you down—"

"—you dance your way through it."

She nods and smiles softly. "That's right. Don't take anyone's shit and don't give up when the chips are down." She swirls a chip in the salsa. "Remember when you were bullied on the bus on the way home from school?"

"I remember. You made me go to Tiger Cub Academy Karate for self-defense."

"Oh, you hated it. You wanted to spend your free time shopping at Bristol's five and dime for yarn so I could crochet sweaters and socks for you."

I raise my pant leg, displaying my hot-pink socks with monkeys on them she knitted for me. "I do love a good pair of fun socks."

"But you never used your self-defense moves on those boys, did you? You went to the prettiest girl on the bus and asked for her help. No way would those losers pick on you in front of Lavonne Shelley and her friends. Oh, she adored you. I ran into her after you moved to California, you know. She said you were the one person she could be herself with. She never had to pretend she was the cool, pretty girl around you."

"That's sweet. It could have backfired if Lavonne had said no."

"My point is, you found a solution on your own. A brilliant one, too. I may have smothered you with kisses and handknit sweaters, but I didn't raise you to throw in the towel when life throws an obstacle in your path. I raised you to stand up for what you deserve. If you want a baby, then you will find a way, Thomas. You always do. You will find your Lavonne."

"Love always wins."

"That's right." She pats my hand and sits back. "What does Dolly Parton always say? 'The magic is inside you, there ain't no crystal ball'."

"I love me some Dolly." I sniffle.

Nana smiles. "Now enough of this moping. Dolly wouldn't sit around eating chips and salsa, wallowing. We have lives to live! How about we go to the community center and see if we can scrounge up some bicycles and head over to the Crab Shack Bar and Grill? We might make it in time for the last hand of strip poker."

"Nana!" I say, aghast.

She waggles her eyebrows and throws the dregs of our drinks down the drain. "Don't sound so shocked, Thomas. I am a sexual being."

I groan and cover my face with my hands. "I'll go, Nana, but I am not partaking in strip poker."

"Oh, before I forget, I need you to remember how to get back here because George asked me to go for a swim later, okay? Normally I'd cancel, but I think you'll be okay on your own for a few hours."

"How many boyfriends do you have?"

Giggling, she grabs her purse. "An old woman never reveals her secrets, Thomas."

I close the front door behind us. "Wait, don't you need a swimsuit?"

Nana Rose lifts her arms in the air, her face to the sky. "Who says I need a suit to swim?" She continues down the sidewalk, and for the first time in days, I can't help but smile.

Chapter 23

Andie

"ANDIE, YOU DON'T look so good. Are you coming down with something?" Sarah sets her chamomile tea on my desk and the smell steaming out of her cup makes the nausea roll through my belly. Before I can reply, I scoot my chair back and run to the bathroom, where I upend the contents of my breakfast into the toilet.

I wash my hands and rinse my mouth, feeling a touch better. When I come back out, Kiki is standing with Sarah at my desk, whispering.

Sarah glances up. "Feeling better?"

"Oh, I'm fine. I forgot to brush my teeth."

"What's going on, Andie?" Kiki asks, sitting on the edge of my desk.

"What do you mean?"

"Uh, well, we just heard you throw up in the bathroom, and it's not the first time I've seen you rush in there."

I sink into my chair and blow out the breath I was holding. *Tell them, Andie, pull it off like a Band-Aid. They make not like it, but soon you won't be able to hide the baby bump.*

"Okay, yes, there is something I need to tell you guys."

"Yes!" Kiki cheers and holds her hand out to Sarah, who sighs and slaps a twenty in her palm. "You're pregnant, aren't you? Gah, I'm so excited!" She comes around the desk and hugs me. I don't know why I was so worried about telling them. They both look genuinely happy for me.

"Wait." I laugh. "Maybe I was going to tell you we're moving and the vomiting was nerves."

"Bullshit." Kiki grins. "How far along are you?"

"Twelve weeks."

"I'm so excited for you and Cam," she gushes.

"Me too." Sarah wraps me in a hug.

"Thanks. I was going to tell you guys on Friday, but then TJ was having that terrible, no good, horrible day and I couldn't bring myself to hurt him."

"Oh no, he'll be thrilled for you," Sarah says, then bites her lip. "At least, I think he will… But I think you were right to hold off the other day."

"Yeah, it didn't feel right to bring it up when he was so down. But there's something else."

"Oh god, you *are* moving," Kiki cries. "You guys can't leave me."

"We're not moving, but…"

"Andie, it's okay. You can tell us." Sarah nods encouragingly.

"I… I'm not sure I'll be able to handle working here five days a week anymore. I don't want to quit, but I understand if you need someone full-time. This baby surprise couldn't have come at a worse time, with all of us being so busy and

Cam opening up a third location…"

"This baby is a blessing. Don't let work, schedules, or my brother rob you of your joy of that."

"Oh no, Cam has been very supportive. He's over the moon."

"I'm glad." Kiki's smile grows. She looks up at Sarah who nods. "Look, at the beginning, when you were single and struggling and needed the money, it made sense. But now that you're married to my brother with two kids and a third on the way, we get your priorities have changed. You have been an amazing office manager and we love having you here, but family comes first, right, Sare?"

"Absolutely."

Kiki and Sarah slide chairs up to my desk. "We need a bigger office."

"I agree, and I think if we're going to be having an open and honest discussion, we need to talk about hiring assistants." Sarah looks from me to Kiki. "I know we said it would always be us and only us, but it's crazy how much business is coming in. We've doubled our clients from last year, and with TJ wanting to dabble in home décor, we'll be overwhelmed. I'd be willing to train someone underneath me to cover when we're on tour with the band." Sarah holds up her hand as Kiki opens and closes her mouth. "Kiki, you're burning both ends of the candle. You know it, we know it, hell, the cleaning crew that comes in the middle of the night and finds you here knows it. TJ's been urging you to get an assistant. Stop being so damn stubborn."

Kiki's face crumples. "I'm so tired, you guys. I've been trying to hold it all together, but I'm not freaking Superwoman."

"No one is asking you to be," Sarah says gently, stroking her back.

"I really want to try for a baby girl, but Tatum thinks we have our hands full with Chase and Drew. With my luck, we'd have another boy. I just don't want to wait until it's too late, you know? Sorry, Andie"—she sniffles—"we should be celebrating your news, not talking about my problems."

I shake my head and smile. "Kiki, please, vent away. It's long overdue."

"I agree," Sarah says. "Kiki, you've kept this bottled up for too long. We've seen the stress you're under and the pressure you're putting on yourself. First, hire an assistant, and then you'll be in a better headspace to have the baby talk with Tatum. I feel like I'm being pulled in five different directions with flying to LA and Vegas for award shows, touring with the band, and local clients here… I'm going to burn out if I don't get some help."

I nod and give them a watery smile. "Damn these hormones. I love you guys so much. You gave me my start here, but I need to be more present at home."

"Us too." Sarah and Kiki both sniffle.

"Okay, then it's decided," Kiki says. "We're each in charge of finding an assistant. Andie, you tell us what hours you want to work and we'll work with it. We don't want to lose you, either." Kiki stands and hugs me. "I'm so happy I'm going to be an auntie again."

"What about TJ?" I ask.

"TJ's going through a crisis right now." Kiki bites her bottom lip, tapping her fingers on my desk.

"I think we should put him in charge of finding a new office space for us because let's face it, as much as I love being above The Social Hour, we've outgrown it here," Sarah says.

Kiki snaps her fingers. "Brilliant, Sare. He'll love that assignment. Cam has always wanted the upstairs for storage anyway, so he'll be ecstatic."

I chuckle. "Yes, he will be."

"But first things first, you guys. We need to go help our friend, Tammy Jean. He needs us more than he's willing to admit."

"Road trip?" Sarah suggests.

"I'll reschedule the appointments," I say, flipping open the book.

"Too bad Mandy isn't still here. She could shave two hours off the drive time." Kiki winks.

"Oh lord, I think we should fly." I laugh.

Kiki claps her hands. "Wait, I have a brilliant idea."

"Oh boy," Sarah mutters. "This never ends well."

"Andie, look up Nana Rose's number. I'm going to see if the guys are free for a little impromptu concert down in West Palm. Sarah, go call Connor and let's go get TJ."

Chapter 24

TJ

IT'S BEEN A week since I landed on Nana Rose's doorstep and I'm exhausted. Nana has had me biking, swimming, playing croquet, learning to knit, baking, and partaking in craft hour every day. Some old hag named Joan has it out for me during crafting hour. She calls me Carrot Top and always insists on sitting next to me, putting a timer in front of us to see who can finish faster and do it better. Yesterday I had to yank my kiln-dried, painted teapot away from her when she tried to hide it in the trash because all the ladies were ooh-ing and ahh-ing over it. Nana says she's like this with everyone and not to take it personally, but I'm on to Joan. That geriatric won't beat me. Today we're making chunky knit blankets and I already have a plan to mess up her count.

I know I need to head back to Nashville, but this week, although tiring, has been very therapeutic. Nana and I have had lots of laughs over her delicious margaritas, and I even got to meet her pool boy, Sven, which is ironic because Nana doesn't have a pool. It's obvious I'm cramping her style, not that Nana would ever tell me, but I'm finally ready to go home to Connor and face the music.

Nana opens the sliding-glass door and sticks her head out. "Thomas, dear, can you come here for a moment?"

"Nana, can it wait? I'm so tired from our spinning class this morning. I can barely move my pinky finger and I need all my strength to out-knit Joan this afternoon."

"I have Connor on the phone, dear."

That's odd. Why didn't he call my cell? I check my phone. Fully charged, no new calls. "Well, why didn't you say so in the first place?" I heave myself out of the cushioned lounge chair and hobble up the steps.

"Thomas, you really should stretch more."

"Nana, I normally drink lots of coffee and complain at work every day. This whole exercising-every-day thing has awoken muscles I didn't even know existed."

I grab the phone from her and smile. "Hi, handsome."

"Hi, Love, how's yer day so far?"

"Nana tried to kill me with her sadistic spinning class, and I'm gearing up to show Joan that I can chunky knit blanket her under the table any day of the week. I've watched some YouTube videos and I think I've got my technique perfected."

"Wow, that sounds…fun."

"Joan messed with the wrong gay."

"Right, well, I hate to mess up yer afternoon, but I need ye to open yer front door."

"What?" I rush to the front door still holding Nana's cordless phone to my ear. I fling it open. There on her doorstep is Connor, holding a bouquet of cream freesia, my fave. "What are you doing here?"

"You can hang up the phone, Love."

I lower it and fling myself into his arms. "I've missed you so much. I'm sorry for leaving so abruptly and for getting so upset." I tenderly kiss him. "I'm sorry for everything. Nana called me a buffoon and she was right. Can you forgive me?"

"Always." He kisses my lips. "I know ye wanted some time to get over yer hurt, but we missed ye, too."

"We?" I ask, leaning back, pulling the flowers to my nose, and inhaling deeply. Connor gives me his sexy smile and motions with his chin to look behind him. I hadn't even noticed the executive coach parked across the road and its occupants. "Is that…"

Leaning against the luxury bus are Kiki, Sarah, and Andie. I shade my eyes.

"Yep, we decided we needed to come get ye and while we were here, the boys are promoting their new album with their first stop in West Palm Beach before they hit the big tour in June."

"The guys are here too?"

"Yeah, they are doin' a sound check over at the gardens as we speak. It took a lot of moving parts to throw this together so quickly, but we had your nana's help."

"Nana knew about this?" I ask incredulously. "Wait, is that Mandy driving?"

Connor grimaces. "She insisted when Andie told her the plan. I've never rolled down a highway going a hundred miles an hour in a coach before. I didn' know they could go that fast."

"You guys came for me?" I look up into his beautiful

blue eyes, the color of the ocean behind us. Tears pool in mine.

"We did." Connor leans in and kisses me again. Then he raises his hand and waves everyone over. Kiki comes running and leaps into my arms.

"Turd Jam, are you okay?"

"I'm okay, Kinky."

"Goddamn it, don't ever leave me standing in the middle of a nightclub again."

"I'm sorry. Total breakdown. It won't happen again, I promise."

"Cross your heart." She makes the cross-motion with her finger over her chest and I do the same.

"Cross my heart."

"TJ! Your nana's house is so beautiful!" Sarah pulls me into a hug.

"Thanks, Sare Bear. Thank you guys for coming here. It means so much to me." I swipe away a tear. "I'm so embarrassed."

"TJ, you are always there for us. It's our turn to return the favor. Besides, we couldn't let you go on vacation without us." Kiki pats my back. "Nana Rose? It's your favorite person in the whole world! Open up the photo albums and pour the margaritas!"

"Bitch please, I'm her favorite person," I spout out.

Nana Rose stands in the open doorway with her arms open wide. "How's my favorite girl?"

Kiki gives me an I-told-you-so look over her shoulder and hugs Nana. "Have I ever shown you the picture of Thomas in his yellow crochet daisy vest?"

"What?" Kiki squeals. "You have not. I'm dying to see it."

"Nana, no!"

"Come on, everyone, come inside." Nana waves everyone in behind Kiki. "Oh Sarah, I love the natural blonde, but the purple was so much fun."

"I'll change it again soon, Nana Rose. Thanks for having us."

"Of course, dear. Oh, Anderson, you look like you're positively glowing. How far along are you, dear?"

"Oh uh, I'm…uh—"

"Oh my god, hold the hot sauce, you're preggers?" I squeal.

Andie's eyes dart between me, Connor, and Nana. "I found out a few weeks ago. I didn't want to upset y'all."

"Upset us? Honey, we're thrilled for you and Cam." I pull her into a hug and squeeze. "I'm so sad you thought it would upset me. Andie, just because it may not work out for us, don't ever think I don't want it for you guys, okay?"

She nods and bursts into tears. "I'm sorry. Damn hormones."

"We're so excited for you and Cam, Love." Connor pulls her into his arms.

"Come on, honey, come inside and get yourself together. Are we waiting for your friend on the bus?"

"Mandy?" Andie turns. "She's giving a tour. Your neighbors wanted to see inside the coach."

I cup my hands around my mouth and shout, "Hey Mandy, are you coming in?"

She waves. "Be there in a sec! Showing Rita and Ed

around!"

"Well, wonderful, everyone's here." Nana smiles, hugging Connor. "Especially my handsome Irishman."

"Hands off my man, Nana." I follow Nana and Connor into the house and see my three besties gathered around the kitchen table. "I can't believe you guys are here!"

"We're here because we wanted to show you we've got your back, even when you're feeling low and don't think you need your friends."

"I always need you guys." I pull out a barstool from the small kitchen island and sit down while Connor helps Nana gather food and drinks. "I'm in a much better place than I was a week ago, thanks to Nana Rose."

Kiki exhales. "Good, we're glad, because there are going to be a few changes at work, and I think you'll be excited about them."

The three of them share their plans and we chat about different locations for the new office. I'm thrilled to hear she and Sarah will be hiring assistants. She's right. This is the perfect distraction to take my mind off our baby struggles.

"So does this mean I get to interview and hire the new office assistant to help Andie?" I clap my hands giddily.

"No," Connor, Sarah, and Kiki shout simultaneously.

"Rude much. I did okay with Andie, didn't I?" I smile affectionately at her.

"That was an asteroid-hitting-the-earth kind of rarity. A winning ticket for the million-dollar Powerball kind of lucky," Kiki says. "Might we remind you of the disasters that came before her? I sometimes see the guy who was always crying at the coffee shop and it is *so* awkward. Let's leave this one to Andie, 'kay?"

"Fine." I pout.

"Good. We better get ready." Sarah beams. "We've got a concert to get ready for!"

"Wait, what time is it? Did I miss craft hour?"

Kiki raises an eyebrow. "Craft hour?"

"I can't wait to see the concert, and I'm so happy you guys are all here, but first, I have to out-knit Joan during our chunky knit blanket class. She's this miserable woman who has it out for me. I'm taking her down."

Kiki rubs her hands together. "Ooh, this sounds fun. We'll make time for it."

Outside, the bus horn blares. "Was that Mandy?" Sarah asks.

"I think she was letting Ed and Rita test-drive the bus." Andie dips a carrot in hummus.

"I hope not. Ed is legally blind and Rita lost her license after an unfortunate golf-carting accident involving daiquiris and an alligator," Nana says casually. "Ed almost broke his hip."

We all look at each other and jump up, running outside.

Chapter 25

Tatum

KIKI SLIDES THE sheet back and crawls into bed. She snuggles next to me and lays her head on my bare chest. Her fingertips draw lazy circles on my abdomen, causing my muscles to ripple. I breathe in her wildflower scent and gently thread my fingers through her silky brown hair.

"Mmm, that feels nice. You guys were amazing tonight."

"I never thought a sixty-and-over crowd could get that rowdy."

"I'm not sure who thought it was a good idea to serve them alcohol. I was dying when that old lady threw her bra at you."

I grimace. "It's really disturbing having someone your grandma's age throwing her undergarments at your face."

Kiki giggles. "Grannies get to have their fun, too. I guarantee I'll be throwing my panties in your face when we're eighty."

"God help me." I laugh.

"I thought Nana Rose was going to need a hip replacement the way she was showing Mandy how to swivel her hips."

"I'm glad she had a good time."

"We all did. Thank you for doing that, babe. I know it wasn't in your schedule and it took a lot for you guys to pull together at the last minute, but it meant so much to TJ and me."

"Anything for you, CG." I kiss the top of her head. "We had fun."

"Do you ever get tired of it all?" she asks after a few moments.

"No, it's such a rush. I love the fans, the crowd, the music, playing onstage with my best friends… I'm one lucky son of a bitch." I shift my body so that I'm lying down beside her, gazing into her eyes. "The moment it gets old for either of us is the moment I hang up my guitar. Do you get tired of it?" I ask, lifting an eyebrow.

"Never. I love watching you perform." She brushes her fingers through my hair.

I smile. "What's your favorite song for moments like this?"

"You mean the half-drowsy, should I go to bed or should I make a move on my man kind of moment?"

"Yeah, sure, that."

She rolls her eyes and taps her finger to her lips, thinking. "Are you going to steal my phone again and go through my playlist, embarrassing the hell out of me?"

My grin grows wider, remembering the night I first tried to kiss her. "Answer the question, Coffee Girl."

She grabs her phone off the side table and opens her

playlist. "For moments like this, I would play 'My Man' by Maddie and Tae."

She plays the song.

"Look at you picking out a country song about your man. I'm so proud."

"Oh, it's my song for TJ."

"What?" I sit up, pretending to be offended. She holds up a finger, smiling. She switches to a Spice Girls song. I grab the phone from her. "'Wannabe'? Really? This is the song for when we're lying in bed gazing into each other's eyes whispering sweet nothings?"

"It's catchy and tells you what I want." She rips it back from my hands. I lie back, flinging my arm over my face as Mel B sings about what she really, really wants. She switches the song to Taylor Swift's 'You Need to Calm Down'.

"Ha-ha, very funny. I am calm."

She grins toothily at me and plays "Don't Stop Me Now" by Queen. She mouths, *don't stop me now*, arching an eyebrow. I snatch the phone and tickle her with my other hand.

"Oh my god, okay I'm sorry! Gah! Please stop tickling me," she gasps in between laughter. "I can't hold my pee like I used to after two kids. Tatum James Reed, I *will* pee on you!"

I immediately withdraw my hand. "Well, that was a mood-killer." I grin. She snatches her phone and scrolls through her songs.

"Okay, okay. Here's your song for whenever I think of you, or when I'm half asleep lying in bed with you." Taylor Swift sings and I look over at her, my brows scrunched together.

"I don't know this song—" I grab the phone back.

Kiki giggles as Taylor sings, "I Forgot That You Existed".

"Oh really? It's like that, is it? Don't make me change all your car stations to honky-tonk radio."

"You wouldn't dare. Not that twangy shit."

I nod sagely.

"Fine." She grabs her phone back and scrolls through her music. "This song game of yours is so weird."

"You love it. It's what made you fall in love with me when we first met."

"I believe it was your butt in Levi's that made me fall in love but think what you want, Tater Tot. I don't want to be a killjoy."

I lean up on one elbow and gaze down at her. She's so beautiful and stubborn. "I'm trying to get to know you, Coffee Girl."

She arches an eyebrow. "After two kids and living on the road in a tiny bedroom, for weeks on end, I'm pretty sure we know each other better than most."

I kiss her full lips and she smiles softly before playing our song, "Songbird" by Fleetwood Mac.

"I knew you'd play this."

"Then why the hell make me go through all the song hoops?"

"Because I love you and I enjoy driving you crazy." I wrap my arms around her and pull her on top of me. "I also like to keep tabs on what questionable music you're listening to."

"Hey, those songs are awesome. I could be listening to

that bum, Tatum Reed. He's so pitchy and full of himself. How he got a recording contract is beyond me—"

I capture her lips with mine, effectively shushing her. Kiki's fingers thread through my hair, and I groan, wanting more. She breaks the kiss, gasping for air.

"Tatum, I'm not on the Pill."

"Then I guess we'll leave it to fate," I say, knowing how badly she wants to try for another baby.

She rears back. "Wait, are you serious?"

I tuck a lock of hair behind her ear, her eyes searching mine. "Kiki, at the end of the day, all I want for you and the boys is to be happy. If that means another baby…" I shrug. "But don't be mad if we have another boy. These swimmers of mine are hellbent on creating wild boys, not sweet baby girls."

"I don't care what it is. I really don't." A tear rolls down her cheek and I swipe it away with my thumb. "As long as it's healthy, right?"

I pull her back down to me and make love to her without interruptions, without babies crying or kids climbing into bed, knowing this moment of quiet won't last long. Life is funny like that. Just when you think you've got a handle on things, you make a decision that complicates the hell out of everything. But one thing I've learned in all this is in the end, it doesn't matter, because it always somehow works out.

Chapter 26

THE ELEVATOR DOORS open and I hop off feeling refreshed and renewed. Connor and I had a long talk when we got back from Florida. He's worried I had become obsessed over trying to start a family, and he's right, I had. We decided to take a step back and take it as it comes, if it ever comes. I still cling to the hope that someday we'll be able to have a baby of our own, but I'm no longer hellbent on making it happen as quickly as possible. We did agree to contact Gloria and finish our application to be foster parents just to have that option in our back pockets. Classes start in a few weeks, and I'm actually looking forward to it.

"Shorts, you're looking breathtaking this lovely spring morning." She looks pasty and her hair looks limp and unbrushed, but no need to get her spirits down. I throw my coat and bag on her desk and she subtly slides them right back off.

"I just threw up, but thanks, TJ."

"Oh hon, TMI," I stage-whisper. "When do we start

interviewing for your position?"

"I have some applicants already, but—"

"Please let me help you! Please, please, pretty please? I mean, what if you vomit during the middle of an interview?" I hold my hands clasped together under my chin.

Andie twists her mouth. "Fine, if you'll stop doing that creepy smile."

"Yay, it will be so funsies, you and me interviewing together!"

"Yeah, funsies." Andie flattens her lips and covers her mouth with her hand.

"Kiki, Sare Bear, can you come out here, please?" I shout.

Kiki and Sarah come out of their offices. "Morning, TJ. You're here early. Is there a meeting I forgot about?" Sarah checks her watch.

"Girls, I got my hands on the new *Nash News* magazine and you are *not* going to believe the article inside."

The girls look at each other curiously. "What is it about?" Kiki asks.

I flip open to the page I have tabbed and place it on Andie's desk for everyone to see. "It's a piece on Sonja King."

"Oh no, TJ. Maybe you shouldn't read this."

"Too late, Shorts."

Kiki picks up the magazine and reads the article out loud.

"Sonja King announced she was having a baby with her reality TV costar, Simon Brown from *Love Lost and Found* last month, but love may be permanently lost for these two as they were seen arguing outside their Nashville home. Sources say that Simon was caught *in flagrante delicto* with

Sonja's best friend, model Amanda Pierce. Not only has Sonja's love life gone sideways, but so has her decorator, famed Nashville designer John Paul Pierre Luc. According to our sources, *People Magazine* was supposed to do a spread on the nursery, but pulled out when they found out it was decorated like a Moulin Rouge brothel. One source called the room 'extremely troubling and satanic' and 'they would never put a baby in that room'. Our sources say this is where her bestie and her baby daddy were caught in the act. Investigators found gum in the carpet belonging to Amanda who is often seen chewing gum. Sonja is devastated and due to give birth this June."

Kiki looks up from the page. "TJ, you can't seriously believe this load of crap. Investigators at the scene? Like it's a crime scene?"

"Amanda *is* always chewing gum," I say.

"Yeah, but this is a gossip rag. It's filled with half-truths and garbage," Sarah says, picking up the magazine. She looks at the cover showing a grainy photo in the corner of Sonja arguing with Simon. "Although that looks real."

"Doesn't Sonja yell at everyone?" Andie cranes her neck to look.

"True." Sarah bites her lip. "I don't know if I buy it."

"Well, because I knew you three would be total Debbie Downers, I called JPPL's assistant, Claude, to confirm the story."

"And?" Kiki waves her hand when I pause for dramatic effect.

"He confirmed it's all true. *People* pulled the story and JPPL is devastated. He thought Moulin Rouge was *très magnifique*. Allegedly, Sonja has been trash-talking him and said he took advantage of her, and she did not approve of the theme. She's refusing to pay. Only time will tell about Simon, Amanda, and Sonja."

"Well, I always say, what goes around comes around. Good thing you dodged using Jean Luc Poop as your designer." Kiki winks.

"Yes, I think Connor would have had a coronary if he came home to a Moulin Rouge-themed nursery."

"Any news from Gloria?" asks Kiki.

"No news, but I'm okay with it." I sigh, then clap my hands. "Because we've got a baby shower and reveal to plan for Andie!"

"Oh, oh no." Andie's eyes double in size. "I'm good. Cam and I don't need a reveal, or a shower, or any kind of party for that matter."

"Now, Shorts, I realize Kiki's baby reveal for Drew didn't go as planned…"

"You smoke-bombed the entire party with green and purple smoke. Tatum's great-aunt almost passed out."

"I hear you, we'll forgo the smoke. Ooh! What about glitter bombs in pink or blue?"

"No!" all three of them shout as one.

"You guys are no fun. Don't worry, Shorts, I'll keep this sharp wheel turning and figure out something spectacular. Oh, and get ready because my doula gloves are on. We'll start practicing our breathing techniques in a few weeks."

"Oh man, good luck with that." Kiki laughs. "TJ, maybe you should have smelling salts with you in the delivery room this time."

"God help me." Andie puts in her head in her hands.

"One time, Kinky. Are you ever going to let me live it down?"

"Never."

Andie smiles. "Here's hoping I have another cesarian section."

These girls don't realize it yet, but they need me. "You guys, listen up! Who's ready to go look at some properties?"

"Ooh, me!" Sarah pops out of her chair.

"Me too," Kiki says. "Andie, you coming?"

"I think I'm going to stay here in case anyone calls. I'm still feeling kinda nauseous."

"As your doula, I insist you stay and rest." I boop her on her nose before turning to survey our loft. "I can't believe I'm saying this, but I'm really going to miss this place."

"Well," Kiki says, pressing the elevator button, "luckily your husband runs the bar downstairs and you can come up here and reflect any time you want."

"You're telling me you're not going to miss it? So many memories here. It's where we first started."

"Are you crying?" Kiki asks.

"No." I quickly swipe the tear away. "Dust mote."

"We outgrew our space, Teej. I, for one, will not miss sharing my office space with you when you take off your shoes and prop your nasty socks on my desk."

"Or when he steals all your pens, takes the last of the copy paper and doesn't replace it, or eats your yogurt that has your name in bold letters on it," Sarah adds unhelpfully.

"Sounds like a you problem, Sare Bear."

Andie calls out from her desk, "Or when he pushes you

out of the way, so he's not the last to arrive to clean out the kitchen fridge!"

"You guys act like I'm a nuisance when, in reality, I keep this ship chugging along."

"Pretty sure Andie is the captain of this ship," Kiki says.

"Well, I'm the cute sailor making sure all the knots are tied." I wink.

Kiki side-eyes me.

"You love me."

"We do." Sarah pulls me into a side-hug as we step on the elevator.

"We do?" Kiki raises an eyebrow as we turn around in the elevator and wave goodbye to Andie.

"We do!" Andie shouts, and the doors close.

I love my three bitches, too.

Chapter 27

Cam

ANDIE'S EYES ARE closed when I return from tucking Enzo into bed. Poor Andie has been so sick with this pregnancy. Hopefully, now that she's in the second trimester she'll start feeling better. I lie down next to her and put my hand over her rounded belly. It's so fascinating to watch the baby grow. He or she's the size of a mango now.

Andie startles awake and blinks her eyes open.

"Shit, I'm sorry, babe." I kiss her lips.

"Did I fall asleep?"

"Yeah. I put Enzo to bed and checked on Charleigh, who is fast asleep. Dishes are done. All is good."

"Oh no, I'm so sorry. I meant to do the dishes. I sat down for a second to change clothes…"

"Shh, babe, it's okay. You're tired. You're growing a baby, take it easy."

"I put my phone in the fridge the other day and didn't realize it was in there until dinnertime. Then yesterday, I took the kids out of the car and left all the doors open and the car running in the driveway. For an hour, Cam. Thank God it wasn't stolen. I'm a mess."

I chuckle. "Awe, honey."

"I'm fat and tired and I miss drinking coffee and wine."

"You're gorgeous and perfect and wine gives you hangovers. Totally overrated."

"Says the guy who can have some."

"So I've been thinking." I rub my palm over her belly. "I'm going to put off opening the next location."

She sits up. "But why? You've been so excited about it."

"Not really. I haven't found the perfect spot for it yet…"

"I thought you were going to put it in that strip mall?"

"That was the plan, but a Chick-Fil-A was going in the same area and we would have been sandwiched between a hair salon and a UPS store. The location didn't fit our branding."

Andie nods. "But that doesn't mean you have to scrap it altogether, does it?"

I lean down and kiss our growing mango. "I'm happy with what we have, Andie. If I expand too fast, I could lose it all. I'm okay with waiting a year or two. I need to make sure my family is secure before I throw more fuel on the fire."

"I'm sorry, Cam." A tear rolls down her cheek.

"Babe, why are you crying?"

"You could open a third if I wasn't pregnant."

"Andie, stop." I hang my head as I gather my thoughts. She runs her fingers through my hair. I look up into her sad eyes. "I need you, Enzo, Charleigh, and little one more than another location, more than the success, more than anything. You three are what matter most to me."

She leans forward and touches her lips to mine. "I love you, Cameron Forbes," she whispers.

"I love you more," I whisper back.

"TJ wants to throw a baby reveal shower for us."

I groan and lie back. "We were having such a peaceful, loving moment."

She giggles. "I know. He wants to do pink and blue glitter bombs for the reveal."

"Yeah, and he probably wants to have the party at The Social Hour so he can grind glitter into everything. Hell no. Do you know how long it took me to get the glitter out of everything after Tatum's birthday party a few years ago? I was still finding glitter in my hair after a week of showers. No way."

"Well, I didn't say he could. I told him I wanted to ask you first if you wanted to find out what the sex is, or if you want to be surprised?"

"Surprised," I blurt.

"Wow, no hesitation there. Is that because TJ wants to throw us a party?"

"Yup." I grin and turn my head to look at her. I link my fingers with hers and gently squeeze. "Let's be surprised. Not because of TJ, although that is a big factor, but because the anticipation of finding out if it's a boy or girl will be fun."

"I like that." She smiles and nods. "There's something different about you, Cam. I can't quite put my finger on it, but you've changed. Remember when you used to be terrified of kids?"

"I was never terrified of kids."

"Okay, maybe terrified isn't the right word, but they

definitely weren't your favorite. You were always so worried Sarah or Kiki's kids would wipe something on your Hermès tie. You used to talk to Enzo like you were trying to impress one of your business partners."

"I did not," I scoff.

"Remember when I walked in on you the second time we met and you were taking care of Sarah and Kiki's kids all by yourself? Hair mussed, baby food all over your face and shirt… You've come a long way, handsome." She threads her fingers through my hair and kisses my lips. I look into her eyes and think about what an asshat I used to be before I met Andie.

"I love kids. Especially ours. My nephew can be a little challenging at times."

Andie laughs and it makes my heart flip.

"You're an amazing dad."

I pinch my brows together. "I don't feel different. Is it a good or bad change?"

She looks at me and contemplates. "Definitely good. You're softer around the edges. It suits you."

I nuzzle her neck and kiss her, drawing her closer to me. "I love you, gorgeous."

"Love you more," she says, followed by a yawn.

She's right. I am different. Ten years ago, I would have never put work on the back burner for personal matters. I would have spent all my time finding a new location for the third bar. But now that I have a family and a baby on the way, opening a new Social Hour just isn't a priority anymore. Andie, Enzo, Charleigh, and this baby are my number one in my life.

I slowly place soft kisses behind Andie's ear. "Babe…now that the kids are asleep, want to get naked?" Soft snores break the silence in the bedroom. "Andie?" I sit up on my elbow and look down at my beautiful, passed-out wife. I kiss her cheek and pull the covers over her.

"Come on, Vader, let's go grab a beer and catch the end of the hockey game. We'll make it a guys' night," I say to our dog, who pops up out of his dog bed and trots after me.

I settle down on the couch after grabbing two beers, and pop the tops. Vader jumps up on the couch next to me and I clink my bottle with his. "Cheers, buddy."

If twenty-five-year-old me could see me now, having a guys' night with my dog, he'd be laughing his ass off, calling me a pussy. What that stupid-ass punk didn't know back then is that love changes everything.

Chapter 28

Lex

JAX STROLLS INTO the kitchen and grabs a can of sparkling water from the fridge. He turns around, and I peer at the doll strapped to his front in a baby carrier.

"What the feck are ye wearin'?"

He pops the top of the can and takes a drink. "Mom is making me wear this stupid doll of Uncle Connor and Uncle TJ's."

I squint my eyes and scrunch my nose. "What the feck is wrong with it? Why is it wearin' a sequined eyepatch?"

Jax shrugs. "I guess it's missing an eye. I don't know, nor do I care."

Sarah walks in and smiles, checking her watch. "Hey guys. Jax, have you fed BB-2 before baseball practice?"

Jax groans. "I was just about to."

I track my wife's movements around the kitchen. "Sunshine, why does Jax have a wee baby strapped to his front?"

She turns around and grins. "Oh, well, you know how we gave TJ a baby to practice with and what a disaster that turned out to be?"

"Connor mentioned something about a scary Chucky doll TJ was taking care of."

"Yes. When I tried to donate it to Jax's school's home-ec class, the teacher politely declined, saying it was too frightening for the kids. So, I thought it would be good practice for Jax, since he's a mature adult now, right?" She lifts a brow and her smile spreads. I've learned to never argue with her when she does that.

"Yes, right."

"Oh come on, Dad, not you too. I hate this thing. It cries all the time. Mom made me take it to Will's soccer game the other day. It was so embarrassing. It wouldn't stop crying and all my friends kept asking why I was carrying around a baby with duct tape on its arm and an eyepatch."

"Why *does* it have tape on its arm? Is that marker all over its head?" I ask.

"TJ broke it when he slammed it in the car door." Sarah frowns, peering at the doll. "I thought I got the marker off with rubbing alcohol. Jessica and Matt? Jax, did your friends sign the baby's head?"

"Well, it already had marker on it." Jax shrugs, moving away from Sarah.

As if on cue, the baby emits a strange, garbled howl.

"Jesus, what's wrong with it?" I ask.

"It's possessed," Jax whispers, his back to Sarah.

"I'm pretty sure TJ dropped it or spilled liquid on it because its voice box is messed up."

"I'm pretty sure it's possessed," Jax mumbles.

"How long does he have to carry this thing around?" I

ask Sarah, smirking at Jax and his terrifying baby.

"He has to be BB-2's baby daddy for two weeks."

I fold my arms over my chest. "Well, I think it's a solid plan. If yer gonna have sex, then ye should know yer consequences."

"This is the worst." Jax takes the bottle Sarah hands him and shoves it into the crying baby's mouth. A loud gas-exploding sound emits from the baby. "Oh no, not again!" He runs out of the kitchen with a look of pure disgust on his face.

"What just happened?" I ask Sarah.

"I think BB2 had an explosion in his diaper."

I grimace and then chuckle, rubbing my hand down my face. "Sunshine, have I ever told ye how brilliant ye are? He will never want to have sex again."

Sarah smiles knowingly. "I'm not sure what model Kiki ordered, but that thing is Satan's spawn. He may want to try and have picnics again, but he'll always remember to keep his salami wrapped."

"Look at you using my sex lingo." I reach for her and pull her to me, kissing her lips. "He's gonna hate us."

Sarah loops her arms around my waist. "Maybe, but someday he'll thank us. The weird thing, though? Wyatt loves the baby. I caught him carrying it around the other day and watching TV with it. Like it soothes him."

"Yer tellin' me, our anxiety-ridden son is calmed by a creepy baby with an eyepatch? He's more fucked up than I thought."

"Lex!" She pushes my chest. "He is not fucked up."

I lift her up onto the counter and step between her legs,

smirking. She links her arms around my neck. "I'm teasin', Sunshine. Honestly? I haven't heard him cry over something for the last couple of days."

"BB-2…" Sarah smiles up at me. "He may be the answer to all our problems."

"Let me get this straight. We've spent hundreds of dollars on some therapist who wants him to draw fucking doodles when he gets anxious and all we had to do is get him a scary-ass doll?"

"Apparently."

"You've killed two birds with one stone, Sunshine." I grin in awe.

"I'm fucking brilliant if I do say so myself."

"Brilliant and sexy. How did I get so lucky?"

Sarah shrugs and grins, our noses touching. "I waited around a long time for you to come to your senses."

I touch my lips to hers and pull back a breath. "Good things come to those who wait."

Sarah tilts her head back and laughs. "You're so full of yourself, Lex Ryan."

I growl. "Where are the kids?"

"Well, Jax will be trying to figure out how to change BB-2's diaper for the next half hour until he has to go to practice and the twins are shopping with your mom."

"So we've got plenty of time." I capture her lips in a hungry kiss. She pulls back when we hear Jax curse and the robot baby's weird crying sound again.

"Should we help him?"

"Love, no amount of BB-2 crying will stop me from making love to my woman."

I wrap her legs around my waist and carry her to our bedroom, where I triple-check the door is locked. I've had enough picnic talk to last me a lifetime.

Chapter 29

Kiki

WE LEFT THE Academy of Country Music Awards after-parties early tonight because I was beat, and Tatum didn't feel like partying into the wee hours of the morning. He spins me in a slow circle and gathers me in his arms as we dance to a slow song on our back porch, the twinkle lights strung above creating a magical glow. I smile up at him in wonder. I don't know how I got so lucky to have this beautiful, talented man as my husband and best friend.

"I'm so proud of you, Tater Tot. Winning another ACM."

"It wasn't only me. I wouldn't have won tonight without Lex, Matt, and Will."

"I know." Smiling, I search his eyes. "That's what I love about you. So many other artists would have wanted to go off on their own, but not you. You love your people fiercely."

He squeezes me tight. "The guys make me a better singer, a better artist, a better person. I'd be an idiot to think otherwise."

"Well I, for one, as your biggest fan, think you could make anything happen on your own." I curl my fingers into his hair at the nape of his neck. "But I know you'd be lost without them."

Grinning, he spins me around. I laugh, holding onto him, burning this moment into my forever memories. I close my eyes and lean my head against his chest. We sway to Kane Brown's song, "Thank God", and I can't help but think how true the words ring for us.

"I love you, Tater Tot."

"I love you, Coffee Girl."

"Oh my god, I love you both," a third party cries out, arms encircling us, causing me to scream. *TJ?*

Tatum steps back. "What the hell?"

"Jesus, TJ, I almost kicked you in the nuts. What the fuck are you doing here?" I yell.

TJ wipes a tear from his cheek, standing with his arms crossed. "Seriously, you guys are the most adorbs couple I've ever witnessed."

"How did he get past security?" A bewildered Tatum shoves his hands in his hair.

"I have a key, and Brad was out there and waved me in."

"Brad is so fired," Tatum breathes out.

I grind my teeth and look over at TJ. "You have until three to explain what you're doing here. Dammit, TJ, you know this is the first minute we've had alone in days. Shouldn't you be at home redecorating or something?"

"Wow, Kinky, that is so stereotypical. Oh! By the way, that reminds me, Connor and I are going antiquing Saturday if you want to tag along."

"I'm in. You know I can't turn down a day of antiquing." I shake my head. "Dammit, you're purposefully getting me off track! Tammy Jean, what are you doing here?"

"Oh, well, Drew-bear forgot Bankie, so I told Connor I'd run and grab it. Lord, that little mini Tatum gets worked up at bedtime if he doesn't have it. So, here I am, looking for Bankie, minding my own biz when I see you two out here slow-dancing in your fancy clothes and I just couldn't help myself. You looked too cute not to hug. Oh Tatum, congrats on the win tonight. Looking extra fine in that tux. Of course you do, I picked it out," he titters. "Honestly, I thought you guys would be out partying. But I've got Bankie, so…yeah." He stands and grins at us like a complete loon.

"You snooped through our bedroom, didn't you?" I raise an eyebrow.

"Define snoops?"

"TJ…"

"I mean I might have peeked in and happened to notice a t-shirt of Tatum's lying on the chair, and I *might* have smelled it."

Tatum looks like he's about to blow a gasket, so I take TJ's arm and spin him toward the door. "Thanks for coming to get Bankie. We appreciate you watching the boys tonight, but it's late so—"

"Oh, totes, totes, I got you, boo." He waggles his eyebrows. "I'll let you two get back to making babies."

"We weren't making babies—"

"Later, Taters!" he shouts to Tatum and blows an air-kiss at me. "Kinky, looking fetch girlfriend, don't let it go to waste tonight." He winks and disappears inside.

I sigh and whirl to Tatum.

"I'm still trying to figure out how the hell he got past gate security. I told them not to bother us tonight unless it was a serious emergency."

"TJ is very resourceful and persuasive."

"It scares me he has a key. Do you think he truly left the house, or is he going to jump out and hug us in the middle of the night? I could picture him hiding under our bed like Chase does."

"It's a definite possibility." I shrug and smile. "I might have given TJ and Connor a key in case of emergencies."

"Kiki." Tatum pinches the bridge of his nose. "That's why I have Brad and a security team. In case of emergencies."

"I'm old school, I can't help it. I mean, why wouldn't I give my best friend a key to my house? He's always had one."

"Because he's certifiable."

I wrap my arms around his waist and laugh against his chest. "I know, but I love him."

"I know you do." Tatum lifts my chin and kisses my lips.

"I'm sorry he interrupted us," I whisper.

"It's okay." Tatum's hooded eyes lower as he dips his head and captures my lips with his. Swiping his tongue over mine, they tangle together as he presses into me, his hardness making my knees buckle.

He breaks the kiss, pressing his forehead to mine, both of us gasping for air. He swipes his thumb over my lips. "I'll never get tired of kissing these bee-stung lips."

I look at him tenderly and brush a lock of hair off his

forehead. "Good, because you're stuck with me."

"There's no one else I'd rather be stuck with." He kisses my nose.

"Even when your pants ripped in the crotch on stage and I gave you my Mr. Kitty tank to wear, causing a social media circus that plagues you still to this day?"

He smirks. "Even then."

"Even when I dye your favorite shirt pink?"

"It's a jersey, not a shirt."

"You know what I mean. Even when I dye your jersey?"

"I mean, that sucked because it was an original, but yes, even when you dye my beloved signed Wayne Gretzky jersey pink."

"Even when I accidentally broke your favorite guitar and blamed it on Chase?"

"Hold up. *You* broke it? You blatantly lied to my face and blamed it on your firstborn?"

I nibble my lip. "It was an accident. I was dusting and it fell off the shelf."

He arches an eyebrow. "You don't dust, and it wasn't on a shelf. It was hanging on the wall with the others."

I blow out a breath. "Fine, I was getting it down to use as a prop in one of my pictures, and I accidentally knocked it off the wall. I didn't mean to."

He bites his lip and hangs his head, shaking it. "Even when you break my favorite guitar, I'd still want to be stuck with you." He sighs heavily and looks me in the eye. "Any more confessions you'd like to share tonight, Coffee Girl?"

"Would you still want to be stuck with me if I told you a little white stick showed two little pink lines?"

He swallows and cups my face with his hands. "You're pregnant?"

I nod, tears filling my eyes. "Yes, six weeks."

He smashes his lips to mine, surprising me. I widen my eyes, and then slowly close them as I fall into the kiss. He pulls back, his eyes darting between mine.

"You sure?"

"Pretty damn sure." I laugh.

He chuckles, swiping the tears that have leaked down my cheeks. "Kiki Forbes Reed, you are stuck with me even if you're questionable at fixing wardrobe malfunctions, horrible with the laundry, and break all my favorite guitars. You are stuck with me every day until I take my last breath. I am the luckiest son of bitch on this earth to be stuck with you."

"And me you, Tatum." I lift up on tiptoe and kiss him.

He swoops me up into his arms, the train of my beaded gown dragging along the floor as he carries me to our bedroom.

"Did you light candles? It's beautiful. Are those white rose petals?" I ask, noticing there are about a dozen candles lit around the room and petals on the floor and bedspread.

"Uh, Kiki, it wasn't me. But remind me to thank our stalker later. Come to think of it, he wasn't holding Bankie when he left." He quirks his lips and I giggle against his chest.

"Drew never lets Bankie out of his sight."

He stands me in the middle of our bedroom and unzips my gown. It pools at my feet. He holds my hand as I step out of it.

"It's so damn quiet." He smiles while I unbutton his

tuxedo shirt.

"Too damn quiet." I hum, flinging it back to reveal his tanned muscular chest.

His hands smooth around my waist and draw me to him. "Thank God."

I place my hands on his chest, the heat seeping through my fingers, his heartbeat steady. "Wait."

"What's wrong?" He rears his head. "Kiki, what are you doing?"

I get down on my hands and knees and look under the bed and then make my way over to our walk-in closet. Both are blessedly TJ-free. "Just checking." Smiling, I slide back into his arms.

"Good thinking."

"Remember, you're stuck with me—and TJ."

Tatum nods, leaning down, and kisses me until I forget about TJ, guitars, pink shirts, and even babies.

Chapter 30

"LADIES, IT'S A big night!" I singsong, plopping down on my couch with a bottle of water. Bartie jumps on the couch and head bumps my arm before climbing into Kiki's lap. Tonight the girls are joining me in a little TV-watching entertainment of *Nashville Next*'s latest documentary.

"Some people call me the space cowboy, some call me a rocket of love? Is that a direct quote?" Kiki looks up from the article she's reading and raises an eyebrow.

"I thought it was catchy."

"First of all, no one has ever called you that. Second, that's not the correct lyrics from 'The Joker'. It's gangster of love."

"Do I look like a gangster to you?" I ask, pointing the remote at the flat screen.

"Well, you definitely don't look like a rocket of love."

I roll my eyes and wave my hand for her to continue reading.

Kiki sighs before picking back up where she left off. "TJ

Ryan may be a jokester in his own right, but when it comes to running Nashville Style, he walks the straight and narrow." Kiki glances up. "Seriously? Who wrote this crap?"

"Kinky, don't be jelly. I can't help it that I get requests for interviews."

"Did TJ offer their journalist a free makeup session with Sarah again?" Andie sits down with a bowl of popcorn.

"TJ, seriously?" Sarah shouts from the kitchen. She sits down with another bowl of popcorn and hands Kiki a bottle of water. "You have to stop offering our services for free so you can get your name in a magazine."

"Ladies, chillax. It's called free advertising."

"I don't see you offering up your services," Sarah says pointedly.

"Sare Bear, I don't have time in my busy day to offer free consults. You be talkin' crazy, mon."

"First of all, you're not Jamaican," Kiki says. "You're a white guy from New Mexico with flaming red hair. Second, you need to ask us permission first before doing any more of these horrible interviews." Kiki turns up the volume. "Now everyone, quiet."

Nashville Next's opening credits roll.

"On tonight's episode, Josie Jansen from *Nashville Next* will be interviewing Nashville's very own reality TV star, Sonja King."

Video clips of Sonja play from her reality show, *Love Lost and Found*, where she's kissing her baby daddy Simon, to her and her best friend Amanda on the red carpet posing for photographers.

"Sonja, I want to say congratulations on the pregnancy."

Josie smiles brightly at Sonja.

"Whoever did the fillers in Sonja's face should have their license taken away," Andie says. "She looks like she's forty, not twenty-eight."

"Her makeup is awful." Sarah nods in agreement. "Look how shiny her forehead is. She looks like she came from the gym."

Sonja smiles at the camera. "Thanks, Josie. I love being pregnant. It opens your eyes to a whole new world you didn't know existed."

"What's wrong with her voice?" Kiki grimaces. "Why does she sound like a breathy six-year-old?"

"Shush, you guys," I scold, shoving popcorn in my mouth. "I can't hear."

Sonja does look awful. Her hair is up, but not sleek like her signature look. She has dark circles under her eyes that even makeup can't cover and the fillers have made her look like a pufferfish.

"Rumors are that you were supposed to host season two of *Love Lost and Found*. What will happen now that you're pregnant?"

"Wow, look at Josie Jansen asking the hard-hitting questions. Of course, she can still host, you twit. Just because you're pregnant doesn't mean you can't do anything else," Andie gripes. We all look over at her in shock and then start laughing. "Sorry, y'all, but I'm so tired of everyone thinking your life is doomed if you get pregnant. I had a lady come up to me in the store the other day and literally tell me my life is over. It's ridiculous."

I pat Andie's knee. "Don't listen to the haters, Shorts."

Sonja purses her puffy lips. "I plan on taking a little time off with the baby and hosting in the future."

Josie's smile drops and she looks at Sonja with concern. "There have been rumors that you and the baby's daddy have split. Can you confirm this for us?"

Sonja's eyes dart from the camera to Josie and then to someone off-camera. She laughs nervously, rubbing the palms of her hands over her thighs. "Just rumors, Josie. Simon and I are happily awaiting for the baby to arrive."

"Bullshit," Kiki crows. "Did you see her eyes? She's lying like a whore in church."

"Is Simon here today?" Josie asks.

"Um, no, he's on location."

"Yeah, on location in Amanda's pants," I say. Kiki high-fives me.

"You guys." Andie frowns. "Be nice."

"Andie, you know she's an awful human being. Otherwise, I would feel really sorry for her," Kiki says.

"Totes agree. Remember a few months ago when Sarah did her makeup and Kiki designed that dress for her and when they asked who she was wearing, she suddenly had amnesia and couldn't remember who the designer was or where she got her lip color from? Then when another interviewer asked, she said someone over at The White Bird. She couldn't even get the name of The White Dove correct, not that they had anything to do with it. She sucks."

"Oh yeah, I forgot about that."

"I haven't." Kiki crosses her arms tight. "She is *non gradito* at our studio. I don't care how many reality shows she's starred in."

A video clip of Sonja with her best friend, Amanda, plays on *Nashville Next*. Sonja looks pissed, distancing herself from Amanda on the red carpet, while Amanda smacks her gum, looking lost without her bestie.

"Some have said your reality TV best friend, Amanda Pierce, is the reason for the alleged strife between you and Simon. Is this true?"

"Sonja looks like she's trying to hold in a fart," I observe.

"Amanda and I are fine. There is no strife."

Josie leans forward, a wicked smile replacing her concerned expression. "So how do you explain this photo of Simon walking hand in hand with Amanda leaving a pizza restaurant called Jackaroos the other night?" Josie hands her a photo.

"If Sonja had laser beams for eyes, that photo would be on fire." Sarah giggles.

"They're just friends." Sonja shoves the now-crumpled photo back at Josie. "I knew they were going to dinner." The screen shows the photo in question.

"Mmm-hmm, sure you did," Kiki says.

"I don't hold TJ's hand like that when we leave a restaurant," Sarah says.

"Mmm, girlfriend, that is not a good look for your man," I say. "He looks like he wants to twirl his meatballs with your bestie's spaghetti."

"Yeah, Sonja's not happy. Look at her expression." Andie shoves more popcorn in her mouth. "And gross, TJ."

"Leave a little for us, Shorts. Is someone feeling better?"

"Yes. Y'all I finally turned the corner, thank God," Andie says around a mouthful of popcorn. "I'm always hungry now."

"Tell me about the controversy behind Jean Paul Pierre Luc's unfortunate nursery design," Josie prompts.

Sonja squirms in her seat. "I'm sorry, but I thought we were going to be talking about *me*."

"We are." Josie smiles. "You hired JPPL to design your nursery, did you not? Sources have told me you don't even own the house and that you refuse to pay JPPL for services rendered?"

"Look at Josie Jansen thinking she's an investigative reporter." Kiki cackles.

"I hired him to design my nursery. I didn't like his ideas so I fired him. That's it. There's no controversy."

"So he didn't design a French brothel under your supervision?"

"What? No. I would never approve of that."

"So these pictures obtained by *Nashville Lifestyles* don't show you standing in the middle of the nursery, smiling?"

"Ooh, she's in the hot seat now," I titter.

"Ah, that." Sonja looks like a deer caught in headlights. "That was a promotional thing. That wasn't *my* nursery."

"So you didn't threaten to sue *Nashville Lifestyles* to destroy the pictures and spread defamatory rumors about JPPL, which in turn, drove his company into the ground? Is it not true that you are now in a lawsuit with JPPL?"

"I'm not commenting." Sonja stands. "This is not what I thought it would be. We're supposed to be talking about *me*! This interview is over. I'm done." Sonja rips her mic off. Josie looks a bit stunned but recovers quickly. The camera crew follows Sonja to her dressing room. She whirls on them.

"I will sue you if you don't get this camera out of my face! I'm done here!"

"Well, that was unexpected." Josie clears her throat. "I'm Josie Jansen, and this is *Nashville Next*."

"Well, that's not good PR for her." I look over at the girls who share the same stunned expressions as me.

"Good thing you didn't do *Nashville Next*, TJ. I don't think they would have shown you in the golden light you were hoping for," Sarah says.

"Yeah, you guys were right."

"Again." Andie grins. I stick my tongue out at her.

"Well, it's a good thing you didn't. I don't think *People Magazine* would have liked it," Kiki says casually like she didn't just drop a bomb in my lap.

"What do you mean by that?" I turn toward her.

"You're not the only one who can get free advertising." Kiki smiles.

"Kiki, what are you talking about?"

She smiles at Andie and Sarah before answering my question. "The guys are going to be in an article in the June edition. Well, they're on the cover actually, and I may have put a little bug in Tatum and his publicist, Kimberly's ear that it would be cool if they could do a piece on the struggles you and Connor have been going through. Gloria said she'd be willing to give some facts and statistics. That is, if you would want…"

My mouth opens and closes like a guppy fish. "Would I want? *Would I want*? Of course, I want!" Thoughts race around my brain like what I would wear for the photo shoot and we'll have to throw a party, of course. Would we have finger food or a sit-down dinner? Can Andie capture me throwing glitter in midair? I wonder if those purple suede shoes are still on sale at Barneys. I have to call Nana Rose, and Connor will be…

Shit. Connor. I clear my throat and take a deep breath. *Slow down, TJ. Take the crazy to the curb. Think about Connor.*

"You guys, this is amazing and I'm so honored, but I need to run it by Connor first. If we do this interview, we both have to agree."

"Well"—Kiki throws her hands in the air—"good thing Connor already said yes."

I hop up and shout, fist-pumping the air. Popcorn spills all over the couch. "The guys were okay with this?"

"Look, I know I said it would never happen, but we all agreed this was important. Laws need to change and be more accepting of gay couples adopting and fostering. TJ, you and Connor are our family, and when one of us is struggling, we find a way to hold each other through it. We all agreed your story needs to be out there. But just so we're clear, you're a sidebar story, not the front page."

"I totes understand. Still, it's exciting." I wipe the tears from my face. "Group hug," I blubber, waving them in and holding them tight in a circle. "You guys are literally the bestest friends a gay kid with bright orange hair from Albuquerque, New Mexico could have ever dreamed about. Thank you for always having my back."

"TJ, we can't imagine life without you," Andie sobs. "Damn hormones."

"You bring the shine to my sun." Sarah smiles and kisses

my cheek.

"I'm pregnant," Kiki blurts out.

"What?" Sarah screams.

We break apart and stare in astonishment at Kiki who looks like she's about to vomit. The girls hug her and chatter nonstop, ecstatic for Kiki. I can't help the stupid grin from spreading across my face. "Lord, help us all." I squeeze her into a hug and whisper, "I can't wait to be Uncle TJ again."

Chapter 31

Connor

IT'S BEEN MONTHS since we returned from Nana Rose's house in Florida and things have settled back down in our lives. TJ is no longer baby crazy like he was before the Penny incident and we agreed to take a step back and live every day in the moment. If it's meant to be, then it will be, is our new mantra.

After a long discussion with Nana Rose, we decided it couldn't hurt to finish the foster application and take the necessary classes, just in case. We turned in our health records and background checks, took the classes, which took a couple of weeks, and then that was that.

It's been a blessing, honestly, because between the *People Magazine* interview and both of us being swamped with work, finding time to relax and breathe has been few and far between.

I flip off the movie and gently remove Bartie from my lap. TJ is softly snoring next to me. I gently shake him. "Love, let's go to bed."

"Do you like sparkles? Do you have access to lighters?" he mumbles in his sleep. He's been doing that a lot lately since he offered to help Andie hire a new receptionist, much to the girls' dismay. "Harry Styles is a sex god…"

"Thomas, wake up." I shake him.

He sits straight up. "Nana, I swear I didn't steal your legwarmers."

"TJ, it's me, Connor." I chuckle. "Come on, ye fell asleep during the movie again. Time for bed."

TJ groans, pulling himself off the couch. "I was awake. Watched the whole thing this time."

I shake my head. "I think I logged you in at ten thirty for snorin'. Go to bed. I'll lock up here."

As he shuffles down the hall, yawning loudly, my cell phone rings. I look at the number but don't recognize the caller. I pocket my phone and turn off the kitchen lights. My phone buzzes again with a voicemail. I pull it back out and hit the voicemail button when the same number calls again. This time, I pick up.

"Hello?"

"Connor? It's Gloria. I'm sorry to bother you. I tried calling TJ, but it went straight to voicemail."

"Oh, no problem. How can I help ye, Gloria?" I glance at my watch. It's 12:30 a.m.

"It's last call." I can hear the smile in her voice.

A few seconds tick by as the words seep in. *Last call.* "What's goin' on?" I ask gruffly.

"We have a situation. One of my foster kids was pregnant. A teenager. She's about to age out of the system when she turns eighteen next month and doesn't have a place to go. She doesn't want the babies and the father is not in the picture. She doesn't want her babies to end up in the system like she did. I told her I knew of the perfect couple who could handle the job. I told her about you and she agreed to do a private adoption." Gloria waits as I try to process what she's saying. "Let me tell you, this never happens, Connor. Once-in-a-blue-moon kind of moment."

"I…" My throat is parched, emotion clogging my throat. I grab a bottle of water and take a sip. "I'm floored, Gloria."

"The babies have to stay in the hospital for one more day. Can you get your lawyer to draw up the papers?"

"I think so." I glance at my watch like a dumbass, wondering if the lawyer is up.

"This is it, Connor. Last call. I need to know or else I'll have to put them through the system. Do you and TJ want to adopt the babies?"

"Yes," I breathe out, without even thinking. "Yes, we want them. TJ!" I shout down the hall.

"Okay, come to Nashville General first thing tomorrow morning with your lawyer. We'll be waiting for you."

"Gloria, can she change her mind?"

"Absolutely she can, but Connor, she's scared. She doesn't have a family. No one to turn to but me. She needs you both. She won't change her mind. See you in the morning."

"Gloria, wait."

"Yes, Connor?"

"What do ye mean babies?"

"Oh." She chuckles. "I forgot that tidbit. She had twins…girls. See you tomorrow." Gloria disconnects.

"Twins?" The phone drops to my side. "TJ!"

"Cheese and rice, stop yelling. I'm right here, boo," he says right behind me, making me jump.

"That was…" I swallow dryly.

"Yes?"

"You need to cancel the trip to Greece next week."

"What? Why? I'm supposed to monitor Andie's every movement while she's there. As her doula—"

"She'll have to find someone else," I say distractedly while I slam open drawers trying to find paper and a pen. I have no idea where to begin with what we'll need for infants. We're totally unprepared for this.

"What are you looking for and why are you mumbling?"

"Help me find a pen!"

"Connor, you're not making any sense and now I'm irritated you got me out of bed in the middle of the night to help you look for a pen and to tell me I have to cancel my trip. Can we please talk about this in the morning?"

I slam more drawers and spin in a circle. "Shite, we're in over our heads. What did I do? I shouldn't have said yes right away. I should have consulted with ye. I did exactly what I asked ye not to do. I'm so sorry."

"Are you on drugs?" TJ pulls a face. "Because you're seriously acting mental and I'm worried."

"That was Gloria." I look at TJ. "We're having twins."

"What are you talking about?"

"Gloria. She just called. Last call. There's a teen at the hospital who delivered twins and she wants us to take them."

"Oh my god, oh my god, this is it. Code Red alert. When, are we taking them? Now? I need to get dressed. Is she dropping them off? She said it could be anywhere from a ten-minute warning to two hours. Oh my god, I'm hyperventilating."

TJ spins in his boxer shorts and colorful socks, and I know I will never forget this moment. "Love, calm down." I grab his arms and force him to look into my eyes. "This is it. It's not a foster situation. The mother is a teenager and wants to give them up for adoption. *Twins*, TJ. We'll have to contact our lawyer in the morning. We'll need diapers and formula, clothes…" I wipe the tears leaking from his eyes and touch my forehead to his. "We had twins."

TJ squeezes my neck and pushes away. "We don't need any of that stuff. We have all of it from when we had Benjamin Blueberry!" He walks down the hallway toward the spare bedroom.

"What are ye talkin' about, Love?" I follow him down the hall and into the bedroom. He opens the double doors of the closet I never go into and I'm stunned by the amount of baby formula, diapers, clothes, blankets, and toys on the shelves.

"I think I went a little crazy before." TJ nibbles on his fingernail.

"I think yer feckin' amazin'." I pick him up and whirl him around. "It's like ye knew it was goin' to happen for us."

"I didn't know, but I hoped. Are we really having twins? Did she say what they were?"

"Both girls." I can't stop the permanent smile on my face if I tried. "We're so in over our heads, ye know that, right?"

"I'm not going to be able to sleep tonight. I want to go see them now!"

I sit down on the guest bed and run my hands through my hair, my adrenalin high taking a nosedive. "TJ, I'm scared," I admit. "I almost shat in my pants when Gloria said last call. How are we goin' to handle two babies? We could barely keep a doll alive."

TJ sits next to me and takes my hand in his. "It's normal to be scared. I am too, but my excitement definitely trumps being nervous. Benjamin Blueberry was the devil incarnate and a defective doll that needed to be burned at the stake. Trust me, if we could keep *him* alive, these babies will be cake. We're going to be the best damn dads to these two little girls. They don't know it, but they won the lottery with you and me."

"Ye think?" I arch an eyebrow.

"I know." TJ squeezes my hand. "We're it, Connor. We can't let them down. Gloria and their mom are counting on us."

I shake my head. "Yer right, Love. We can't, and we won't."

Because TJ *is* right, we're the last line of defense for these babies. We're their last call.

THE NEXT MORNING, we contact our family attorney and he agrees to meet us at the hospital at ten. TJ and I barely slept a wink last night. He was on his laptop ordering two cribs, changing tables, and more girl clothes than we could know what to do with. I'm pretty sure our credit card is smoking from all the purchases.

We race to the hospital and meet Gloria in the waiting room of the NICU. She gives us a hug and a huge smile. "Congratulations, dads."

"She still wants to go through with it?" I ask, a lump the size of the Cliffs of Moher jamming my throat.

Gloria nods. "Yes, I spoke with her a few minutes ago and she wants to sign the paperwork. She asked if you would be willing to have an open adoption."

"You mean where she can have contact with the babies?"

"You can set up parameters," Gloria says. "You are in control. She can't see them or contact them without your permission. She's young and immature right now, but I think she's got a good head on her shoulders. I truly believe she'll make something of herself one day."

"Can we meet her?" TJ asks.

Gloria's smile dims. "I'm not sure she's ready for that."

TJ and I trade a look. "I'm okay with open adoption if you are."

"I am. I want to make sure she can't take the babies away from us once she gets back on her feet."

"No, she can't. Once she signs the adoption papers, the girls are all yours. Why don't we meet the babies first, and then you can decide, okay?"

"Yes, of course." TJ claps his hands. "Oh, Gloria, I was thinking about this at four in the morning. What is their ethnicity? Not that it matters one iota, but I was watching YouTube videos on girls' hair textures and learning how to do cornrows. Hair textures for girls are so complicated. Some require special solutions, some need heat treatments or can I just do braids?" TJ looks at me as I roll my eyes. "What, is that wrong to ask?"

"I think we have time before we have to worry about doing their hair."

"I want to be prepared because we both know that's my department."

Gloria chuckles and squeezes TJ's arm. "The mom and father are mixed race. So you'll probably have to wait and see. The good news is, both babies are healthy and have strong lungs."

She leads us to the nursery where we are required to wear masks and gloves. A nurse then takes us into the room. She walks us over to two beautiful baby girls bundled in small plastic bassinets with heat lamps over them. "Can we touch them?" I ask her.

"You can hold them." The corners of her eyes crinkle. "They will be ready to go home tomorrow."

She hands me a baby and I'm scared to breathe. Her head has a small patch of dark hair and her eyes are squeezed shut. TJ and I stare down at her with complete adoration. "She's so tiny," I say.

"Everything about her is amazing."

I look up at TJ, tears glazing my eyes. "She's perfect."

"She's five pounds and her sister is four." The nurse hands TJ her twin and we stare down at both our babies in complete awe.

"I guess this means we're not naming one of them Bartholomew," TJ says.

"No, thank Christ. Nor are we naming one of them Lomew."

"I'd like to name one of them Cara. That was my mom's name. What do you think?" TJ asks thoughtfully as he rocks the baby in his arms.

"I think that's a beautiful name. It means 'friend' in Irish." I smile. "How about Rilee, for the other? It means 'courageous' and 'brave'."

"I love it." TJ gazes down at Cara. "I think we should do an open adoption. What if they want to know who their mom is one day? I can't imagine ever denying these two babies anything."

"I agree. It would be important to know her medical history too. But I think we need to set strong boundaries from the get-go. We have to think about our families since they now have a famous uncle."

"Agreed." He nods as we stare at our beautiful baby girls. "I never thought I could feel so much love," TJ whispers.

"Me, either." I trace Rilee's tiny eyebrows with my index finger. How did we get so lucky? "I'm smitten, TJ."

"Me too, babe. Me too. Oh god, you know what this means?"

"No?" I look over at TJ.

"I'm going to have to get a minivan."

I chuckle. "Yeah, probably so, Love."

We look up at Gloria, who waves at us through the window. We proudly hold the twins up and she takes a picture. This is decidedly the best day of my life.

Chapter 32

I WHEEL THE double stroller into our spacious office we moved into a month ago and wave hello at the new girl who will be working part-time in Andie's position. Her name is Claire. She smiles too much and doesn't get my sarcasm, but she's nice enough and does a good job.

"Are those the babies?" Claire squeals, hopping out of her chair.

"Pipe it down, they're sleeping." I frown at her. "Come on, Claire, it's baby one-oh-one not to wake a sleeping baby. They have literally been up all night long. I'm exhausted."

"Oh, sorry," she whispers. "You poor thing. Kiki asked me to do a coffee run and she ordered you a mocha Frappuccino with extra whip and the cute little sprinkles you love so much."

"You're an absolute doll, Claire, but I quit the coffee crack. It was messing up my sleep schedule, and that's a no-go when these two wake up at all hours of the night. But please, I insist you have it. I'll be happy knowing someone will appreciate my former addiction."

"Oh, okay." She warily looks over at the venti cup. "It looks like it has a lot of sugar and calories, and I'm not sure about sprinkles in coffee..." She frowns before popping her smile back into place. "Can I help with anything?"

"Just here to do a little work for a client and then the girls and I have a top-secret special meeting. You can't tell anyone."

"Ooh, sounds dangerous." She waggles her eyebrows and beams. "Lips sealed." She pantomimes zipping her lips. Normally, I'd love Claire's gusto, but I'm dog-tired and it's a little too much juice in the blender this early in the day. I feel a headache tapping my brain as she sits and stares at me like a serial killer hyped up on Red Bull.

"Kay, well, I'll be in back with the girls. Toodles."

"Toodles." Claire laughs too loudly, making me cringe. "You're hilarious, TJ!"

Cara stirs in her sleep and I'm about to go mama bear on Claire's ass for making dolphin chattering noises when her phone rings. I quickly wheel the sleeping babies into the back and knock on Kiki's door. Sarah and Andie are in there helping Kiki hang dresses. I hold my index finger to my lips and point at the babies.

"Yay, I was hoping you'd bring them in today," Kiki squeals.

"I swear to God, if you wake them, you're changing, feeding, and burping them."

"Uh, okay, you don't have to ask me twice." She swoops in and scoops up Cara. "I love that their bows are bigger than their heads."

"I want one!" Sarah makes a grabby hand gesture and carefully picks up Rilee. "Hello, my little niece. You are so beautiful!"

My jaw hangs open in shock. "Um, hello? Have we all forgotten the handwashing rule?"

"Oh, Sarah and I used the restroom a minute ago." Kiki rocks Cara. "They are so beautiful, TJ."

"And?" I fling out my arms in exasperation.

"And…smart?" Kiki looks at the other two, perplexed.

"And did you wash your hands after going to the bathroom?" I stand with my hands on my hips.

"Ew, gross. Of course we did," Sarah says. "Look at TJ being all Mr. Germaphobe Mom. It's so cute."

I flop down onto the couch and let the girls fawn over the twins.

Andie coos at Cara over Kiki's shoulder. She's due in two weeks and we can't wait to find out what she's having. She looks up at Sarah and smiles. "Are you feeling the baby bug, Sare?"

"Nope. But I love my nieces to pieces. Have you found one to be easier-going than the other yet?"

"Rilee is definitely the louder of the two." I rub my eyes. "She's more demanding than Cara."

"How are you and Connor doing?"

"Well, the first four weeks were awful. No one told me how much babies cry. I thought they'd be sleeping all the time like the precious little angels we met in the hospital. I swear, Rilee's scream can reach decibels I didn't even know existed. And Cara likes to throw-up formula on me every chance she gets. She ruined my fave cashmere sweater. I locked myself in the laundry room and cried. We didn't know what the hell we were doing. Luckily Nana Rose was there helping us, and Maggie has been a godsend. But the real MVP has been Connor. There is no way I could have done this on my own. He's been amazing."

"Yes, Maggie was wonderful when Alexis and Wyatt were born." Sarah smiles. "But I'm sure Connor would say the same about you, TJ."

"Well, I didn't tell you all, but I was depressed the first few weeks. I mean, don't get me wrong. I was so happy to have them…ecstatic. But I wasn't prepared for the reality of having twins. I cracked under the pressure. It's a lot of responsibility raising two human beings that you have sworn you'll never let down. Between the crying, the diapers, the feedings and lack of sleep, I crumbled."

"Awe, TJ."

"Gloria gave me the name of a therapist and y'all won't believe her name. Dr. Bart! Isn't that wild? It was meant to be, like sprinkles on caramel mocha lattes. She's amazeballs and has helped me when I feel panicky or feeling uncertain in situations. Connor has been super supportive through it all. Everyone has made me realize I can do this."

"You totally can, TJ. We're here for you." Andie hugs me. "I'm so happy for you and Connor!"

"Thanks. We have a routine now. They are…a lot of work. But totes worth it."

Kiki, Sarah, and Andie smirk at each other.

"We tried to warn you with BB-2," Sarah singsongs.

"Oh please, the only lesson that thing taught me was to sleep with one eye open in case it tried to smother me in my sleep."

"Your daddy's silly," Andie baby-talks to Rilee, who has opened her eyes. "How is Bartie doing with all the chaos?"

"She loves the twins. We'll find her sleeping under their cribs or on their changing table. She's always watching over them. It's really sweet."

"Oreo and Furball were like that with the boys. Once they got mobile, the cats knew to hide out in their cat trees if the kids got to be too much.

"That's a great idea. We'll have to get her one. Thank you guys for trying to help me. I'm sorry I didn't treat Benjamin Blueberry very well."

"You're forgiven." Kiki hands Andie Cara and sits down next to me, pulling me into a side-hug. "We're proud of you, TJ. We weren't sure you could handle it, but look at you. A daddy to two girls. And you finally got to use a version of the name Bartholomew."

"Thanks, K-Bestie. I'd try to come up with something fabulous to say, but I'm brain-dead."

"Sometimes silence is all that's needed." She winks.

Andie and Sarah place the babies back in the stroller while Kiki stands and stretches.

"I swear your stomach has doubled in size since I saw you last. Did you eat the whole box of Snickers bars from Costco again?"

"Rude!" She swats my hand away and runs a hand over her growing belly. "You know by now I'm not a cute pregnant person. And that only happened one time."

"Sure, it did. Okay, ladies, ready for our soiree?"

"Where are we going?" Andie asks.

"Jazzy hands! It's a surprise. We're walking there."

"Oh great," Kiki mumbles, grabbing her purse. "What are you afraid we'll mess up your new beloved minivan?"

"Don't be hatin' on Vinnie Van Gogh," I say. "That baby purrs like a kitten, and the sliding remote doors are the bomb. It has video monitors, and sensors so there's no chance of me leaving something on the roof or hood. It also has backup cameras so I don't have a chance of running the stroller over when I accidentally leave it behind the car. It happened with the Range Rover and I have learned my lesson. The babies weren't in it, of course."

"Jesus, how do you survive?" Kiki smirks.

"You named your minivan Vinnie Van Gogh?" Sarah asks, placing a blanket over Rilee in the double stroller.

"Cutsies, right? Vinny for mini and Van Gogh because it's a van and it goes places. Connor came up with it and I thought it was *trés magnifique*."

"Let's go. I'm hangry and I'm about to lose my shit over a van named Vinnie." Kiki grouses.

"Someone's G to the rumpy." I say to the twins, turning the stroller around. "Auntie Kiki needs a Snickers bar."

The other two grab their things and we head out into the late-summer sunshine over to the park.

"We're going to a park for lunch?"

"Kiki, can you just flow with the moment for once in your life?"

"I think you mean go with the flow," Andie chimes in.

"Okay, world traveler." I spread a large blanket under a shade tree in the grass and take out a to-go bag from our favorite deli.

"I can flow, but someone is going to have to help Andie and me off the ground."

"I'm not a sadist, Kiki. Andie, I brought a deluxe folding chair for you. It even has a footrest. Isn't it darling?" I unfold the chair and pat the cushioned seat.

"Wait, where's my chair?"

"Well, Kiki, if you were half as big as Andie, I would have brought one for you too."

"I'm not sure that was a compliment, but I'll take the chair," Andie says. She helps me pass out the drinks and sandwiches while Sarah and Kiki lay the babies on the blanket. "This is so fun, TJ!"

"Well, I have the babies today since Connor is working, and I thought a restaurant would be too loud for them, and too crowded. And this is probably the last time we'll be together like this before Sarah jets off to some award show and you guys have your babies."

"I canceled the Vegas trip." Sarah smiles nervously.

"What? Why?" I gasp.

"Because I need to be more present here." She looks over at Kiki, who nods. "I'm thinking of starting my own makeup line."

"Oh my god, Sarah, that's amazing!" Andie gushes.

"Sare Bear, I love this idea," I tell her.

"You do?"

"Yes! Do you know how many people asked Sonja for her lipstick color at the Teen Choice Awards?"

"Yeah, and she claimed she had no clue." Kiki rolls her eyes.

"Well, she's a snap, crackle, pop now." I snap my fingers.

"What does that mean?" Andie whispers to Sarah.

"She's a has-been, Shorts. Which I called from day one."

"I heard she moved back home to Kansas and is living with her parents. Sad." Sarah frowns. "Anyway, that's the plan."

"Well cheers, to new plans, babies, and friendship."

"Cheers!" The four of us clink our glasses of sparkling cider.

After lunch, I grab another bag from the stroller. "Because you bitches wouldn't let me throw you a shower, I got you a little something. Sare Bear, one for you too."

"Awe, TJ, that's so sweet," the three of them say, greedily grabbing the little box shaped like a Chinese take-out container.

"Now wait. You have to open them together on three. One, two, three."

They open the tops of the boxes and a little pop sounds while a poof of Tiffany-blue glitter rains down all around them.

"I so hate you right now," Andie grumbles.

I take out my phone and snap a picture. "I know, but to see the expressions on your faces right now. So worth it."

"Some things will never change." Sarah sighs.

"TJ, I have a meeting with a client this afternoon. Now I look like I've been at a strip club getting lap dances."

"Everyone needs a little sparkle, Kiki. There's something else in the box."

The girls look warily in the box and each lift out a silver bangle with a charm for each of us on them.

"I have one too." I lift my sleeve and show them.

"It's beautiful," Sarah says. "Oh my gosh, look at the charms. A camera for Andie, a dress for Kiki, a sun for me, and a diamond for you? I'm confused, what does the diamond stand for?"

"Hello? Shine bright like a diamond? The most dazzling, sought-after gem in the world?"

The three of them burst out laughing.

"Okay, Rihanna. Shine bright." Kiki smirks and leans in to kiss me on the cheek. "Thank you, it's beautiful."

"Don't mock me, sluts. It's a real diamond, and those are semi-precious garnets, onyx, and citrine."

"We love you, TJ. It's perfect and beautiful." Andie beams, clasping her bracelet and admiring the charms.

"We'll never take it off," Sarah says.

"I love you three bitches too, even though you mock my diamond. I couldn't do life without you." I walk over to Kiki and help haul her up. "Oh, one more thing. As your doula and midwife—"

"Nope, not happening, Turd Jam."

"—I persuaded the nurse to tell me the sex of your baby after your ultrasound the other day when you and Tatum were being gushy and annoying saying you didn't care what the sex was, you just wanted a healthy baby."

"I remember..." Kiki eyes me suspiciously. "What do you mean you persuaded? Wait, you know what it is? Tell me!"

I stroke my chin and look up at the sky. "But you said you didn't care."

"I don't." She noncommittally shrugs, but by the way she's chewing her bottom lip, I know it's killing her not to know. She spins in a circle looking to Sarah and Andie for help, but they just shrug, bemused smiles on their faces.

"Are you sure?"

"Okay, fine. Tell me. I need to know. No wait, don't tell me. Tatum should be here for it. But I've got to know. Dammit, TJ," she yelps. "Why do you do this to me? Don't stand there smiling like that, tell me!" She stomps her foot, her hands clenched. The glitter in her hair catches the sun. I adore her to pieces.

"Hello? Isn't it obvi? I mean, I nailed it this time if I do say so myself."

"TJ!" the three girls shout.

"The blue glitter bomb? You guys are covered in blue."

Kiki stares at me in shock, not processing what I'm saying. Sarah covers her mouth and squeals. I guess I have to spell it out for her.

"Kiki, you're having a boy." I take more glitter out of my pocket and throw it in the air. "Surprise!"

"Wait, are you sure? A boy?" She runs her hand over her stomach. "I'm having another boy? But that's not what I...I mean, of course I want a healthy baby, but I *really* wanted a girl, you guys. Like, really, truly, madly wanted a girl."

"Awe, honey." I wrap her in a hug. "You're the best boy mom I know. No one else could put up with their shit like you do. God must have known you could handle another."

"I do love my boys." She laughs through her tears. "Well, fuck. Here we go again."

Chapter 33

Andie

MY HAND RUBS my belly in a circular motion as I breathe through my nose. Shit, this is it. The baby's coming early. I walk down the hallway to the kitchen. I need to call Cam. Looking down at my watch, I whimper. He had a meeting on the other side of town and it's rush hour. Stabbing pain has me grabbing the edge of the countertop. "Oh god, that fucking hurts. Call Cam," I say to my watch. Cam's voicemail picks up.

"Babe, it's me. Uh, I think the baby has decided to come two weeks early. Meet me at the hospital."

Next, I call Kiki, but her phone goes straight to voicemail. Same with Sarah's phone. Shit, shit, shit. I don't want to bother TJ because he has the twins to deal with. I call the office. My replacement, Claire, picks up.

"Nashville Style, Claire speaking. How can I make your day better?"

"Claire, it's Andie," I pant as another contraction rolls through me. Shit, they're close. Too close. "Can you have

Kiki call me ASAP? It's an emergency."

"Oh, sure thing! I'm pretty sure she's in her office. At least I hope she is, or I totally zoned out when she walked by my desk." She snorts. "Oh, no. Don't mention I said that to Kiki. She kind of scares me. Um, so now that I have you on the phone, I'm looking at the computer and wondering…are the client files supposed to be alphabetized—"

"Claire! I can't right now, please go interrupt whatever she's doing!"

"Oh, um, okay, no need to get snippy about it, I'm only trying to learn and do a good—"

I hang up on Claire and call TJ.

"This better be important. I literally just finished changing both twins' diapers and one had the most horrific-smelling green sludge ooze out. You know what I'm talking about right? It's like—"

I moan and keel as another contraction grips my insides and twists them tight.

"I know, gross right? I made the same exact sound. Seriously Andie, don't tell anyone, but I think I might have blacked out for a few seconds. One minute I was holding a diaper and the next I was down on the ground. Don't worry, no babies were in danger. What a doozy! Anyhoo, what's your sitch?"

"TJ," I cry, "I need you to get your butt over here ASAP. I can't get a hold of anyone and I'm having this baby. It's coming fast!"

"No, no, no, no, no! You're not due for another two weeks. I'm not wearing the right clothes to help deliver a baby. Where's my doula outfit? My Mr. Miyagi bandana? I wonder where Connor stored it—"

"TJ, I'm going to have this baby by myself if you don't leave now," I growl. "Fuck the bandana and doula outfit. I need you!" I scream, another contraction tightening my abdomen.

"Shit. I'm coming, Andie! Don't move!"

"Call an ambulance," I pant. "And don't forget to bring the twins with you."

"Right, right. Shit. I almost ran out the door without them. I'll send out the bat signal for everyone."

I hang up the phone and look over at the baby monitor. Charleigh is taking her afternoon nap and should be waking up soon. Enzo is over at Sarah's house with her kids. I brace myself for another contraction and that's when my water breaks all over the kitchen floor.

Chapter 34

"CAM, WHERE THE hell are you? You know what, never mind. Get to the hospital as soon as you can. Andie's in labor. I'm on my way to your house to get her. Call me back!"

I hang up and race toward Cam and Andie's house. Sarah went to my house to grab Chase and Drew and take them to her place and then she'll meet us at the hospital. I call TJ but it goes straight to voicemail. I call Connor next.

"Hey Kiki, what's the craic?"

"Have you talked to TJ?"

"No, what's wrong? Is it something with the twins? He was texting me about a diaper blowout earlier, but then I didn't hear from him again."

"Andie went into labor and I'm meeting him over at her house."

"Shite, okay. Lemme see if I can get someone to cover me here. Does Cam know? He had a meeting this afternoon across town."

"I can't get a hold of him."

"Okay, I'll keep tryin' him. I'll leave here shortly to come help."

I pull into Cam and Andie's driveway and throw the car in park behind TJ's beloved minivan. The side doors and driver's side door are open as well as the front door to Andie's house. It looks like a crime scene. I duck my head into the van, making sure he didn't leave one of the twins out here. I run up the front steps and into the house.

"TJ? Andie?" I shout, quickly moving toward the cries of babies in the kitchen. I walk in and freeze. "Oh my god."

TJ has one of the twins in a Baby Bjorn on his front and another is in a bassinet, fussing. Charleigh is in her high chair crying, while Andie is on a blanket on the floor, moaning.

"Kiki, don't just stand there, help me with the babies."

TJ's stern voice spurs me into action because frankly, he's never stern. "Let me help Andie, since you already have one strapped to your body."

"But I'm her doula."

"Well, you're gonna have to take a back seat, doula. Andie, do you think you can get up so I can drive you to the hospital?"

Andie's glazed eyes slide over to mine. She grips my hand. "Kiki, thank God you're here. There's not enough time. I'm having this baby now."

"Oh shit. Okay, Teej, talk me through what you know."

"I'm a doula, Kinky, not a midwife."

"Oh my god, I'm going to die," Andie whimpers.

"No, no, don't say that. We've got you." I press a cool

cloth TJ hands me to her forehead.

"I tried singing to her but she threatened to cut off my testicles. She's scarier than you are during labor." TJ stands and picks up the other baby out of the bassinet and then hands Charleigh a sippy cup of milk.

"Andie, how close are the contractions?"

"About five, I think. Maybe less. I can't do this, Kiki…"

I look up at TJ, feeling completely helpless.

"I've already called the paramedics, but there's a big accident on the highway, so they're delayed. But don't worry, I've got this," he says, sounding way more confident than I feel.

"You almost threw up when you saw the water on the floor," Andie pants.

"Andie, we're going to do this and I'm going to need your help." *Think, Kiki.* "I need you to take your leggings and underwear off so I can see how many centimeters you're dilated, okay? I'll cover you with a blanket. Do not push, okay? TJ, google how to deliver a baby at home."

I race to their bedroom and fling open the doors to their linen closet. I grab a blanket and several clean towels, then run back to the kitchen. TJ is pacing back and forth mumbling about smelling salts. Charleigh is watching us curiously while she sucks on her sippy cup.

"Teej, I need you to keep it together, okay? I cannot have you fainting while holding two babies. In fact, why don't you sit on the floor in case you drop on me."

"I'm not going to faint, Kiki."

Andie strips off her clothes and I check to see how dilated she is. "Holy shit, you're crowning. There's no time to think. We're delivering right now."

"I need to push," Andie cries.

"I feel dizzy." TJ slumps down against the cabinets next to Andie. "I don't think I'm ready for this. I mean we've practiced, but when it comes down to D-day, I only know breathing techniques. I've never delivered a baby before—"

"Jesus, Tinker Jam, please stop talking and hand me Rilee before you pass out."

He hands the baby over and I place her in the bassinet. Cara is fast asleep in the Baby Bjorn and seems okay at the moment, so I leave her with him.

"Okay, Andie, hold TJ's hand and take a deep breath."

TJ takes a dramatic deep breath next to her and holds it while looking at me expectantly.

I roll my eyes. "On the count of three, you're going to push, got it?"

Andie and TJ both nod.

"One, two three, push!"

Chapter 35

Sarah

WYATT JOSTLES IN my arms as I run into the waiting room with Enzo gripping my other hand. I spot Kiki and TJ sitting by the window, with their heads down. Kiki looks like she's been crying. "Guys, are you okay? I got here as fast as I could. What happened?"

Kiki looks up, her eyes glazed with tears. "She had a little boy. Cameron Thomas Forbes. Eight pounds and six ounces."

I sink into a seat across from them and put Wyatt and Enzo in the chairs next to me. "That's incredible—"

"He didn't make it."

I gasp and my lip trembles. "The baby didn't make it? Oh my god." I sit back in shock, not sure how to process this news. I look over to see if Enzo is paying attention, but luckily he's talking to Wyatt.

"No." Kiki shakes her head. "My brother, Cam. He didn't make it in time for the delivery. He got stuck in the wreck traffic. He literally rolled up fifteen minutes ago."

"So wait, the baby is okay? Andie's okay? Everyone is alive and okay? Because your delivery right now really sucks."

"Yes, healthy baby, mama is recovering well, and Cam is with them."

I deflate against my seat. "I seriously hate you right now. You literally made my heart stop. Why are you crying?"

"I was laughing about walking in and seeing TJ with Andie on the floor, and all the babies are crying, doors open. TJ's mumbling about smelling salts. I can't stop giggling."

"It's super annoying." TJ side-eyes Kiki. "It wasn't *that* funny. I think she's still on an adrenalin high."

"Why are you on an adrenalin high?"

"You won't believe it, Sare, I delivered a baby! A fucking baby!"

"Hey! Language." I frown, nodding in Wyatt and Enzo's direction. "What do you mean you delivered a baby?"

"I mean, I brought a baby into this world in Andie's kitchen."

"What?" I ask, my jaw dropping. "Are you serious?"

"Yep, it was the most incredible thing I've ever witnessed. I think I'm going to enroll in medical school and become an obstetrician."

"Oh goodie, here we go again." TJ rolls his eyes.

"Hey, just because you passed out during a live birth, *again*, doesn't mean you have to kill my dream."

"Kinky, do you know how many years it takes to go through medical school? And I hate to point out the obvious, but baby number *tres* is going to pop soon and then you're going to wish you listened to me and hired an assistant."

"Dream killer." Kiki sighs and looks over at Wyatt. "Uh,

Sare? Where are all the kids?"

"Lex is watching them. Wyatt didn't want to miss out on the action. In fact, he told me on the way over he wants to be a doctor someday."

"Maybe by the time Kiki gets her shit together she and Wyatt can go to school together."

"Very funny, Tammy Jean."

"Sare Bear"—TJ leans forward and stage-whispers—"why does Wyatt have Benjamin Blueberry?"

I look over at Wyatt rocking BB-2, and smile. "It's the strangest thing, you guys. He's come out of his shell because of this doll. He feeds it, changes its diapers, and takes care of it. It's the cutest thing. I don't know if it's feeling responsible for something, or taking care of a baby, but it has certainly reduced his anxiety."

"It's weird and creepy," TJ whispers. "It's not a real baby. I'm pretty sure it just blinked at me."

"It probably remembers your voice and is going to come and strangle you in your sleep tonight." Kiki smiles evilly.

"Well, thanks, Kinksadoodle. As if I'm not sleep-deprived enough, now I have to worry about Chucky doll, Benji Blue, killing me in my bed."

I roll my eyes at my two best friends and chuckle. Connor rolls the double stroller off the elevator and strides over to us. I stand up and hug him. "Were you a part of the circus?"

He smirks and shakes his head. "By the time I got to Andie's, the paramedics were there taking care of Andie and the baby—"

"And giving TJ oxygen," Kiki chimes in.

"And giving TJ oxygen, so I grabbed everyone while Andie went in the ambulance with TJ and we all came here."

"I can't believe I missed out on all the excitement," I say sadly.

"Sare Bear, be glad you missed out. When I saw that head crowning, it was lights out for me, and thank goodness because I probably would have puked if I saw all that stuff come out with the baby."

"You mean the placenta?" Kiki arches an eyebrow.

"Don't go all *Dr. Quinn Medicine Woman* on me now because you delivered *one* baby, Kinky."

"Uncle Coco, can I see the babies?" Wyatt asks Connor.

"Of course, little man." Connor wheels the stroller around so Wyatt is at eye level with Cara and Rilee. "Mama, are these my cousins?"

"Yes, they are." I smile proudly at Wyatt. He's changed so much in the past few months. He's curious now instead of afraid. Smiling instead of crying.

"Here, Cara, this is Benji. He's your cousin too." Wyatt angles BB-2 to kiss Cara's forehead. TJ swoops in and picks up Wyatt, while Connor swiftly maneuvers the stroller away.

"Whoa there, little buddy. I'm not sure your cousins are prepared to meet your voodoo doll yet. They're sleeping right now and if Benji cries, it might wake them up."

Kiki giggles. "I don't think I've ever seen TJ move that fast."

Wyatt nods his head sagely and then sticks BB-2 in TJ's face. "He wants a kiss from Uncle TJ."

TJ rears his head back, his eyes panicked. "I'm gonna pass, buddy."

"Please, Uncle TJ?"

"Yeah, Uncle TJ, kiss the doll," Kiki prods.

"You're dead to me, both of you." He points to me and Kiki before screwing his eyes tight and quickly kissing BB-2's head. He puts Wyatt down and wipes his mouth on his sleeve. "Probably cursed now."

Cam appears from around the corner, holding Charleigh.

"Daddy!" Enzo runs over and flings himself against him.

"Hey buddy, Mommy's been asking to see you. Ready to go meet your baby brother?"

"Yes! He can fight bad guys with me."

"Yeah, bud, he can. Hey guys, thanks for waiting. Ready to meet baby Cam?"

"Yes!" we all cheer.

"I'll wait out here with the kids," Connor says. Cam looks like he's going to argue, but then takes a look at BB-2 and grimaces.

"I think that's wise."

"Don't you guys think you're being a wee bit dramatic? It's a doll." I laugh.

"Sare Bear, I'm pretty sure it moved by itself to that other chair. Connor, keep an eye on that thing. Don't let it get near the twins."

Connor nods and guides the stroller with Charleigh and Wyatt over to the waiting room chairs.

We walk into Andie's room and she looks up from the hospital bed, looking tired, but elated. We all wash our hands and gather around her. Enzo climbs up next to his mom.

"Hey guys. Meet Cameron Thomas Forbes."

"I'm so honored he has my middle name." TJ leans in and kisses Andie's cheek. "Are you going to call him CT? Because that might sound weird. It reminds me of a CT scan or ET the alien. Oh my gosh, wouldn't it be cute to ask him to phone home?"

Cam clears his throat. "Just Cameron."

"How much oxygen did they give you on the ride over?" Kiki side-eyes TJ.

"Without you and Kiki, I would have been in a lot of trouble. Thank you both so much." She passes the baby to Cam, who hands it over to Kiki. I look over her shoulder in awe of the tiny little miracle.

"You don't owe us a thing," Kiki says. "I am honored to have been the one to deliver my nephew."

"That's so cool." I squeeze Kiki's shoulders. "Are you ready for yours, Kiki?"

"No." She laughs through her tears. "But I will be. Here, hold him. It will make you want another."

I take the baby from Kiki and smile down at the tiny bundle. "He's beautiful, but just like when I held TJ's babies, I don't have the tug."

"What's the tug?" Cam asks as he perches next to Andie.

"I'm happy with Jax and the twins. I don't feel the tug to have another. I'm good."

"Me too," Andie says. "We're done, Cameron Forbes."

TJ comes over and squeezes us both into a hug. "We did it, you guys."

"What did we do?" Kiki asks.

"We came full circle," TJ says. Kiki arches an eyebrow. "Cheese and rice do I have to spell it out for you? I'd definitely rethink the medical school angle. Sare Bear has an amazing family. Sure, her kids struggled a bit, but what family doesn't? She's got a new makeup line in the works. Kiki, you're preggers with baby number three and have a successful line of wedding gowns. Andie has an amazing family and took the most beautiful photographs in Greece for her new book. And I'm a new dad to twins. I mean a year ago, who the hell would have guessed this? We did it. We beat the odds and came out on top."

"We did it." Kiki sniffles, handing her nephew back to Andie.

"We did it." Andie runs her finger down the baby's cheek and looks up at Cam with tears in her eyes.

"We did it." I squeeze Kiki and TJ's hands, finally feeling free from all the metaphorical ropes that had me in knots for the past year.

The door to the room slams open with a bang. Mandy holds onto the doorjamb, panting. "I just sprinted up five flights of stairs. I think I broke the minivan's speedometer. Who knew that thing could get up to a hundred and twenty? I went balls to the wall to get here. I even shaved an hour off the regular time. I wore an adult diaper so there would be no pee stops like that crazy astronaut killer lady. Don't worry, I didn't need it. Give me that adorable bundle of sweetness. Auntie Mandy is here!"

"Wash your hands!" we all shout as she reaches for the baby.

"So, what did I miss?"

Epilogue I

TJ

SOMEONE ONCE SAID everything happens for a reason. I think about that often since we adopted the two little miracles in our lives. I smile, watching Maggie lift Cara in the air and twirl her around while Nana Rose stuffs a piece of cake into Rilee's mouth. Gloria tickles her little feet and coos at her. Andie, Sarah, and Kiki pass out cake to everyone, while Mandy tries valiantly to make a balloon animal hat for Charleigh. The kids race around the playground with half-popped balloons on their heads like sugar-crazed banshees. Mandy belly laughs at something Kiki says and it makes me smile. I truly am blessed to have these wonderful women in my life, helping Connor and me raise our babies.

We invited their adoptive mom to the party, through Gloria, but she elected not to come. I was bummed for our girls at first but came around to accepting that it was her decision. Maybe someday, when she's ready, she'll want to be a part of their lives.

"You did it, TJ. We didn't think you could, but you

proved us wrong." Kiki slings an arm around my neck and hands me a champagne flute. Sarah and Andie flank my other side. We watch everyone enjoying the twins' first birthday party at the park.

"Thanks, guys. There were some touch-and-go moments, but we survived the first year."

"It only gets harder from here." Sarah laughs.

"Yeah." I sigh. "I know."

"Hey, at least you didn't shut a limb in the car door or spill hot coffee on them," Andie says brightly.

"Or drive off with them on the roof of the car or leave them in a car seat for more than an hour." Kiki smirks.

"Yeah, and they aren't missing an eye or have to wear an eyepatch," Sarah adds helpfully.

"Cheers to that." I laugh. We knock our champagne flutes together, our bracelets glittering in the afternoon light. "I know I'm biased, but they are beautiful babies. Cara is so sweet and Rilee is a spitfire. We're going to have our hands full when they get older."

"They are gorgeous," Sarah says, "but don't worry, their cousins will keep them in line and chase all the boys away."

"Congratulations on the second *People Magazine* article." Kiki winks. "The pictures of you, Connor, and the girls are amazing."

"Couldn't have done it without our amazing photographer." I kiss Andie's cheek. "I think it will give hope to those families who are struggling."

"For sure," Sarah agrees. "We're so proud of you and Connor for putting your story out there."

People Magazine had such a positive response from our

sidebar story with the band, that they asked to do a full-page cover story when they found out we adopted Cara and Rilee. Connor and I held hands during the whole interview and I let him do most of the talking. He was candid and talked about the highs and lows of raising twins.

I always knew he'd be an amazing dad, but he breathed life back into me when we first brought them home. It was scary and challenging with two babies, and I had no clue what I was doing. Between the daily panic attacks and the feeling undeserving of these babies, the cracks in my facade were starting to show. But Connor kept us glued together and said that not knowing how everything is supposed to go will make us better parents. For once in my life, I took a step back and let someone else take the reins.

"I know this isn't your usual style for a party, but I'm glad you decided not to go with the over-the-top circus theme with the bearded lady and the dancing bears and dogs. I know you were chomping at the bit to wear the ringmaster outfit with the tophat—"

"And sequined coat."

"And the sequined coat, but this is nice," Kiki says.

"Yeah, it is nice. I'm glad you and Connor shot down pretty much all of my ideas."

Tatum jokes with Cam while they both hold the newest additions to their families. Kiki may have griped about not having a little girl like she hoped, but little Jake Reed has both of them wrapped around his little finger. Chase runs around the playground with Drew's bankie tied around his neck like he's Superman, while Drew chases him. Alexis and Enzo compete on who can swing the highest, while Wyatt pushes BB-2 in a baby swing next to them. Jax, Lex, Connor, Matt, and Will play a game of football while Finn referees.

"You know, I've always wanted a big family." I smile, looking around at our friends and family. "And that dream finally came true."

"We may not be perfect," Kiki says.

"Or sane." Andie laughs.

"But we've got each other." Sarah hugs me.

I grin and wave them into a huddle. Kiki groans and I give her the stink eye. "On three, you guys. Give me a razzle dazzle, snizzle my shizzle, sparkle, pop, and fizz. TJ's the best!"

I dip my hands into my pockets and throw glitter in the air, the sparkly fragments raining down all around us.

"TJ!" the three of them yell.

Life is always better with sparkle.

"Cynthia Rusli once said, 'Everything happens for a reason. Every person we meet has a role in our life, whether it is big or small. Some will hurt, betray and make us cry. Some will teach us a lesson, not to change us, but to make us be a better person.'

"I wholeheartedly believe this to be true. If I didn't have to go through the hard stuff—if I didn't fail, then I wouldn't be the man I am today. People come in and out of our lives, challenging us to look deeper within ourselves. My Nana Rose always said, you have two choices in life. You can either dance with the two left feet you were given or give up and go home. I'm going to choose to dance. I apologize to no one, bitches."

—TJ Ryan, *The Nashville Spotlight*

Epilogue II

Connor

"HEY GUYS!" I shout, but no one pays me any attention. Looking around The Social Hour, I'm surrounded by all my friends. Tatum and Kiki, Lex and Sarah, Cam and Andie, TJ, Mandy, Matt, Will, and their girlfriends. It's been a long day of festivities celebrating our beautiful daughters' first trip around the sun. The grandparents brought all the kids back to Sarah and Lex's house for one massive sleepover. Luckily, Kiki had the forethought to hire a few babysitters to help out.

It's often said that the Irish are known for their luck, and I'm gonna have to agree with whatever drunk curmudgeon came up with that theory. We're strong-willed enough to always land on our feet, even when the chips are down. Whether the theory is true or I'm just a stubborn arse, I'm grateful for the people here tonight.

TJ is animatedly talking with Mandy, his cheeks flushed and hair mussed. Damn, he's as adorable as the first night he walked into my bar looking like a sequined leprechaun. I had my doubts after the first couple days the twins were home that we would make it to their first year. TJ would go from crying to laughing, back to bawling within a thirty-second conversation. I thought I was going to have to raise them on my own when he locked himself in the laundry room after Cara projectile-vomited all over his new Burberry sweater. But after a week of me and Nana Rose patiently talking him off the ledge, and a little help from Gloria and Dr. Bart, he came back swinging, ready to be the dad I knew he could be. Mum was right, life is about pivoting, and I just had to patiently wait for him to turn full circle back to me. I'm so damn proud of my man.

My brother snags Sarah as she walks by, dipping her into a kiss. They've had a tough year with their kids, but their love is strong and true. I learned a lot from watching them navigate everything, from Alexis's habit of parroting adults, to Wyatt's anxiety and Jax's sex education. They tackled it together and came out on the other side closer than ever. Most couples would have folded, but not Lex and Sunshine. I shake my head and chuckle. I can't believe the wanker is still standin'.

Cameron catches my eye and raises his beer. I lift my chin in return. He was so worried everything would crash and burn this past year, but the jammy sod has it all—a beautiful wife who thinks he hung the moon, three healthy and incredibly sweet kids, a smashing successful business, and me as his best friend and business partner. Like I said, he's a lucky chancer.

Tatum wraps an arm around Kiki, who looks like she's about to pass out. The boys adore the new baby, but have not calmed down by any means as Kiki had hoped. She has officially announced she is done having babies. I guess three boys is enough to wrangle. I told her she could get her girly fix with the twins anytime she needs it. But like everyone here tonight, the chaos seems to have made them stronger. Tatum kisses the top of her head and snuggles her closer.

We have Kiki and Tatum to thank for all of us being here tonight. If it weren't for them getting together, I never would have met TJ in Ireland, Sarah most likely wouldn't have had the *cojones* to kiss Lex, and Andie would have never applied for a job at Nashville Stylists. Funny how one little chance meeting changes everything.

I get up on the bar, put my fingers in my mouth, and whistle loudly. Everyone looks up in my direction. "Sorry for that, but I need yer attention."

"Well get on with it, ye gobshite," Lex yells.

"Shut yer bake, ye muppet." I smile. "First, I'd like to say thank ye to my husband for helpin' raise the two most amazin' girls. I love ye, *mo shíorghrá*."

Everyone cheers while TJ blows me a kiss.

I raise my glass. "Whiskey all around for an ol' Irish toast."

Our server, Mac, passes out whiskey to all my friends and family. Everyone raises their glass.

"I love ye guys."

"Awe! We love you, Connor," they shout. There are some hoots and whistles. I wave my hand to settle them down. I wink at my husband who whistles the loudest.

"There are good ships, and there are wood ships, and the ships that sail at sea. But the best ships are friendships, and may they always be. Slainte."

"Slainte!" everyone calls out, downing their whiskey shots.

"It's last call, ye lovable muckers. Ye done have to go home, but ye can't stay here."

The End

A Note from the Author

I always knew I wanted to write TJ's book, and I KNEW the fans wanted another book, but I couldn't figure out what his story would be. He had already met and married Connor in book two, so it wasn't going to be their whirlwind romance story. And then I thought, they're getting older, what if they tried to adopt a baby? But it had to be done in typical TJ fashion: complete zaniness. What started out as a sweet, fun idea about adoption quickly grew into concern for the LGBTQ community. Although Mississippi was the last state to overturn laws banning LGBTQ couples from adopting in 2016, discrimination among the community still exists in several states. So much judgment and ugliness in this world when deserving human beings have so much to give. If you live in a conservative state, I hope you implore your elected officials to stand for equal rights. It shouldn't be left up to government officials to decide who can have a family. For more information you can visit www.americanadoptions. com.

I wish there were more Glorias in this world.

Acknowledgments

Thank you to everyone who has loved this series from the start. I wouldn't be here writing this without your love and support. I hope I did this series justice with this last book. To my core group of die-hard readers who made these books possible, I adore you. Thank you from the bottom of my heart. To my sister Allison, thank you for always being my sounding board. There were a lot of times you've talked me off the ledge. I appreciate you and love you. Stephanie, thank you for offering to Beta Read and take the time to give me feedback. I SO appreciate you. To Lisa for always being my cheerleader, thank you. To Josie for making us sing Gloria at the top of our lungs with our heads out the window. Never take life too seriously, right? To Michelle for being my editor on this series from the very beginning. Little did you know what you were getting into with that first Zoom call back in 2019. I know it's a lot of brainpower to edit TJ, so I thank you for hanging in there with me. Your support means everything to me. To my family, for your love and support and insisting on reading my books, thank you and I love you. To my husband and kids for putting up with my: just give me one more paragraph, one more minute, one more second! Your patience made this book happen. To Josephine and Richard, thank you from the bottom of my heart for all your love and support.

Other Books by Sophie Sinclair

The Coffee Book Series
Coffee Girl – Coffee Book 1
The Makeup Artist – Coffee Book 2
The Social Hour – Coffee Book 3

The Love Series
Lindsey Love Loves
Patrick Loves Love

The Greyson Gap Series
Where The River Takes You – Greyson Gap Book 1

About the Author

Sophie Sinclair lives with her husband, two daughters, a boxer-mix named Dunkin Donuts, a chi-pit named Moki, and a cat named Pickles in Davidson, NC.

You can find me on my website:
www.sophiesinclairwrites.com
Social Media:
Instagram: @sophiesinclairauthor
Facebook: Sophie Sinclair Writes
Twitter: @authorssinclair

If you enjoyed this book, please leave a review!

Thank you,
Sophie